The Sacrificial Man

The Sacrificial Man

A Thriller

Ruth Dugdall

ARCADE PUBLISHING
NEW YORK

Acknowledgements

This novel has been several years in the making and in that time I have benefitted from the generosity and support of many people. My heartfelt thanks to Helen Miles, who was first to offer *The Sacrificial Man* a publishing contract and generous enough to agree a move to Legend Press when it became clear that the 'Cate Austin novels' belonged together; to the team at Legend—Tom Chalmers, Lauren Parsons, and Lucy Boguslawski—who are nothing short of amazing in their dedication and energy. Belated thanks to Elaine Hanson whose generous setting up of the Luke Bitmead Bursary resulted in the publication of *The Woman Before Me*, the first Cate Austin novel.

For their professional expertise I am indebted to Nigel Stone, Senior Lecturer in Law at the University of East Anglia and Dr. Bodhan Solomka, Forensic Psychiatrist at the Norvic Centre.

This novel was partly funded by an Arts Council grant and SCAN grant. These enabled me to benefit from a year of mentorship with Michelle Spring. My writing friends Liz Ferretti, Morag Lewis, Sophie Green, and Jane Bailey have given me direction when I wondered where I was heading. Our monthly meeting have saved me from a dead end many times! I am also grateful to Maureen Blundell for her candid advice and keen eye.

A personal note of thanks to my family, Margaret and John Dugdall and Peter and Beryl Marshall, for keeping the faith even on days when I had lost my own.

And finally a big cheer for my husband, Andrew, who has believed in this novel from the outset and has made many sacrifices in the name of writing. None involving any pot-bellied pigs, thankfully!

Thanks to you all.

To Andrew, for all your sacrifices and support.
With love.

Now more than ever seems it rich to die,
To cease upon the midnight with no pain . . .

John Keats

1

Trains terminated here. It was the end of the line.

Only just past nine, and I waited for the last train to arrive. A sharp breeze made me nip my jacket close, turn my collar up. I was alone on the platform. A mere shelter. No café, not even a chocolate machine, just a bench and a timetable screwed by cracked Plexiglas to the crumbling brickwork. I was on the edge looking down, fighting that familiar urge to jump that some commuters experience. On the track were discarded cans and wrappers, the litter of those who had also waited for trains. I was an actor in the wings of an unlit stage, apprehensive before the audience arrived. The wind picked up in bitter gusts. I turned my face against it, looking down the track into the dark tunnel. Lights would come, then noise. Then him.

I checked my watch. Seven minutes past nine. Eight minutes to go. Not long. Too long. I stamped my feet, fidgety with nervous energy, hands curling and uncurling in my pocket, chilled to the core by the thought of what was to come. I didn't know what he looked like. I'd seen a picture, but how often do people use a photo that reveals the truth? Being beautiful, I didn't need a flattering image, but the picture I sent him was also a lie. My hair looked over bright in the sunshine, light lifting my features as I smiled to someone off-camera. In it I looked carefree. After, I regretted sending it, thinking I'd lured him to me under false pretences. Worried he'd be disappointed when I wasn't as easy-hearted as I'd appeared in the snap. This was one of the advantages with meeting in cyberspace; we could hide our neuroses.

I tried to relax; after all, he'd picked me. He said he'd had quite a choice, more replied to his advert than he would have anticipated. I looked into the dark sky and thought of all the others out in the world seeking the same thing. I wasn't alone in my desire.

Stop. I'm going too fast. There's another story to tell, before he arrives.

1

Others are coming to judge me. Professionals will come and demand that I tell them my story. Whatever they conclude, bound by conventional thought, by their own mediocre experience of love, my deed will outlive me. Time alone will prove what is right. They can't force this tale from me and I won't trust them. But I've chosen you. You will listen. You are my judge, the true arbiter. And we have time, yet, before the train pulls into the station.

My Internet name was Robin, like the bird, but also because it made me think of American cheerleaders with tanned tennis legs and blonde hair. Wholesome. When I was Robin my world sparkled new and I could do things differently. I could be someone else.

We didn't use our given names on the site. It was part of the unspoken deal. And anyway our parents named us. Our avatars, picked by us, revealed something truer. I liked his. He was Mr. Smith.

To me, Smith was beautifully anonymous—an Everyman. I didn't want the unique or standalone; I sought the mediocre, the average, the one lost in a crowd. I wanted the man who worked behind a desk, who microwaved cardboard meals, who rubbed the sore grooves down his nose, scored by his glasses. Mr. Mousy Hair, Mr. Nylon Shirts. Strange, that I sought the ordinary when I'm anything but. I've never met a man who didn't desire me, at least at first, but my own taste is modest.

Robin wanted safety. Predictability was more important than fun, and I quickly deleted adverts from men who smugly announced they had a GSOH. I like to laugh, but not on demand. I wasn't seeking a cabaret act.

His was a simple enough advert. He'd been a fan of Morrissey in his teens and I imagined a melancholic youth with floppy hair smoking dope. He said he was a Catholic and, however lapsed, the faith was in his blood. I suppose that attracted me, too, that tenuous link to my mother's religion.

Yes, others replied to his advert as well as me. Some men and several women. But I was his choice.

I had to hunt. I'd meet other men before Smith. After all, finding love is never easy. I was making a commitment for life, and these things can't be hurried. Also, I wasn't quite ready. If Smith had come to me before that time, I'd have let him slide through my fingers like sand.

I didn't respond to his advert straight away. I looked around first, visiting chat rooms and surfing the web. Staying silent, a wallflower. It's easy on a computer screen. Your entrance is only noticed when someone types:

Hello Robin! I see you've just joined us. Welcome.

If you stay silent long enough no one bothers you. After a page of conversation your arrival is history and people forget. I learned how relationships could be built by words. Biding my time. Browsing Facebook and Twitter, searching special sites, cruising in and out of chat rooms. I didn't know what I was waiting for until I found his advert:

MAN SEEKS BEAUTIFUL WOMAN FOR THE JOURNEY OF A LIFETIME: I WILL LIFT MINE EYES TO THE HILLS, FROM WHENCE COMETH MY HELP. WILL YOU HELP ME TO DIE?

I read it over and over, keeping it on my screen until I finally logged off. I needed time to think before I replied.

But I'm rushing again. Always my failing, that I head for the summit before charting the course. I must resist. It's important to start at the beginning. And doesn't every story begin with the mother?

My mother's name was Matilde Mariani. This is her story, too.

2

1977

Matilde walked slowly, scuffing her patent shoes on the pavement and hauling her school bag, letting it bang against her legs, marking the white kneesocks with dust. It was a sticky day and her blazer was tight across her chest. She undid the single button, took off the straw boater with her free hand. No one would be home when she arrived and she could be happy, but first she had to pass the row of shops. The boy who delivered the meat was loitering outside the butcher's, his bike thrown on the pavement. Behind him, through the window, animals hung in halves. She was careful to keep looking ahead, waiting for the jeer. "What, ain't yaw gonna talk to me now? Posh cow! Stuck up spic! Ain't I good enough for yaw, then gal?"

Letting the Norfolk drawl wash over her, she told herself she was used to this and, after all, it was only words. She kept walking, holding her breath against the iron stench of pig's blood in the air. The house felt empty. Her father mostly worked late; he had three factories now and didn't trust the managers so he was always on site, checking the fabrics and the orders, making sure no one was fiddling him. 'I will always be a foreigner to them', he said. 'I cannot expect loyalty.' Matilde's mother was better at fitting in, and belonged to many local groups ran by women with money who needed an occupation. She kept busy so that she did not have to endure the lonely house, but for Matty the hour between arriving home and her parents' return was when she found peace. She preferred to be alone.

She climbed the stairs to her room, shrugging off the blazer, and undid the top buttons on her shirt, still carrying the school bag and boater.

Her bedroom door was ajar. She knew she had closed it that morning. Her heart sunk: Papa was home after all.

Ruth Dugdall

He sat on her bed, a great walrus of a man with slackened jowls and eyes like beetles, green-black and shiny. Above him Karen Carpenter, her favourite singer, gave a sad, watery smile.

"You're late. Where've you been?"

She could hear it, the threat. She knew it was there, just under the surface. Karen's smile was hopeless. "Papa, I walked too slowly. I'm sorry."

"Don't lie to me. You've been with a boy again. Look at your shirt!" Her hand rose to cover her collarbone. "Come here." She did not move. "I said, come here." She walked forward, watching Karen's resigned smile so she didn't have to see her father's eyes. Knowing the beetles would crawl all over her flesh if she looked at him. "Closer." She could smell the alcohol on his breath. He spat words that pricked her with moisture, "You are a filthy slut. You are a disgrace to this family." He waited until she was crying, then struggled up from the bed and left the room.

Karen Carpenter was trying to smile, but her eyes remained sad and dark. It was Matty's fault, she was too pretty. She saw herself in the mirror and winced; hair too light. Not the brunette of the Mediterranean, but blonde. And green eyes, not blackened like her father's, but light green like fresh moss. Too striking. If she wasn't so pretty it wouldn't happen, that's what she believed. But how do you make yourself ugly if you're not? How can you still be beautiful when everything inside is ugly?

At school the other girls avoided her. Only the boy who worked at the butcher's showed interest. And Mr. Ferris, the Latin teacher. He spoke to her in a way that made her shiver and shrink back. She was afraid that he could see through her, to the truth. That she was a slut.

She was seventeen. Not an adult, but not a child either, so she knew what it meant when her period was late. There was always the pill to stop babies coming, but how could she get that? She was so young, and not even married. How could she admit her sin to a doctor? Instead Matilde, or Matty as she wanted to be called—at least in her head where she had friends who understood—tried to pretend it was not happening. It would not happen again. Mostly, she tried to ignore it and concentrate on books. All types of books, but especially those about people.

She did well in her studies. Even her mother said so. The previous year she had passed all her O levels, with high grades. So she stayed on at St. Alban's, with the other girls in straw hats who talked endlessly about boys when all she wanted to do was read. And learn. She was studying for A levels. Latin, of course. Papa insisted. It was a part of their heritage, he said, and anyway she was good at it. Mr. Ferris said it must be because of her Italian father, her knowledge of a romantic language, but he was wrong; her father almost never spoke his mother tongue. And music, another good thing for a lady to learn. But what she really wanted to study wasn't on the syllabus. Her choice would have been psychology. She read books that weren't in the school library, only in the big library in town, searching for answers. It was the closest she got to knowing why. She read Freud, his diagnosis for hysteria, and thought she understood. Hated him for naming it, for making it bigger than them, for putting it in every home. She felt sick, but couldn't stop reading about Dora K and she wondered if that is what she was, a hysteric, and if that was why she must keep her mouth shut. Why she must study.

And now, one year into her A levels, one year from the exams, she had stopped bleeding.

She'd felt sick since she woke, and the smell of incense was making it worse. In all of Matty's seventeen years she had only missed mass twice, once when she caught measles and once when her grandfather died and they had travelled to Italy. Other than those rare exceptions, the Mariani family sat in the same pew each Sunday and listened to Father Michael condemn the world.

The wooden pew was like a box that she just couldn't fit into and the effort of trying to sit so straight made her sweat. Her father's huge body was pressed against her right side, and he noticed her fidgeting. "Keep still!" he demanded, and the woman in front turned around. Her father nodded back apologetically. To Matty's left sat her mother, her contained shape as immobile as a sepulcher, staring at Father Michael as if he held the answer to all questions. Perfectly presented, Matty's mother was devout in her attention.

The priest's voice rose, loud and sonorous. The flames of the candles twitched, as if called by his certain proclamation, "Sin is a disease of the soul. And the only physician is Our Lord. And the only medicine is to repent. Do you repent?" he asked, "Do you?" It seemed to Matty that his eyes sought her out and she looked at her knees, overcome again by the wave of nausea that turned in her stomach like a tide. She clasped her hands together, seasick, tried to concentrate on the horizon, but could only kneel. She was forced to lower herself onto the pew cushion. The wool was red and scratchy under her naked knees. She couldn't pray.

Closing her eyes made the sickness worse so she concentrated on the effigy of the Virgin Mary. The irony struck her, as she suffered on her knees before the unmarried mother, bile in her throat.

"Our Father," intoned the congregation, "who art in heaven. Hallowed be thy name." Matty lurched forward, tried to resist, but as the congregation spoke of forgiving those who trespass against us, she knew she could fight it no longer and finally gave in to natural force, vomiting all over the polished floor.

Her mother thought it was food poisoning from the fish they had eaten the night before and Matty was excused from confession. She couldn't have told Father Michael the truth anyway. She knew about Mary, about Jesus' birth, and about things that are sinful. But in the books, the ones in the town library filed under health, the ones with pictures, she knew, too, that a baby could be removed, taken away, like a tumour that needed cutting out. Her mother once had a lump on her breast that was cut away, to make her well again. That was what Matty needed; she wanted the bad bit severed, but knew it was impossible. It was a sin. Even if a cure was possible, she would never recover. How could she when the sickness was within her? When it was her fault for being too pretty. Too lovely. She hated being lovely, but pregnant women weren't lovely. Maybe the baby would make her fat and ugly, too. Maybe it would keep her safe. She didn't know what to do, and there was no one to tell. The blood just never came, and she kept studying the books, and still she was woken too early, because she was too lovely, and all she thought of as she was forced onto her back, was the milk van in the street, glass on glass in the doorway. She rose above herself, tried not to look down, and wished she was fat and ugly and not there at all.

She was so small, Matty Mariani, that her clothes still fit even when the books said they shouldn't. And the rounding of her breasts was just assumed to be puberty by anybody who noticed, like Mr. Ferris, who failed to observe anything else. She walked around on her own, and the other girls called her weird or stuck-up, but mostly they didn't know what to make of her so they didn't try.

But Papa knew she wasn't sick because of the fish. Even though the change to her body was slight, he could tell.

He took her to a doctor. "I do not wish her mother to know. You understand: the shame would kill her."

The doctor nodded sagely at her father, then asked Matty to climb on the couch. It was a narrow couch, and a dark room. She hadn't been there before, the man was not her usual doctor, and her father had driven to a different town, out of the city. They may not even be in Norfolk.

She suspected that it was not the best practice in the area by the stained walls, the receptionist's bleached hair. Her father had already paid—she'd seen him remove his wallet and peel off notes. She heard him give a false name; he was ashamed, of course. Cheap doctor for a cheap whore.

The doctor lifted her shirt, her school one, and pulled down the waistband of her skirt. She looked away, to the wall that peeled paint like a snake shedding skin. At the end of the couch stood her father. Watching.

"You're a good way along." He pushed hard on her stomach, two fingers pressed into her flesh until she wanted to wriggle. She lay still and endured the examination. The doctor finally stopped prodding and said to Matty's father, "She's too far gone."

"She can't be," her father's voice was almost begging, his face red and the beetles blacker than ever. He tipped into anger so easily and she prayed the doctor wouldn't provoke him. "If it's a question of money . . ."

The doctor pulled down Matty's shirt and turned fully to her father. "It is not money that's the problem, sir. It's the law. And it would be dangerous to do it now. There could be complications. Your daughter could die."

Her father's face turned from pleading to fury. He grabbed her wrist, wrenched her from the couch as if he would dash the baby from her if he could. "You stupid girl. Why didn't you say something earlier? You could have had an abortion."

She shuddered to hear her father say the word. Abortion was a sin. But then, as Father Michael said, one sin made the way for another.

There was no choice. It was too late. My mother's fate was already sealed along with my own.

3

Lifting her head from the safety of her duvet cocoon Cate Austin blinked at the white-bright bedroom, her breath drifting like smoke on the cold air. Through the window she could see snow falling, heavy floating flakes bumping against the glass and landing on the ledge. Closing her eyes she could still see the brightness, and knew how cold and clean the world would seem outside, but it was an illusion. Just a few drops of rain, a slither of sun, and the ground would be slushy with ice and grit, the mud and grime winning yet again.

She checked the clock—it was still early—so she snuggled back under the duvet, feeling the warm skin of her daughter's leg. She hadn't heard Amelia join her in the night and never really minded even though she felt obliged to make some show of telling her to stay in her own bed. But Amelia was lovely, especially asleep when her long eyelashes brushed her pale skin, her face so peaceful and content. Cate cuddled her daughter gently, kissing her shoulder, but the girl didn't stir. A shard of anger pricked under her skin; Tim had brought Amelia home late last night. It wasn't fair, it left her exhausted the next day at school. But she also knew she couldn't complain too loudly because without Sally, Tim's girlfriend, Cate would have to find a childminder. She hated to feel gratitude to the woman who had stolen her husband, but there you have it. Life.

At the kitchen table, Amelia toyed with her Coco Pops while Cate gulped down some toast. Christmas cards were still blue-tacked to the cupboards and the forgotten advent calendar, its windows all open, was propped against the window. Amelia was rosy cheeked and sing-song voiced, quicker to shake off sleep than her mother.

"Mummy, am I going to Daddy's today?"

"Yes, poppet. Now hurry up and eat your cereal."

"And will Sally pick me up from school?"

"She will. Drink some juice, please."

"Will Father Christmas come again tonight?"

"No, Amelia. He only comes once a year. Thankfully."

"But it's still Christmas!"

"No, not really."

Cate followed Amelia's gaze to the Christmas tree in the lounge, now stripped of its chocolate baubles and shedding copious amounts of needles from its dead boughs. The needles would be around for months, with her crappy Hoover. She made a mental note to get an artificial tree next year.

"We'll take it down tonight."

"Awww! I like the tree."

Cate looked at her watch—it was time they weren't there. She began the daily search for her car keys—why did she never put them in the cupboard, where they should be?—when the telephone interrupted. Amelia abandoned her untouched cereal, running to pick it up.

"Hello? Daddy!"

Cate listened to her daughter's eager reactions watched her wide smile and wondered why Tim was calling so early.

"Mum—Daddy wants you!"

Not anymore, thought Cate dryly, as she took the outstretched receiver. "Yes?"

"Hi, Cate. Look, don't go getting het up, but Sally's really tired with the new baby, and it's probably best if Amelia doesn't come to stay this weekend."

In the pause of the moment Cate saw Amelia dig out the lost car keys from her doll's pram and jangle them like a musical instrument.

"And have you told her that?"

Tim cleared his throat. "I thought it'd be best coming from you. But don't make it sound like I don't want her, okay? Just do me a favour, and tell her you want to take her somewhere or something."

Cate was aware of her daughter listening. "Okay, Tim." Fucking Tim, letting Amelia down again. But he had a new family now, a new child; she could hear it squawking in the background.

"I'll call sometime over the weekend okay? Look, I've got to go."

The baby's crying intensified and she was about to ask how it was when the phone went dead.

"Morning, sunshine! How was Christmas?"

Cate swivelled her chair to face Paul Chatham, leaning against the door-jamb at the entrance to her office. He was wearing a red waistcoat and a novelty tie, no doubt presents from Santa.

"Not good. It was Tim's turn to have Amelia this year so I had a pre-packed Sunday roast for one with the Queen's speech and a side order of self-pity. Yours?"

"Wonderful, of course! Sam cooked a fabulous goose for Christmas day—terribly fattening, I'm afraid." He lifted the waistcoat and pinched his side, revealing a comfortable amount of flesh. "Now, this isn't just a social call, Cate. It's work, I'm afraid. One of the trials of accepting a manager's job in the community is allocation."

He showed her a bundle of papers which he had been hiding behind his back, waving them in the air with a flourish.

Cate kept her groan inside. "Not a new case, Paul. You know I'm snowed under as it is."

"Then another snowball won't hurt, will it? A month is all I need—it's a pre-sentence report, to be completed by January 27th. They've requested a psychiatric report."

"Oh good, he's a nutter."

"She, actually. Alice Mariani. And I'm not so sure she is. I'll be honest, Cate, if you don't take this case I don't know who else to give it to. It's a weird one."

"And you thought of me?" smiled Cate, sweetly. "Thanks."

"After the work you did with Rose Wilks, this has got your name written all over it."

Cate stilled and she felt her heart hammering in her ribcage, speeding just at the woman's name. "If you think I'm such an expert why won't you let me supervise Wilks' parole licence when she gets out?"

Paul sighed, leaning back against the door in an exaggerated show of impatience. "Cate, we have gone over this again and again. And she's not even out for another year."

"Which will fly by! I *know* her, Paul. I know what she's capable of! I could keep an eye on her . . ."

Paul raises his eyebrows. "I think the further away you stay from Rose Wilks the better. Now—about this new case . . ."

Cate shook her head slightly, relieved that her heart was now beating its usual rhythm, and focused back on Paul. "Okay. Tell me."

"She's in her thirties, an academic. Lectures at Essex College in English Literature."

"Not our usual punter, then."

"No. But then, neither is the case. She helped her lover to commit suicide. He left some note saying he wanted to die. The court didn't know what to do with her—he took a lethal drug overdose and had a heart attack. She didn't call the police until it was too late. Eventually she was convicted of assisted suicide."

"Like euthanasia—was he ill? Something terminal?"

Paul shrugged. "Doesn't say so, but then we haven't got the Crown Prosecution papers yet. He was only twenty-seven, some paper pusher."

"Sounds a sad story."

"You haven't heard the worst. Brace yourself. Before he died she ate some of his flesh."

"What do you mean?"

Paul, slid his hand into his trouser pocket and whistled. "Probably tastes like chicken."

"Oh please. Now I definitely don't want this case. How come it wasn't in the papers?"

"It was. Don't you watch the news?"

"Not if I can help it."

"Well, it was all over the press last summer."

Cate thought back. Last summer she'd been quite preoccupied with Rose Wilks and all the problems in the prison. No wonder she hadn't seen anything about this case.

"And another thing. Alice Mariani has attracted a lot of attention from one of those groups that campaign for legalised euthanasia. The Hemlock Society are supporting her—they've got some petition going, arguing that she shouldn't be charged with anything."

"Great, I'll be heckled in the courtroom."

"So, will you take it?"

Cate looked at Paul's expectant face, the thin file of papers in his hand. "No, Paul. I'm sorry. But I don't think I can. I've got reports coming out of my ears and I don't want to take on something like this. Give it to someone else, someone looking for a challenge. But leave me alone."

Paul skipped towards her, dropping the file on her desk, and tiptoed back to the doorway. "No can do, I'm afraid. I know you Cate—I need you on this one. Anyway, it'll be a piece of cake. Probably just some bizarre sex game that went wrong."

Famous last words, thought Cate, looking down at the file which has fallen open at a newspaper article. She reads the headline: *Victim enjoyed dying, claims Suffolk Cannibal.*

4

Cate grit her teeth to the endless shriek of violins playing in her ear, jumping as a hand appears on her shoulder. Paul.

"Coffee?"

She nodded, holding the earpiece away. "They've still got me on hold. Bloody psychiatrists—don't they know that listening to this drivel could drive someone mad?"

"Hang up."

"I would, but I want to speak to Dr. Gregg before I meet Alice Mariani this afternoon. I'd like to know if I need to take a bodyguard. If so, you're it."

"Me?" Paul backed away. "I'm far too busy! It's not like the prison, you know; I've actually got work to do."

He disappeared just in time to avoid the balled-up paper she threw at him, whistling his way down the corridor.

"And don't forget that coffee!" she called. It was the least he could do for stitching her up with this case.

"Ms. Austin? Sorry to have kept you. I'm putting you through now."

About bloody time.

"Dr. Charles Gregg speaking."

"Morning, Dr. Gregg. I'm Cate Austin, Probation Officer. We have a case in common. Alice Mariani."

He chuckled, "Robin to her friends."

"I understand you're going to be writing the psychiatric report. I was wondering if you've met her yet?"

"I have. Just yesterday, in fact. She lives in a very nice house. Georgian. Very well-appointed."

"Really?" Cate deadpans. Maybe Dr. Gregg had misheard and thought she was writing a report for *Homes & Interiors*. Or maybe he was just a snob.

Oblivious to her thoughts, he continued, "She's a lecturer at the local college. English literature—not a subject I ever got on with, but she spoke most animatedly about it. Almost made me want to read a novel."

"Did you make an initial assessment?" She tried to sound light, but was so tempted by sarcasm that she bit her pen nib.

There was a beat of silence and Cate imagined him fiddling with something on his desk, not really concentrating.

"Not yet. It was a brief meeting. I will start with the clinical investigation next time. It's always an advantage to get to know the patient first, build an understanding. But my initial view is that she presents as highly intelligent, if a bit cool. No signs of psychosis."

Cate started to write with the bitten pen. "So she's sane? We're not looking at a hospital order?"

"As I say, I need to see her again. One mustn't rush these things."

"What's your view on the nature of the case? I imagine you haven't come across many cannibals before?" she joked, tasting her own revulsion as she said the word.

"I think the eating of the flesh—and we are talking a very small amount—is not the defining feature of this case." It defines it for me, thought Cate. "Eating human flesh does not *ipso facto* define psychiatric disturbance—I believe she asserts that it was not her decision, but a request she complied with for the victim. It may be bizarre, but one cannot assume pathology. I think when you meet her you will feel more assured of that."

Cate was unconvinced—*Victim enjoyed dying, claims Suffolk Cannibal*— she wished she could get that line out of her head. "Okay, well I'd appreciate a call when you've completed your assessment."

Cate put down the receiver feeling that the conversation had been a waste of time. The only thing she'd learned was the period of Mariani's home. And she would be seeing it herself soon enough. But Dr. Gregg seemed to like Mariani; he didn't think she was mad. That must count for something.

"Coffee. As madam requested."

"Cheers, Paul." She stirred the drink with her pen, and took a sip. "Christ, how many sugars did you put in?"

"The usual. One."

"Must be my taste buds—maybe I'm coming down with something stress-related."

"If you're going to start moaning I'm going."

"Okay. Would you prefer gory assisted suicide details?"

"Hmm. Point taken. Maybe we'll just talk fashion—so, is faded navy in this season, or is that suit one your ex left behind? You're hardly going to get a boyfriend to play with going around like that, now are you?"

"You know what, Paul, I'd appreciate it if you'd fuck right off!"

"Say no more, sweetheart, I'm outa here. But at least do something with your hair."

Cate's car skidded on black ice, forcing her to pump the brake before she got it back under control. She'd underestimated the time it would take to travel from the probation office in the center of Ipswich, to Alice Mariani's home in Lavenham. She looked at the clock on the dashboard; she was already fifteen minutes late and the last sign told her she still had five miles to go. The miles took forever on winding icy roads, steep hedges obscured the view and daylight was fading. She daren't drive fast and kept both hands on the wheel, braced for another skid. It would be dark when she drove home and none of these roads had any lights. Plus, everything in life was more reliable than her Volkswagen, whatever the advert claimed.

Cate carefully turned a corner, passing a remote pub that was still advertising Xmas Lunch. The paintwork was dirty and the car park empty. Living in the sticks was only a dream if you had cash and a car, she thought as her headlights hit another dilapidated farmhouse.

Recently she'd worked with a young man whose girlfriend was pregnant. They had been offered a council property in Lavenham and turned it down. Cate had been surprised, thinking that this village, which she hadn't actually visited but knew to be attractive and wealthy, would be a great environment to raise a child. 'Yeah,' her client had said, 'But how would I get a job out there? Miles from anywhere, we'd be bored out of our brains. Besides, it's full of tourists.' Remembering his comment she smiled and hoped they were happy in the roughneck estate where they eventually moved. At least there would be no tourists there.

The tiny villages that she travelled through had their share of run-down properties with mouldy For Sale signs, cheek by jowl with a handful of chalky pink cottages, selling root vegetables on wooden crates by the road. Thank God for towns. Cate couldn't see the appeal of a low roof, of having to drive every time you wanted a pint of milk. Especially not in this weather. The last forecast had predicted snow.

Finally, a crested sign announced Historic Lavenham. Please Drive Carefully.

Cate pulled the Autoroute printout from her bag, holding it over the steering wheel as she drove. She had highlighted Church Street and saw that it was an extension of the main road she was on. She drove past The Swan, a large hotel featured in the local paper's food review. That would be a nice place to go sometime, she thought, knowing that she never would.

She squeezed into a gap behind a sporty car the colour of a ripe tomato and looked up at the house. Laburnham House was white and large, heavily framed with the bare overgrown plant that gave the house its name. Carefully maintained paintwork, gleaming windows.

Victim enjoyed dying, claims Suffolk Cannibal . . . The thought arrived again, and she wiped her palms on her trousers. Cate concentrated on arranging her face into its professional pose as she left the sanctuary of her car, her empty notepad held tight in her fist. She climbed the steps to the door she saw into the front room. A woman was standing, framed by the arch of the window.

5

The probation officer should be here by now. My story is about to begin. She's late and I can't abide poor timekeeping. There are always consequences to any action, of course; I know this. I anticipated the meetings, the interviews with those who will judge me. By whose authority? I'd like to ask, but I'll stay silent. My fate is in their hands. I must be alert to the game that's being played. When your power is limited, strategy is everything. I've been waiting for a long time for this to be at an end, but it can only finish when I've been sentenced. I just have to see through nineteen days and all of this will be over. But she is late, damn her.

Finally, a car. A car for a woman who doesn't care about such things, a run-around in dull green with a dent in the wing. She drives too close to my MG Midget. If she hits it, I'll sue.

Of course, that's a lie. There's more at stake here than scratched paint-work. As she steps out of the car I'm reassured; she matches her motor. I'd expected more presence from someone who holds my future in her hands, but it's a relief that she will be easy to manage. She's so average: brown hair, pale skin, a worn winter coat flapping over a navy suit with a white shirt. Predictable. Smith would have liked her simplicity. He was straightforward in his tastes, in all but his choice of me.

She looks up to where I'm standing at the window and I smile. I open the door and watch her reaction. I see my beauty is a surprise. I'm tall and blonde, and I often use this to my advantage. Had she been a man I would've chosen a skirt, but instead I wear trousers, my hair is pulled into a ponytail, sequined Moroccan slippers on my feet, my face subtly made up. We shake hands, hers is slightly damp. Her nametag matches the name on the letter, Cate Austin. I find abbreviated names so trite.

I lead her to the back of the house. It was once two rooms but I had it knocked through, choosing space. I've created a large kitchen and eating area with a pale leather sofa against the far wall. The floor is slate, and her low heels click as she walks. I direct her to an old pine table, the bench alongside. Fiery snapdragons dominate the table, yellow-red petals like sunset.

"Pretty flowers," she says. "And what a lovely vase." One hand reaches out to touch the handcrafted swirls of white and blue glass in a delicate funnel, beautiful and fragile. "Thank you. It was very expensive." She pulls her hand away but I lift it myself, holding it up so she can see the fine glass, the deep sea blue running through it. "It's my favourite possession," I tell her, "If it broke I know I'd never be able to replace it." Carefully, I place it back on the table positioned in front of glass doors, through which the daylight can be seen dying. It's a small garden full of terracotta pots and a wooden bench, on top of which the black cat grooms himself, oblivious to the weather. It's cold outside, bitter chill, but the cat won't come in. He's suspicious of strangers. Feeling himself observed he stops, paw still raised, and glances up, before dismissively returning to his ablutions.

Cate Austin is pulling a jotter from her bag. "Is it yours?" she asks, indicating the cat.

"By default. He belongs to a neighbour but she's often away, so he comes here for company. Would you like some tea?"

"Coffee, please. Black, one sugar."

"I don't have coffee. Been having a lot of headaches recently, so I've given it up. Gunpowder tea is the closest I've got."

"Thanks." I see her glance at the novel on the table, *The Collector* by John Fowles. I move the book away. "Do you read, Ms. Austin?"

"Not much. No time." Everybody's excuse. But we all have the same amount of time, don't we? The only difference is how we use it. "I suppose you must do a lot of reading in your job?" "It's one of the perks. Reading is classed as work in academia."

"How have the college taken your conviction?"

"University," I correct. "It's affiliated now." I fill the kettle, flick the switch hard. "I've been suspended from any contact with students. The authorities have allowed me to keep my office, and have agreed I may mark essays, but that's all. If I get a community penalty, they'll consider reinstating me. That's as far as they will commit."

"You're lucky they didn't sack you outright."

The cup in my hand clashes with the granite counter. "Lucky? Is that what you call it? I'm a first-rate academic, and they're not letting me have any student contact. It's ridiculous! As if I'm a threat to anyone." I feel heat bloom in my cheeks, and remember that it isn't wise to be so transparent. I have to turn away, back to the kettle. My face is distorted in the stainless steel. We say nothing more as the water boils. I fill the two cups.

At the table, seating myself opposite her, I say, "So, what do you want to know?"

"As much as you want to tell me. More, probably. I have to recommend a sentence to the judge. The courts aren't obliged to follow the proposal of a pre-sentence report, but they usually do."

"That must make you feel quite powerful." I push a cup and saucer across the table. "Mind, it's hot."

She sips her tea. "It makes me want to be sure I'm right."

"And do you always get it right?"

She doesn't answer. Instead she says, "Did your solicitor explain what a pre-sentence report is, Alice?" I notice she uses my name without asking. Impolite. "He did, Cate. But I'd still like to hear it from you."

"It's a report that can be requested by a judge after a conviction has been secured, and it's to help him, it usually is a man, decide on an appropriate sentence. My job is to make enquiries and assess the case so that I'm able to propose a suitable outcome."

"Suitable for whom?" I ask, taking a careful sip of my drink smelling the rising aroma of lemons.

"For everyone, hopefully. I have to consider what is commensurate with the crime. I look at what is usual for similar cases, and consider the victim, and his family . . ."

"There was no victim!"

At my outburst, her face nips into itself, her mouth tight. She doesn't believe me. Why is it so hard for her to understand? "It was a voluntary death. He was the one who sought me out. Don't you believe in the right to choose life or death?"

She speaks slowly. "In the eyes of the law, David Jenkins is a victim. You may feel that helping him to commit suicide was morally defensible, but it was illegal."

Are we not to question laws, which are made by people we elect? Who is to say that laws must always be obeyed? I don't say this. Not yet. I bite back the words I would have used in a different place and time. Instead I say, "And what is the usual sentence for a crime like this?"

She lifts her biro from the table, moving it between her fingers. "Well, this is not exactly a common crime, so 'usual sentence' doesn't really apply. Most cases of assisted suicide concern a partner, or other relative, helping a loved one who is terminally ill to die, as a release from suffering. Euthanasia, if you like. Since the 2009 laws on assisted suicide cases like that don't result in any prosecution."

"I shouldn't have been prosecuted either! You've just described the situation between Smith and myself . . ."

"Why do you call him that," she frowns at her jotter, reads her notes, "when his surname was Jenkins?"

"It was what he wanted me to call him—but you interrupted. We may not have been married, but we were in love. It was euthanasia. The term derives from the Latin. It means an easy death. And last June that is what I gave him, just by being with him when he overdosed."

"But he wasn't unwell," she clarifies. "That's what makes this case different. As well as the way he died. That's why you were prosecuted."

"He may not have been ill, but there are more reasons to wish to leave this earth than physical suffering. You must try to think more creatively, Ms. Austin." Her hand tightens on her pen. I've said too much but I can't stop. "You said there were other considerations in deciding a sentence. What might those be?"

"Well, your needs for one. It's routine to consider if specialist treatment or therapy is required as part of any sentence. If any issues are pertinent, such as alcohol or drug misuse, any past trauma that may require counselling, anger management, sex offender therapy, anything like that."

"Well, none of those apply." Surely she can see that? "I rarely drink and don't touch drugs. And I'm no sex offender." She remains maddeningly silent, watching me carefully.

"Any mental health needs will also be considered, in conjunction with the psychiatric assessment ordered by the court. It'll be completed by Dr. Gregg, who'll decide if you require treatment after he visits you. And if the judge feels you need a custodial sentence, his report may send you to a secure hospital rather than prison." My hand stills on my cup, the only warmth as my body turns cold. Prison? "It may be possible to consider a community order, which could include a variety of conditions. I'll go through my proposal with you before the sentence date, when the report is finished. But in order to write it, Alice, I need to ask you some questions."

How can she carry on as if she hasn't said that word? I can't go to prison. Something hot rises in my chest and I want to shout, 'How dare you suggest such a thing? I've done nothing wrong!'

"Alice?"

I fight my anger down. "More questions. I had enough of those from the police. And during the court hearing." I can't even pretend a smile now.

"I know that. I appreciate that you've said a lot already, but not to me. And I'm not here to interrogate you. You've already been convicted, and the fact that you pleaded guilty will go in your favour. The question now is how you should be sentenced. I want to know more about why David Jenkins killed himself in your home. How did it come to that? And I need to know more about you, Alice. Mariani's an unusual name."

"It's Italian." I stand, remove the cups and turn my back. "Is that where your parents are from?"

"No. They're Suffolk natives. But that's not who gave me my name. Their surname is Dunn. It was mine, too, until I turned sixteen."

"So you changed it?"

Is this what I have to do to be free? Purge my soul to a stranger? "That's right. Wouldn't you, with an ugly surname like that? I changed it to my mother's surname. My mother had a beautiful name. Matilde Mariani. Taking her name seemed important at the time. I was going through that predictable teenage thing of rejecting those who love you. I know it hurt my adoptive parents, even if they pretended to understand. Now I think it was irrelevant, what was I trying to prove? Changing my name wasn't going to change the past."

"But you say it was important to you at the time. Was it a search for identity?"

"Nothing so meaningful, I'm sure. I was barely more than a baby when I was adopted, just a child. It's so long ago, it feels unreal. It's like a story I made up."

I look into the garden, now in darkness. She nods, an acknowledgment that settles in the space between us.

As a lecturer I'm used to speaking to an audience, and I pull my shoulders back. I mustn't show my fear. "What do you want me to tell you?"

She thinks, looks at her notes. "Can I ask you about your adoption?"

"Is it relevant? What can my being adopted have to do with Smith's suicide?"

"Maybe nothing. Maybe everything."

"That's very cryptic. You're asking me to bare my soul on the basis of a possible connection?"

"Everything is connected," she says, evenly. "The difficult bit is working out how. An adoption is a major event. It must have been traumatic for you."

"Not really. I was so young. I was adopted by a couple who wanted me. As long as you're wanted, what difference can genetics make?"

Cate Austin leans back. She puts down her pen, and holds her hands in her lap. "I think we both know it isn't as simple as that. It seems to me, Alice, that you have a choice. We will have a handful of meetings, at the end of which I will file a report with the court. Now, I'm the one that writes that report but the content, the conclusion, is down to you. So you can talk to me, and I realise this will not be easy, but you must trust the criminal justice system to be a fair process, and in the end the sentence will be one that helps you." She pauses, takes a breath. "Or you can refuse to cooperate. That's your choice. But remember when I come to recommend a sentence you will have forced my hand. And I hate recommending prison, especially for a woman, Alice. I really do."

Neat anger prickles the back of my neck, and my hands are cold. She is threatening me. I look at the clock on the wall. "I'm afraid, Ms. Austin, that I'm expecting someone to arrive very shortly. If you'll excuse me, I need to start getting ready."

She twists her mouth, and her hands rise to the table, to her pen. She had hoped her little speech would have me opening up like a Russian doll. "This feels like a bad point to stop," she says, looking down at her jotter and I see a sentence, a question mark at the end. The tip of her biro draws a star next to it.

"What were you going to ask me?"

"I was going to ask about your situation now. If there's another man in your life?"

I can feel my head start to ache. I stretch my feet into my slippers, and stand. "I think I've said enough for our first meeting. I'd like you to leave now."

She hesitates, and then gathers her things. "Okay, Alice, I'll go. But I want you to think about what I've said. And I'd like to see you tomorrow. I want you to come to the probation office." As I show her the door all I can think is that I must avoid prison at any cost.

6

There are things that I will tell only you. You have chosen to listen, and in return I shall be honest. But I won't tell Cate Austin. If she knew that I have a lover, how could that benefit me? It will be our secret. My body is tourniquet tight, muscles quivering from work, the weight of my recent lover along my thigh and chest. My breath rapid while the evidence of lust spills from me onto the sofa. I luxuriate in the peace delivered only after orgasm. My thoughts, usually scratching tumbleweed, unravel and stretch flat. It's what sex can give, like no other fix.

My lover is not Smith, who arrived on a train. Smith is dead: he died last June. This is another lover, a friend from long ago, someone who has known me since I was a child. Lee always returns. It was a long absence this time, all last year while I was with Smith. But this evening, after Cate Austin had gone, Lee came back to me. A few days ago there was an airmail letter to explain; a holiday, back in the UK, only for a few weeks. I'm always grateful to see Lee. I stroke the shorn head, animal-soft, heavy on my shoulder. Before the heat has cooled between us Lee pulls away, and disappears up the stairs to piss in the toilet upstairs, the noise audible above my head. I remember why Smith came to me. We wanted to avoid this anti-climax and we succeeded. I don't move, refuse to let the spell be broken. I admire my body, one hand caressing my flat stomach. I'm a released trap, a catch undone. I'm all damp velvet and warm leather.

Then Lee appears, ridiculous in my tiny bathrobe, "Can I get you anything?"

"Water," I say, licking my dry lips. "And the packet of paracetamol from my bag." Even though I've given up coffee the headaches keep coming.

The pipes sing as the tap is turned and I hear humming from some faraway place. I'm still deep in my void.

Lee brings the water and I spill some on my chest as I take the heavy glass. I see those brown eyes, so recently heavy with lust, scan the discarded newspaper on the floor, wondering where I keep the remote control for the TV. If I were alone I would lie still for a long time, to keep the spell unbroken. There's only one sure way to hold the magic, maintain the high: death.

I have trouble sleeping, always have, so whilst my lover dreams in my bed I potter about the house in my dressing gown, silk sticking to my thigh, checking my collection of cacti, watching the misty dawning of light. It's cold, even for January, and there's frost sparkling on the tops of cars like glitter. When the dawn is fully broken and I've watched several neighbours de-ice their cars and drive off to work, I return to the bedroom. It's gone nine, but I no longer have anywhere to go. The only work I have to do at the university is to mark a pile of essays on Keats, written by first years. An undemanding task, so I can afford to go back to bed.

Lee breathes heavy with hidden visions and has overslept for the planned morning swim. I don't concern myself with this, it's not my business. I'm a lover, not a wife. I peel off my dressing gown like a shed skin and drop it to the floor, place my feet on Lee's ankles, my knees sliding behind the curve of legs, and allow the heat to warm me. The room smells of the morning after sex. A salty, unclean potion that tastes better fresh. Putting an arm over Lee, I match my breath, trick my body into relaxing and hope my mind will follow.

As I curl behind the sleeping body, feeling the force of life, I think: I won't tell Cate Austin your name. I'll keep you out of this. After all, this return is only for a brief time, and it can't make any difference. Lee is a friend, my best friend. Dependable and loyal. But never my true love, like Smith. This brief time is just a distraction, a respite. That's all it can be when the future is unknown.

I wait for sleep.

When we wake I find myself teasing Lee, as I've always done over the years. It's been so long since our last time together, so I reach, touch, need to be certain that the return is real. "Why do you have to have your hair so short?" I demand, feeling the dark bristles, the bony scalp underneath, "You're like a hedgehog."

"It's just a military cut, Alice. Not everyone has it so short, but I like it."

I like it too but don't say this. Lee moves around my kitchen, opens the fridge, and grabs a mug from the cupboard. "Make yourself at home, why don't you."

"You want a drink?"

"No." I wait until finally Lee sits down, eating a thickly buttered piece of toast. "So tell me about Germany."

"Why would you want to know about Germany?" Lee smirks at me and I think: it's true, I've never shown much interest before. But this posting is farther away, and for longer. Lee left just a year ago. Last January was also the time when I saw Smith's advert. As one lover abandoned me, another arrived. Fate works like that.

"So you aren't married, then?"

Lee swigs tea, then looks at me, a moment too long. "I think you and I both know that's not possible."

I feel blood in my cheeks, but carry on making light of the intensity in the moment, "Oh, I don't know. I'd have thought you could have found a nice Fraulein to keep you entertained. And I could see you being attracted to the German spirit. You always did like to be dominated." It's supposed to be a joke but Lee isn't smiling. I change the subject, "How long are you here for?"

"A few weeks. I've been building up a lot of leave. There was a month-long exercise recently, and they asked for volunteers. Most of the lads weren't interested, and those with families or wives didn't want to leave the base. But me, I'm easy. So I built up a fair bit of extra hours. I reckon I'll stay for three weeks, at least."

The tricky moment is gone, as Lee and I play this easy, teasing game as we always have. It's good for us to be together. Three weeks, though short, is more than enough time. In less than that I'll be sentenced. I can't think beyond that. If only I could tell Lee about the court case. If only I could be certain that Lee would understand. But I don't have faith. I don't believe that any love could forgive such an infidelity. So I'll keep quiet, and tell only you.

Later, I'll set off to visit Cate Austin at her office but for now I want to busy myself with other thoughts. Lee was always able to distract me, and I return to one of my favourite topics: "Do you still enjoy the military, then? All those rules, all that order?"

"Yes." There's a wicked twinkle in those brown eyes, "Being bossed around was something you taught me to enjoy."

"I never would have guessed it, though," I muse, not for the first time, "You going away, I mean. I always thought you'd just get a job around here. I never thought of you joining the RAF. I never even knew you wanted to fly."

"I don't fly. I fix things."

"You always did want to fix things."

Lee wants to fix me, so very much. So much it hurt sometimes. But I resist. You can't fix someone who doesn't want help.

Lee isn't like me, never was. Leaving school at sixteen was a thing I never even considered, but for Lee it was a given. The teachers never rated Lee as a success, but they were wrong. Taking a job as a lifeguard at the local swimming baths may not have been the most auspicious start, but joining the RAF two years later has led to the perfect career. A Survival Equipment Fitter may not sound very glamorous, mainly fixing punctures in life rafts and folding away parachutes correctly, but Lee saves lives. Fixing a life preserver stops a pilot drowning. Getting that parachute to open correctly is vital.

Lee always was methodical, always was a rescuer. If only I wanted to be saved.

7

Notes following interview with Alice Mariani. NB: I have requested the Crown Prosecution summary of evidence, which is yet to arrive. Alice was with David Jenkins when he took a fatal overdose. She pleaded guilty to Assisting Suicide, a crime that can attract up to fourteen years in prison. In interview, she shows no remorse for this act, principally because she believes it is a morally defensible decision as 'everyone has the right to choose to live or die.'

No indication that DJ was ill or in pain. No debts. So why did he want to die? Alice asserts that assisting with DJ's suicide was a victimless crime and that they were in love. She was adopted when she was four years old. Has this any significance??

Cate stopped typing. Alice said she was adopted by a couple who wanted her. Had they provided Alice with the love and stability she needed? Dorothy on reception rang through.

"Cate, your client's arrived."

"Thanks, Dot."

"She's a bit edgy, and she's attracting some unwelcome attention."

"I'll be right down."

*

The probation office is a ghastly place. Stale air and fag ends, even the plastic chairs are filthy. She had no right asking me to come here. Worse, a man in a baseball hat with rotten teeth keeps trying to talk to me.

Cate Austin appears at the internal entrance, and opens a gateway. I'm tempted to run away into the street, but instead I follow her through without touching the door frame. Who knows what germs linger here? When we reach her office I take the seat and try to compose myself after this assault on my senses. "Please may I have a glass of water?"

She hesitates and I gather from this that she isn't supposed to leave me in her office. I'm affronted that she has to think about it, as if I'm a criminal. Like that lowlife in the waiting room. Eventually, she goes and I'm alone in her room. There's a photo of a young girl on the desk, next to the computer. A pretty girl on a swing, legs in the air. How conventional. The computer screen is still on and I lean forward to read.

She returns quickly, and I have to move back into the chair, avoiding her assessing eye, and pretend to notice the photo on the desk for the first time.

"Is that your daughter?"

"Yes."

She takes her seat, touches the picture and moves it slightly away from my gaze.

"How old is she?" I've never been good at guessing the ages of children, it's not a skill that interests me.

She hesitates, "We're not here to talk about me, Alice."

I look again at the photo. The girl looks about the same age I was when my world shattered. Cate hands me the smeared glass of water, and turns to her computer. I note the slight dilation of her pupils as she realises what she left on the screen. Her notes of our meeting yesterday, which I've read. I'm a fast reader, all those essays I've marked over the years. She moves her mouse, and the screen blanks.

I sip water, still looking at the photo. Cate touches the frame again, turning the picture further out of my line of vision. "I'd like to ask about the degree to which you and David Jenkins planned his death. There was obviously a great deal of premeditation?"

I let there be a pause, and remember the choice she gave me when we last met. The option of talking to her, to avoid prison. But I don't want her victory to be so easy, and keep silent for a moment longer. Her eyes flicker with uncertainty. She doesn't yet know if I will talk.

I say eventually, "Yes. There was."

Glad of the drink, I lean back in the low chair, and Cate swivels so she faces me, but at an angle. The desk is against the wall so there is no barrier between us, except for any words that might get in the way. She lifts her pen to the paper. It's my prompt to begin. And I've made a decision. I decide I have no choice; I decide to talk, but in my own way, choosing my own place to begin.

Cate Austin asks too many questions, and I must be careful. Soon she'll ask about the cutting of flesh, the tasting. It's difficult to explain, easier for me to go further back, to another story. She needs to understand where I come from, why love is so fragile. I'll tell my story, and hope that she understands. My freedom depends on it.

I tell her this:

Although there was a lot to think about before Smith's death, I was concerned about my parents. I thought it must be possible to prepare them in some way, as carefully as the situation would allow. If I could speak with them, before the event, then it would surely help them cope when Smith was dead and I was in the media limelight.

It was April last year, just after Mother's Day but before Easter. I'd known Smith for two months. In just two more he would be dead.

I didn't want my parents discovering our conspiracy from some media headline. To find out from a newspaper article that their daughter had assisted a suicide would be horrible, and I hoped to ready them. I knew they would never understand the passion to which Smith and I aspired. The act we were planning would seize the perfect moment, the most exquisite high. Forever captured. My parents lived their ordinary lives without extreme emotion, in a space that had no warmth. No love was left, yet they remained, like two indifferent animals in the same cage. Had they never thought of escape? Had neither of them imagined an alternative?

My love affair with Smith would be beyond their comprehension. Just as I had always been. If they'd taken just the slightest nip of time to understand . . . but that was how they lived. Change is hard. And they lived their lives between emotions, in the safety of hearts stabilised by beta-blockers.

I chose a different way. What was happening between Smith and myself, our evolving symmetry, was more real than art, than books, than all I knew before he came to me. Smith was my answer. Our journey was just beginning but even then I was practical, pulled down by the weight of tedious detail. And one of these was the pressing issue of my parents' inevitable discovery. I had to pre-warn them.

They rarely occupied the same room and I was forced to speak with them separately. I started with my father. This was the interview I dreaded least. It was a Sunday, and we'd just eaten lunch. For as long as I can remember Dad has eaten meals on a tray in the front room, watching TV. After Mum cleared my plate away, I left the kitchen and went in to him. As I opened the door he looked up, a piece of greasy beef on his fork and a drop of gravy fell onto his shirt. I was glad I didn't eat meat. Sights like this had turned me vegetarian long before I developed a moral conscience.

"Alright, love? What's up?"

He assumed that I was there for a reason and I wondered if there had ever been a time when I'd have joined him just for his company, if it had ever been that easy between us. I doubted it.

He watched me as I seated myself in the chair across from his own, the beef still dangling in mid-air. On the TV men in crash helmets and fast cars swooped around a track, the room filled with the whine of revving exhausts.

My mouth was full of gravel. I didn't know where to begin. Facts don't change. What does alter is your perspective on them. What Smith and I were planning would sound, to others, bizarre, brutal. Even murderous. But I needed to portray it for what it was, not how others would interpret it. It was an act of love. Not that I was going to tell Dad that I would help Smith to die, of course. That would be going too far. But I needed to prepare him, somehow.

We both watched the cars screaming around the track, until I sensed Dad's eyes on me. He swallowed his last mouthful and, clattering his knife and fork on the plate indicating his meal was done, placed the tray on the floor for Mum to collect later, and swallowed again. "Is everything alright at work, Alice?"

Work? It was so many miles from my thoughts that the word jolted me. "Fine. Why do you ask?"

"You just seem a bit distracted." He was looking back at the screen, but he fingered the remote control, nudging down the volume a tad.

"I guess I am. But not about work. I've met someone."

"Oh. A man?"

Well what did he think? "Yes, Dad. A man."

He made a sound as if the beef was still caught in his throat. "Serious, is it?" He was staring at the screen as if that would answer him and I wanted to grab the control and throw it at his head.

"Yes, Dad, I think so. He's very special."

"Blimey! Will you look at that . . ." A red Ferrari had crashed into a crowd barrier, sending spectators dashing for safety.

"The thing is, it's not like a normal relationship. We don't plan for the future . . . Marriage, children, it's not like that . . ."

The driver was being dragged from his smashed-up car, a hand to his crash helmet, as if that was what hurt. Dad looked away from the injured man. "Don't you want kids, then? Does your mother know?"

"It's not that I don't want children, but we don't have the luxury of time. You see, he's dying . . ."

"Dying!" His jaw dropped, exposing his stained lower teeth. Then his eyes widened, "He's not got AIDS, has he?"

"No, Dad. God, you always think of things like that."

"Well, how do you know these days? They don't wear a sign, you know."

"It's not AIDS. But it is terminal." I watched him cave back into his worn armchair, a pained look on his face as if it was him that had crashed through the barrier.

"Well, that's a bit of a mess, isn't it? Finally meeting a bloke and he's sick. Cancer, is it?"

I hadn't mentioned a specific disease but I didn't contradict him. It was easier for him to assume illness. It would make death more acceptable.

"Will we get to meet him?"

I shook my head. "I think it's best you don't. Under the circumstances."

"No point, I suppose. Well, it's a shame, but there's plenty more fish in the sea, love. I'm sorry, though. You've never had any luck when it came to blokes, have you?" He pressed the remote control, drowning out his own words.

We watched as the injured driver was strapped to a stretcher by paramedics, and managed to give the camera a thumbs up. "He was lucky," said Dad.

Mum had finished washing up and was bleaching the worktops. The kitchen smelled like a swimming pool. When I stepped towards her she held up a hand. "Don't come in, Alice. I've just mopped the floor." Her feet were in plastic bags, the type you see in operating theatres, blue with elastic around the ankle like over-sized bootees.

"Mum, can we talk?"

"Hmm? Of course, love. Can you ask your father if he wants a cup of tea?"

I watched as she wiped the kettle, her face stretched in the chrome as she filled it too full, and then reached for her large teapot. There was always too much tea.

I returned from the lounge with Dad's tray. "He said yes please," I said, but she had already poured him a cup which, clattering in its china saucer, she carried through to him. The habitual order of daily living. Why did she always ask if he wanted tea, when he never refused? I shuddered, grateful that I would never be caught up in this Groundhog Day. I heard Dad say, 'Ta' and the lounge door being pulled to. The plastic bootees crunched back toward me. I braced myself.

"Sugar?" I hadn't taken sugar in my drinks since I was a teenager. She waited for my reply, her fingers lighting on a spoon propped in a mountain of white crystals. I shook my head, taking the cup and raising it to my lips, the strong tannins of Co-op's own label coating my mouth. Mum was still in the kitchen, walking on water, while I perched on the stool by the door. The tacky stool made the small square of Formica a 'breakfast bar' and it was where my mother took all her meals. She was squelching around in her blue bootees, wiping away crumbs that I couldn't see, her own tea untouched.

"How old were you when you first met Dad?" I asked, as a way to introduce the subject.

"Nineteen. It was a friend's party and he came right over, asked me if I wanted to go to the Locarno with him. I liked dancing then. We both did. I never understand why you don't go dancing. You wouldn't be able to stop me, if I was still young." She shuffled in her plastic shoes, a weary smile on her face, then looked at me in reproach, as if it was me who had aged her. Would it have been different if they'd had their own child, flesh from their flesh? Perhaps many children, three, four . . . I wondered then, not for the first time, if my separate genetic identity caused the gulf. Or do all children become strangers to their parents?

"As it happens, I did go to a dance last week. In the village hall." I didn't tell her that I hadn't actually danced, that I'd left early to visit the allotment because Smith had a test for me.

"Really?" She was suspicious, "How come?"

"I've got a new boyfriend, Mum." I was surprised at how proud I sounded. I don't know what made me use such a twee expression, boyfriend, like I was a teenager, giving in to my mother's language.

Her smile came quickly, falling on me like the sun. "Oh, Alice, have you? Someone nice?"

Another inane question. I bit away the temptation of sarcasm. "Yes."

"Well, what does he do?"

"He's an actuary."

"A what-ary?"

"Actuary. He works out statistics for an insurance firm in London."

"Insurance, eh? That'll come in handy. And is he nice looking?"

"Average, I guess." Mum looked disappointed. "But I think he's lovely." I felt myself blush, and Mum padded over, the floor squeaking beneath her plastic shoe-covers. She put her hand over mine; it was dry and rough.

"And is it serious?"

"Yes. Very." It was no lie.

"So, when do we get to meet him?"

"The thing is Mum, I'm not sure you should. You see, he's not very well." I thought of my conversation with Dad, of his assumption of disease. "He's got cancer."

"Cancer? Oh, Alice. Where?"

I hadn't anticipated that and panicked. "The stomach. There's nothing that can be done. He hasn't got much longer." Mum reached up to envelop me in her arms, and I was smothered by Lily of the Valley. My chin rested down on her shoulder, my face itchy on the lemon wool of her jumper.

"How long has he got?" Mum sounded like she was crying, but I couldn't see her face. I thought about Smith, about how far we had already come. How far we still had to go.

"Not long."

Cate Austin looks up from her notepad, "So you prepared your parents by telling them David was terminally ill with cancer. It would still be a terrible shock for them to discover your involvement in his death."

"Ms. Austin, I'm beginning to feel a bit unwell." I can feel a numbing sensation above my brow which tells me the headache is coming, the dizziness already making me unsteady. It's gone five o'clock, and I'm tired. Tired of my own voice, my own memories.

She reluctantly closes her notepad and reaches for her diary. "I think we should have another meeting on Monday morning, as the court hearing is less than two weeks away. Can you come here again?"

I shudder. "I've a better idea. Why don't you meet me at the university? They've allowed me to keep my office and if you come early I could show you something of interest."

"Oh?" She looks at me expectantly.

"You're interested in getting to know me, and I think much of what you wish to know would be revealed if you saw me lecture."

She frowns. "I thought you'd been suspended from teaching?"

"And indeed I have. But some lectures are recorded for assessment purposes. I'd like to show you a recording of a lecture I give each year, for the English Literature students. It's an introduction to Keats, and I think it will help you to understand what happened between myself and Smith."

"I'm sure it would go over my head. Romantic poetry was never something I studied."

"Don't worry, Ms. Austin. I won't be testing you on it afterwards."

We look at each other, acknowledging that the real test is far subtler. Cate turns to a fresh sheet in her pad and writes down the directions to the lecture hall, then leads me back to the waiting room, now empty but still smelling of fags and booze. I sniff the stale air, stumbling slightly as the dizziness intensifies. I'm not well.

"You're wrong, you know."

"About what?"

"What was typed on the computer screen. About it being significant that I was adopted. You're way off the mark, you can do better than that." I turn and walk out of the waiting room, into the car park, knowing she is staring after me.

8

1977

Matty knew she could never tell anyone her secret, especially not her mother. It was so much easier to keep silent. Far too easy in a large house where company could always be avoided. Though not in the early morning. During the day she was at school, and then she was in her bedroom studying until tea time. Her mother was never at home doing things that other women seemed to do, not like the smiley women on TV ads who cooked and cleaned and cooed over children. Matty's mother had 'help' with those kind of things. Whatever it was that demanded her time, the calls and visits and charity galas, it was never Matty. And her father worked hard, came home late, so dinner was eaten in silence, her mother reading newsletters or her diary, and Matty staring down at her plate. It was easy to be silent when no one spoke to you.

The body is not the same as the mouth. It has a language of its own, and even though Matty's had conspired with her for seven months, it wanted its say. The school broke the silence. Mr. Ferris had been keeping a watchful eye on Matty's growing breasts and he spoke to the Head of Department, who passed it on to the Head of Year who decided not to speak to Matty herself but to write to her mother, a formal invitation to come up to the school for a meeting the next day. The letter was amongst the invites and minutes of rotary meetings and her mother read it, threw it aside and demanded, "Why do they want to see me, Matilde? As if I haven't got enough to do." Matty prayed her mother wouldn't have time, that she would be too busy to go. She knew the meeting could only be about one thing. She'd seen Miss Russell, the PE teacher, watching her in the showers. Even when she was dressed, Matty's skirt was too tight. Mr. Ferris had been watching her too, and last week she saw Miss Russell talking with him in the playground, glancing her way. Her sin was showing.

The following evening Matty arrived home from school and waited in her bedroom, knowing her mother would even then be learning her secret. Matty tried to read but going over the same sentence again and again, tense for the onslaught that would surely come when her mother walked through the door. She dreaded the key in the door, her mother's shrill voice calling up the stairs.

It never happened.

Matty discovered that her mother was adept at silence and hidden secrets, and dinner was served at usual. Her father had already called to say he would be late, so mother and daughter sat together, although Matty had no appetite.

Her mother's expression was the same as always, a formal mask of biscuit and petal, just as she held her body in a stiff control. She wondered how her mother learned to keep so still, to hold a secret so firmly inside. Her mother was chairing their dinner, managing the agenda, like so much charity business. "Well," she said, after the soup, calmly cutting into her chicken, "you've certainly got us in a predicament. We need to think of how we set about rectifying this, Matilde. I don't suppose you've been to a doctor?"

Her mother clipped the words with her cultivated accent, hiding her immigrant heritage, punctuating her received English with the click of steel handles in the vegetable dish. Matty could not say that her father had taken her to an abortion clinic but it had been too late, "No."

"Then that must be our first step. Do you know when it's due?" Her voice was flat but severe like a conversation in the wind. She did not look at her daughter but her mouth chewed quickly, a swallow, some wine, and so on. On her plate was the dead chicken, its flesh stripped away revealing white bone.

Matty knew when she had stopped bleeding. It was seven months ago. Her voice was so low that her mother had to look up to catch the words. "I think I have three months left."

"You stupid girl. How could you leave it so long?" She took more wine, pushed her plate away. Her mouth was wet, and she dabbed at moisture, folded the napkin. "You'll have to go away for a while. I have heard of a place for teenage girls. When you return everything will be as good as new."

"What will?" Her life? The baby?

Mrs. Mariani raised a carefully pencilled eyebrow, a warning. She had finished her meal, and wanted the conversation ended too. "The child will go to people who can care for it. You will finish your studies."

The food she hasn't eaten caught in Matty's throat, or the water did. Or something else. Her heart maybe. She hadn't thought of giving the baby away. But of course, there was no choice. She bowed her head and tried to swallow.

"Oh for God's sake!" her mother shouted, "Don't pull that face. Don't think this is easy for me, you know." She breathed out, composed herself. "Now you've made me shout. I hate shouting."

She rose from the table, leaving Matty alone with her tears.

The doctor's hands were cold. He pressed low on Matty's abdomen and high, under her breastbone. She felt the paper wrinkle up under her legs, under her back. The light above her head was a fluorescent bulb, it hurt her eyes, but she was afraid to close them. The pressure he applied was firm and she prayed she wouldn't wet herself as his hands moved down to where her stomach was hard and round. He looked at her, just once, as if checking something in her eyes, and then pulled back the curtain, speaking to her mother, who was seated on the other side of the room, clutching a patent leather handbag. Mrs. Mariani held a handkerchief to her lips as if she were about to retch.

"She's about thirty-three weeks pregnant. We'll take some blood, and it would be helpful to have a sample of urine."

"What for?" Mrs. Mariani's lips pursed together in distaste. "We need to check your daughter's protein and iron levels and her blood pressure. Several routine tests are outstanding. Since she's so far along I'd like her to see our midwife straight away." "How do we arrange to get rid of it?" asked her mother firmly, the hanky hovering by her chin.

The doctor frowned. "It's far too late for that, Mrs. Mariani. The baby is viable."

"I mean adoption! Whom do we speak to about having it adopted?"

The doctor glanced at Matty with a look of pity and resignation. He cleared his throat and said, "Social Services can organise everything. I'll ask the midwife to make the initial contact." Finally, turning fully to Matty this time, he said, "Does the father know about the pregnancy?"

"He," said her mother, with venom, "knew before I did."

It was the kindness that undid her.

It was being alone in that darkened room with the midwife who apologised for the sharp needle as she took Matty's blood, "That's the horrible bit out of the way. Now, let's have you up on the couch. That's it."

She pressed so gently on the firm bump, feeling for the back, the kicking feet, the smooth head of the baby in her stomach. "It's a lovely size," she said, smiling. It was the first time anyone had smiled at her in her pregnant state. Her father, her mother, two doctors, Mr. Ferris, had all frowned. But the midwife was smiling. She thought it was something to be happy about.

"I'm not keeping it," Matty said, "I'm not allowed." The midwife, still pressing on her stomach, still connecting with Matty, stopped smiling.

"Who won't allow you?"

"My parents." And as Matty said it she felt a pain in her chest, an ache.

The midwife removed her hands. She gently pulled Matty's top down, handed her a fresh tissue to wipe her eyes, which Matty hadn't even realised she needed.

"It's your baby," she said, "and lots of girls have babies at your age. It wouldn't be easy, but it can be done." But Matty knew this was not true. There was only one way for a girl like her and that was her parents' way. To give up her baby.

"It's your choice, Matilde. You're not a child anymore."

"Tell me how," she said to the kind midwife. "Tell me how to keep it."

Matty's newborn baby lay silent beyond the painted bars, the fleece blanket moving up and down to the rolling rhythm of sleep. Matty retrieved her watch from the changing table: it was nine o'clock. How had that happened? Only a minute ago it had been the middle of the night. She looked at the empty feeding bottle on the cabinet and tried to work out when the baby would be hungry again and if it was worth trying to get some more sleep. Her fear of another interrupted dream stopped her from lying back down. She mentally raced through the options for this precious peace: bath, shower, read, food. Remembering that she hadn't had a proper wash for two days, she opted for a bath, grabbed her towel from the top of the radiator and padded quickly to the communal bathroom down the hall, her bare feet pitter-pattering on the cheap, hard carpet.

Relieved to find the room was empty, Matty locked the door behind her and turned the hot tap on full. The old enamel bath was big but the water filled it quickly. Before it was full she had stripped off, her grubby clothes piled on the toilet seat. She had forgotten her soap, but there was a communal bar on the sink, flat and white with a long black hair stuck to it. She threw the soap in the bath and then joined it. Her pale loose skin mottled, lobster-like, in the too-hot water. She welcomed the discomfort.

Later, dressed only in a dressing gown and still damp, Matty reentered the bedroom and saw that the baby had not moved. A few more moments of peace to enjoy. She carefully slid into the bed and prayed for the silence to last.

So lost was she in her thoughts, so dizzy with the heat from her bath, that it took a few seconds before she registered that the knocking on the door was for her. Afraid of the baby waking, she sat up and reached for the door in one movement to stop the intruder from knocking again.

Filling the narrow doorway, bent over as if she had been listening at the keyhole, was the rotund social worker, her ruddy face poised in an expectant question with a smile as phony as a waitress. She mock whispered, "is Baby asleep?" although her eyes had already fixed on the cot, so Matty did not reply. She'd forgotten that this meeting was today.

Seeing the young mother's confusion, the social worker looked apologetic although her tone did not match. "I'm a bit early, but I have some news. Shall we go downstairs and leave Baby to sleep? Come on, get dressed!"

Matty removed her dressing gown, pulled on a loose skirt and a knitted jumper that would at least be warm. She didn't think to brush her hair and there was no mirror in the room to remind her.

Downstairs, the social worker was squashed into an institutional winged armchair. Matty balanced on the edge of the opposite chair, dismayed when her visitor pulled her chair nearer, at right angles, so that she was trapped in a corner. Matty registered the pseudosmile, pitying but professional. Then the inevitable textbook question: "And how are you feeling?" Matty noticed the way she said "feeling," full of sympathy, but ignored the invitation to confide. She shrugged.

"And how is the little one?" The question demanded an answer and she searched for the right response.

"We had a bad night." In return, the empathetic angled head and infuriating smile. Fortunately the small talk soon ended, and the older woman leaned forward, choosing a soft, even tone, likely from the selection she was taught whilst in training.

"I came straight here as I thought you'd like to know that we have had a referral from the adoption team. They've approved a couple who sound ideal. Would you like me to tell you about them?"

Stunned from sleep exhaustion and hunger, Matty tried to grasp what was being said, her brain a hollow vacuum in which the inert words reverberated but made no impact.

"They're in their thirties. They live in the north, no children. Medical problems, I'm afraid: she's had five miscarriages. He's a manager at a power plant. Very well paid! She works as a nursing assistant, but would be at home full-time after the adoption. A very nice couple, they've been married for six years, and they have a lovely home with a garden. Shall I say more or is that enough?"

Matty tried to interpret what she'd been told. Was she supposed to make a decision on these few bald facts? Surely there was only one question: Will they love my daughter? She raised her fingers to her tired eyes and rubbed.

"I know you're feeling vulnerable, but that's to be expected. I just wanted you to know that we are ready to proceed."

Silence reigned, heavy and tangible, and Matty was too tired to think. The thick atmosphere was disturbed by one swift bang on the door and then a hostel worker bustled in, invading the space with her loud singsong voice. "Your baby's crying. I'll go."

The worker was almost out of the door before Matty stopped her, hot emotion rising from nowhere at the woman's presumption. "No. I'll go." Matty launched herself from the chair, pushed past the social worker, past the hostel worker, and up the stairs.

As she climbed she heard the cries of her newborn. Opening the door the cries were louder than ever, until she reached into the cot and picked the baby up. The crying stopped as if a switch had been flicked and the child snuffled its dry tears into Matty's jumper, nuzzling for the milk it could smell.

The prospect of returning downstairs and sterilising a bottle in a saucepan, facing the social worker, was impossible. Matty was desperately tired and her breasts hurt. Two damp patches on her top announced that her milk had not yet dried up. Sitting down, she experimentally raised her top and lowered her bra. Though unpractised, the baby knew instinctively what to do, like any animal trying to feed from its mother. Matty watched its mouth circle and miss. Eventually, uncertainly, she guided it. After some seconds she felt a jolt as the baby latched on, and within seconds her baby was lapping up the warm, sweet fluid for which she had been crying.

Holding her, watching her, Matty thought of the childless couple who would give her daughter a home. She knew nothing about them, but had no doubt that they would love her child. Her daughter who still had no name. Watching her baby's face, eyes closed in concentration, tiny hands curled, she wondered if she was capable of being a good mother. Not knowing the answer she bent her head down, smelt the soft scent of new life and, for the first time since she was born, gave her little girl a kiss.

Matty Mariani finally decided on a name for her daughter. She called me Alice.

9

"I want it all off," Cate said to the face in the mirror. The hairdresser made a non-committal motion and lifted the shiny scissors from a pouch around her waist, chewing vigorously on gum.

"You sure?"

"Yes," said Cate, as the blade cut, hair falling like autumn leaves. She closed her eyes and smelt mint.

Amelia loved going to the hairdressers and buzzed around the teenage staff, filling cups at the water cooler and held the swishy horsehair brushes to her face.

"It's so soft, Mummy."

The hairdresser laughed, still snipping, as Cate looked down at the magazine trying to finish an article on women who used male prostitutes. Behind her Amelia was chatting to another customer, an elderly woman who asked Amelia how old she was and commented on her pretty nails. Cate caught sight of her own nails. She should have put some paint on them when she did her daughter's—since when did a four-year-old get pampered more than her mother? Since forever, probably, she thought, listening to Amelia singing a song to her admiring audience.

The snipping continued around her ears, interrupted with occasional demands to look down. She flicked through the magazine, the litany of sex and glamour and interchangeable skinny bodies and perfect pouts.

When Cate felt the swishy brushy on her neck she folded the magazine and looked in the mirror. The hairdresser was gazing proudly at the reflection and Amelia's new friend had also stopped to see.

"You've got great features," said the hairdresser with expert knowledge, touching the tips with styling wax, "you suit short hair. You should never grow it long—just look at what it does for you."

The hair was brutally short over her ears, tapered into jags at the nape of her skull. Her eyes looked large, exposed by the short wispy fringe, which barely touched her brows. She hardly recognised herself.

They left the hairdressers on a mission. Cate had put it off as long as she could, but Tim's daughter was now two weeks old. She had to go through the motions of civility, even if it was a charade. For Amelia's sake. After all, the new baby was her step-sister.

When he opened the door Tim's mouth fell slack, and Cate's hand went instinctively to her hair, feeling self-conscious. He ushered them into the lounge with reverential silence, motioning to the baby sleeping in a Moses basket be-decked with pink gingham. Cate hadn't been in the lounge before, choosing to collect or drop Amelia off at the front door without crossing the threshold, and she looked around with curiosity. The room was literally swamped with flowers, every surface had a Congratulations card, and a silver balloon announcing *It's a Girl!* bounced on the ceiling.

Sally, Cate was secretly pleased to see, looked on the brink of physical exhaustion. The fatigue of the weary explorer, back from some gruelling expedition; Sally's hair was having a bad day, and she was wearing a shapeless smock. Cate handed Amelia the present and card, which she rushed over to Sally, crawling onto her lap and insisted on opening herself. Sally kissed Amelia then, remembering Cate, blushed before gaping at Cate's changed hairstyle. "How are you, Cate?"

"Fine, ta."

Minimal words. Sally started sleeping with Tim when he was still living with Cate, Amelia was just six weeks old when he left them. How, Cate would love to ask, would you feel if he left you in four weeks time? Abandoned you with a screaming baby, leaking breasts and a sagging stomach just when you most needed to be loved and cared for? It hadn't been the best of times for Tim to choose. She hoped Sally felt ashamed though she doubted it. If she had any conscience at all she wouldn't have slept with another woman's bloke.

Thank God Amelia was oblivious to all of this. Cate didn't want to poison her daughter and did her best to hide her feelings. Above all, Amelia came first. It was only after they'd left that Cate realised she'd forgotten to ask the baby's name.

10

You, who have chosen to listen, will understand this: I've set up the TV in the darkened lecture theatre, and Cate and I sit, side by side, on the front bench. I press play and the screen blinks to life. On it, I'm facing a room full of students.

"Keats was no stranger to death," I announce as the camera pans the whispering, jostling room. They become still and listen. "He cared for his mother when he was only a child and as a youth saw his brother, Tom, fight a long and losing battle with tuberculosis. These experiences were fundamental to his writing. His brother was a young man, in his prime. To Keats, who loved Tom dearly, his death was a loss to the whole world. Young and bright and beautiful. But the grieving Keats had a choice: to rail against God in anger and fury at the injustice of early death, or to transform, to reevaluate, that experience into a blessing. This reaction is not peculiar to artists. We all do it. Take a look in any churchyard at a child's grave and the stone will invariably tell us that the dead baby was too good for this world, an angel. Death of the old or infirm is expected, a normal rite of passage for us all. But the death of a child, or of a young man, is a terrible happening. An error in the natural order of things. It threatens our understanding of life, of death, of God. This is what happened to Keats. The tragedy of his brother's death endowed his work with genius. Keats himself only lived until his twenty sixth year." The camera pans to the front row where, to the left of the screen, an overseas student takes notes with professional speed.

I enjoy watching my performance, conscious of Cate at my side, also intent on listening to this erudite, articulate person on the screen. My onscreen image is beautiful, slim, clever. To Cate Austin, as to the students sitting enthralled, it must appear as if I have it all.

"As Keats said," I conclude, projecting to the camera, "now more than ever seems rich to die. To cease upon the midnight with no pain. A perfect death is a way to cheat the dulling, dumbing effect of time. To die at the height of love is the only way to preserve its purity."

My voice is louder as I say this, cracked with emotion. I look sideways, wondering if Cate has noticed this.

On the screen there is a moment's stillness before the students move and chatter, gathering their belongings as they leave the hall. A few of them slow up, milling around the lectern as if to ask me something but I ignore them, intent on collecting my papers, and eventually they drift away. The show is over.

I stand and switch the tape off, turn the lights on.

Cate remains in her seat, "That was quite something."

As we are making our way out we both realise that we are not alone. There is the sound of snoring and we see a slumped figure a few rows behind us. "Alex?" I say loudly. He must have been here the whole time.

His head lolls up, revealing the whites of his eyes, red marks on his cheeks from where his knuckles have pressed. He's not just asleep, he's intoxicated.

"God knows how he's made it into the second year." I mutter, glancing at Cate, who is studying him closely.

His eyes are dilated and his lips cracked.

"Alex is always like this," I tell her, "apart from when he's hyped and then he won't shut up. I gather from the polarisation in his moods that he varies his drug of choice."

"Can't he get help? Don't you have drug counsellors at the college?" Alex is in a bad way, trying to focus and swaying in his seat.

"Help is available if he wants it, but he doesn't. He'll never pass this year; he'll drop out. No degree ceremony for him. Come on, we can't do anything." I'm already walking towards the exit when I hear him say, "Bitch!" Cate stops, no doubt expecting me to rebuke him. "Let's go." I say, turning to leave, but she is slow and before we have exited the hall he cries out, "You murdering bitch." In the corridor I walk ahead, Cate catching up behind me.

"Do you often get jeered like that? Why didn't you challenge him?"

I don't turn, just quicken my pace. "Come on, Ms. Austin. I only have half an hour to spare before I must get on with marking essays."

My office is a good size, flanked by pristine white shelves, rows of books placed together aesthetically. Orange penguins, shelves of dark older novels, paperbacks in reds and pinks and blues. Green books are fewer, a fact you wouldn't know if you catalogued your collection by author or subject, but my collection is not conventionally arranged. It is a piece of art.

Cate stares, a viewer in a gallery. "How do you find the one you're looking for?"

"I close my eyes, I picture the cover."

Cate sits in the plastic chair used by students before my ridiculous suspension. Her suit is buttoned and it pulls tight across her chest. "I know nothing about Keats, but does his work really mean all that, or is that what you feel? Is that what you think about time? That it has a dulling, dumbing effect on love?"

My own chair is brown leather, an angled back. It leans with me, away from her. "I think it's a matter of fact that time is the murderer of love and beauty. A perfect death, especially a young death, is like a fly trapped in amber. It is beyond time, beyond decay. Like the revellers depicted on Keats' *Grecian Urn,* the deceased will never age. Only death, or art, can cheat time."

"But what about love that lasts forever, couples who are devoted to each other in their eighties, nineties? Isn't that a way of cheating time, too?"

The heating is on high and she looks hot, but doesn't remove her jacket. I pour two glasses of water from the jug and hand one over. "Maybe. But time still ravages beauty. And it is rather a risk to think love can be sustained. In my experience it doesn't last."

She doesn't disagree. She looks beyond this room, out of the large window, to where students will be walking briskly across the cold square. I don't look, I know what's there and it bores me. I pull her attention back. "All of this means nothing to those students. They're still young enough to feel immortal—they know nothing of death."

"That's a bit patronising, just because they're young doesn't mean they haven't experienced grief."

"Even if death has taken someone close to them it will seem remote. Pleasure and sin are the narcotics of the young. They're too busy enjoying life to fear its loss. They can't wait to leave the lecture hall and head to the union bar. That's the main reason they came to university."

"Surely that can't be right, there must be many students who are here because they want to study." Her tone is sharp.

"Ms. Austin, I long for pupils with genuine aptitude, who wish to learn for learning's sake. Sometimes I despise my students. I see them texting on their mobiles in my class, I'm forced to read work plagiarised from the Internet. And not one of them would choose to sit in their room studying when they could be out partying. They think that English Literature is dead and gone, irrelevant to their modern lives of rap and horror films, gadgets and gizmos. They don't realise that nothing they experience is new."

"But on the video the students were totally rapt by your lecture. Not one of them looked distracted."

"Well, I work hard to keep them entertained. That's why it's so wrong that I'm not allowed to teach. This week I was scheduled to give a lecture on *St. Agnes Eve*. The poem is not a romantic love story but a sensual exploration of a rape. That would have gotten their attention. It's not politically correct and I was looking forward to the pseudo-feminists' reaction. But don't be fooled, Ms. Austin. The students that appeared so engrossed on that tape, would shortly afterwards be drinking vodka and snorting cocaine in the union bar. You saw evidence of that yourself."

Cate is silent for a while, "Who was he?"

"No one who matters. Alex won't last long. I failed his last essay and he can't progress into the final year if he fails another. Which he will." I drain my glass and push it aside.

"Doesn't it bother you? It's such a waste. His future . . . he's only, what, eighteen?"

"And not my problem. I didn't force the drugs into his veins."

11

We all have choices. You know that, don't you, as well as I? To exist, to breathe; to nullify life with narcotics. It's all a choice. Choices, of course, don't happen randomly. They come to us at a certain time, in a special way. But still, we choose. Smith made his choice: to submit is also to act. There is always a schema behind actions, behind deeds. You just have to look hard enough. That's how I analyse the dead poets, looking for a pattern behind the words, searching for the themes and messages under the surface. It's how I live, looking for the meaning, the leitmotif of life. So I don't think it was an accident that long before I met Smith I came across the story of Armin Meiwes, who even then was old news and only commanded one column of print, not even on the front page. It wasn't my newspaper, I rarely buy one, but had been left in the staff common room, on a chair, waiting for me. It was unusual to find the staff room empty. Normally several lecturers would be jostling for position by the open window, cigarette in hand, or would be chatting by the coffee machine. But it was approaching the end of term and a warm day. My colleagues would be seated on the grass with their stacks of essays for marking, or in their rooms preparing for the imminent exodus. I was alone in the staff room. And the paper was next to me, already folded at the page, as if to draw my attention: *ARMIN MEIWES NOT A MURDERER*.

The headline was an announcement, a quote from the defence, and I pulled the paper on to my lap to read the rest of the article.

Armin Meiwes killed and partially ate a man he met via the Internet in March 2001. He was convicted of manslaughter and jailed for eight and a half years. Last year, an appeal court ordered a re-trial to establish whether Meiwes was guilty of murder. The 44-year-old denies the charge and says he simply carried out a willing victim's instructions. He admitted killing the German-based computer specialist Bend-Juergen Brundes at Meiwes' home in the town of Rotenburg.

Meiwes' legal team argued the defendant was 'killing on request', a form of illegal euthanasia that carries a maximum five year sentence. They argue that two consensual adults should be able to act in any way they see fit and there is no evidence that Brundes was not of sound mind when he opted to be killed and eaten. Indeed, he had even joked with Meiwes that 'smoked meat lasts longer,' after hearing they were both smokers. The case continues.

Replacing the paper on the chair at my side, I examined my feelings, took the pulse of my reaction. It was racing, but I found no shock there. Instead my excitement was the sweet taste of recognition, of a thought reflected back in an unexpected setting. Killing on request. The idea, then, had already occurred to me. This newspaper article didn't plant the seed. If the idea hadn't already existed I'd have glanced at the article, dismissed it as a sick perversion. But instead it tapped into something inside me, something already alive, a root planted deep began to reach up. The idea began to grow.

So it was possible then, to find someone like Bend-Juergen Brundes. To find a man, a lover, with the same desire. But how would such an advert be worded? Could I post a message on a computer screen, a flare in the sky, a signal across distant waters? A man might answer, it could be the man standing next to me in the supermarket queue. It could be a man from across the oceans. The web could span these distances, make it possible to send a thread, find a fixing point. To weave a home, for a mate to rest in before extinction. The idea excited me. The German case showed me what was possible.

But the time wasn't right. It was years, a whole six years later, that I started to stalk the Web, reading messages, waiting. Lee had gone, posted to Germany, and I was bored. Looking for something. I didn't know what I sought until I saw the ad:

> MAN SEEKS BEAUTIFUL WOMAN FOR THE JOURNEY OF A LIFETIME: I WILL
> LIFT MINE EYES TO THE HILLS, FROM WHENCE COMETH MY HELP. WILL YOU
> HELP ME TO DIE?

Smith placed the advert in January last year, and I replied. He first came to me in the February. He never even told me his real name. He wanted to protect me. That was our agreement. I confess to being with him when he died. I watched him take the overdose, I watched him cut his own skin. Smith wanted to die. It was his free choice. His death was suicide. I was just helping him; he didn't want to be on his own when the end came. Who wants to die alone?

Cate Austin doesn't see this. She can't. She's part of a system that believes in retribution and justice, whatever that means. And she speaks of prison.

Today a psychiatrist is coming. He will also have a hand in deciding my fate. I've made a decision. I'll be the author of my own destiny. I will not submit to the judgment of others; the time has come to act.

I'd not thought about prison before Cate Austin said it. The word is too romantic, a beautiful lie. 'Prise,' a word for open. Said quickly prison could be present—birthdays and Christmas.

How can such a word mean something so ugly, so absolute, as incarceration? I shall say jail. The word is more honest, in it you can hear the clink of keys in locks. I like to be honest with words: jail terrifies me. There. It's said.

Smith has been dead for seven months and never, in all that time, did I think jail was my fate.

You don't believe me. Of course, I knew it was a possibility. Others, my solicitor, my barrister, pointed out it was there like rotten meat at the back of the fridge. How could it be forgotten? And it had happened to Meiwes in the end; the prosecution challenged the initial sentence and he was sentenced for murder. He was stupid though, searching for another victim and thereby inviting prosecution. A serial cannibal, he was a risk to society and his sentence bears no significance to my case.

Why should incarceration concern me as a serious option, when I've done nothing wrong? Nothing! Life, the air we breathe, is random. A happenchance that molecules and genes and chromosomes came together at random and we exist. That flesh and bone grow, that we're allowed to flourish in the womb, that we are not, as a mere collection of cells, sucked away in a tube and discarded in some hospital rubbish bin. Survival is always an outside chance in the game of life, yet we exist. We are alive and, even more wonderful, with conscience and consciousness. Thoughts and actions and choices. Each breath we take is a choice.

Who are they, these people who think they can pass laws against suicide, as if breath can be protected by statute? Life is not a right. It's a choice. Every breath, think of that, breathe it in. Make your choice again and again and know that you are alive, that life is what you choose. Now hold your breath. Do it. Hold, for a second, two. Do I have the right to tell you to breathe in again? Does anybody have that right? So, no, I don't believe jail should be my punishment. If I can see beyond a law that would have me locked away, then surely you can, too? Now, breathe again.

But Cate Austin says it may be so. That I can be locked away. I'm not naïve: I know what could happen to me in prison. Just look at me! Beautiful. Clever. An academic, for Christ's sake. What chance would I have against addicts and thieves, prostitutes and thugs? My face would be shredded, I'd be an object of jealousy, vilified. I can defend myself against words, but not blows. Oh yes, I'm accomplished, but I'm still afraid of the flick knife, the hypodermic needle, the desperate woman with nothing to lose.

I won't allow them to send me to jail. There's always a choice and I choose to live, to breathe. I choose another way.

The psychiatrist, Dr. Gregg, will be here soon. Cate said it was in his power to keep me from jail. He can ask for a hospital order, she said, and unlike a jail term there would be no fixed time that I must serve. Once judged sane, I'd be released. I could be free again in weeks. Days, even.

It makes me furious. How dare a man come here to judge me? So, this is the choice: I must be mad or evil. Sad or bad. It's not possible, apparently, to be sane and to have helped Smith as I did. I'm sick of ignorant people misinterpreting my actions, choosing to label me as mentally unstable rather than facing their bigoted world of sanity. I'm angry, so angry that all I want to do is break glass. All I want to do is scream. No wonder I've felt so ill recently; the headaches, the dizziness.

The anger bubbles inside as I watch his car arrive, a family estate in conservative blue. Dr. Gregg too wears blue, a dogtooth jacket and cords, half-moon glasses that glint as he looks up. I'm standing at the window, looking down as he waves up to me in greeting.

I've been waiting for my audience to arrive.

12

"Ms. Austin, it's Charles Gregg speaking. You wanted me to contact you after my meeting with Alice. I saw her yesterday afternoon."

Cate put down her sandwich and swallowed a mouthful of tuna mayonnaise. "Great. Thanks for calling so promptly. I saw her myself on Monday. We watched a tape of her giving a lecture on time and death. She was rather impressive."

"I imagine she was," he said dryly, "did you show her you were impressed?"

Cate thinks back, "Well, yes. I told her I thought her students were totally engrossed, as I was."

"People like Alice need approval and praise. Tell me, Ms. Austin, has it ever seemed to you that Alice considers herself to be unique? That she considers the majority of people beneath her?"

Cate didn't need to think hard to answer the question, "Well, she's quite scornful of how most people experience love. She thinks that her decision to help Smith die is misunderstood more than anything else. And she definitely doesn't think it's anybody else's business—free choice and all that."

"Exactly. The laws of the land don't count for her."

Cate felt at a disadvantage, as if Dr. Gregg had already reached some conclusion he was now leading her to. "So, how did you find her?"

"Just as you have described. Only more so."

"How do you mean?"

She heard the rustle of paper, as if a file was being flicked through. "Have you ever heard of egomania?"

"Well, yes," she replied cautiously, "but I didn't think it was a medical term."

"It isn't. It's the nineteenth century word for a narcissistic personality disorder, but I think it sums things up nicely. I think Alice is a classic case. There are nine key features to the disorder, and my initial assessment is that she scores high on most of them. She's pre-occupied with power, arrogant and has a feeling of entitlement to act as she feels fit. Another feature is a lack of empathy. You've seen her more than me, have you seen any evidence of empathy?"

Cate thought of Alice's dismissive attitude towards her addict student Alex. "Not a huge amount. But she did go to some lengths to protect her parents. I think she cares about their feelings."

"She needs to show five traits to be diagnosed. Even if she has empathy, her need for excessive admiration is obvious from the way she talks. She showed a great deal of arrogance, demanding what right I had to judge her. It struck me as quite a typical presentation of the symptoms."

There was a pause on the line, but Cate found herself momentarily unable to fill it. "What other traits would she have if she's got egomania?"

"One is envy of others. They're highly exploitative people, they can sniff out other people's weaknesses like rats. In work situations they're often high achievers but also bullies."

"Yes, I could see her as a bully." Cate herself had felt Alice's intimidating presence. "But is she dangerous?"

"That depends. If a person feels beyond the law, if they feel justified in everything they do, and if they lack empathy, then they can be very dangerous indeed."

Cate took a breath, and thought she should have seen this coming. "So, are you going to be treating her? Can egomania be cured?"

"Most psychiatrists think not. A personality disorder is a part of someone's makeup, and very hard to alter. Of course, cognitive behavioural therapy, working on distorted thoughts, can have some impact. But I need to assess her further. She's here at the hospital. I had her admitted."

"She's at St. Therese's?" Cate remembered visiting the psychiatric hospital, its low grey buildings and wandering patients. Alice didn't belong there, surely? "Why?"

"For her own safety. The danger with narcissistic personality disorder, if that's what she's got, is that if the patient feels thwarted, when their power is threatened, they rage. They rage against the world, against others. They can rage against themselves. I saw evidence of self-harm on her wrists. As the interview progressed she was increasingly hysterical. She threw things, she shouted, and then she smashed a vase and held the glass to her neck. I just couldn't take the risk that she wouldn't harm herself or someone else. After calling out the approved social worker, who shared my concerns,

I had her admitted to the secure ward of St. Therese's. She was totally uncontrollable, hysterical to the point of vomiting, until we sedated her."

"But why would she harm herself? From what you've said, she feels justified and certain of her own ability. Why would she be suicidal?"

"She wouldn't, in the usual sense of depression and projecting negative thoughts inward. But an egomaniac would kill themselves to make a point, as a grandiose act. Think of cult leaders who instigate mass suicides. That's typical narcissistic personality disorder behaviour, revenge against the world on a magnificent scale. I couldn't take the risk that Alice wouldn't do something to make a point."

Cate silently cursed. How had she not spotted that Alice was so ill? She had picked up that Alice was arrogant but not that she was a risk to herself. Had she misjudged Alice? Dr. Gregg was obviously more qualified to judge than her, but somehow Alice didn't strike her as a self-harmer or a suicide risk. "So what will you be recommending in your report? A hospital order instead of a prison sentence?"

"It's too early to say. I'd need another psychiatrist to agree, if a hospital order looks likely. But I'd have to be sure I could treat her, and I haven't made a firm diagnosis yet. First, we'll see how Alice responds to the hospital environment."

"I'd like to see her."

"I think a visit from you would be a good idea, so you can see how she's responding. Just don't excite her in any way. She could be violent."

Cate braced herself. "I'll come this afternoon."

"She was very distressed at being sectioned, so we had to sedate her. She was asleep when I did my ward round this morning and will be groggy for a while. Why not wait until tomorrow?"

"Tomorrow, then. Thanks for letting me know." Cate put down the phone. Suddenly losing her appetite she threw the remains of her sandwich in the bin and picked up the case file, wondering if there was a clue, something she had missed, in the witness statements.

The Crown Prosecution papers, bound in a thick red band, had arrived just yesterday. She'd intended to read them over the weekend while Amelia was with her dad, but given the sudden change of events she decided there was no time to waste.

The first thing she saw under the headed front sheet was a photocopy of a handwritten letter. On closer inspection Cate saw it was David Jenkins' suicide note. It was written in small black letters, the hand of a man who uses the left side of his brain, tiny scratches of letters and over-rounded conso-nants. It was dated June 15th last year. The day before he died.

To Whom It May Concern.

This won't make sense to many people, but that doesn't mat-ter. It makes sense to me. Please excuse my crap handwrit-ing. I read on a computer site dedicated to these things that suicide notes are more personal written than typed. Looking on those websites, and there are lots, made me realise how the last words of a dying man can be twisted. This is important. I want to get it right. Not for me, but for Robin. For what she's risking.

What I want to say is that suicide is my choice. No one else is to blame. Robin answered my call, but if she hadn't I would have found someone else to be with me when I do it. Whatever, it would have ended up this way. I couldn't bear to think of her being punished. I just want her to be left in peace.

Robin is no more responsible for my death than a train driver who runs over a guy who jumped on the tracks. She may be driving the train, but she never made me jump. It will be me swallowing the drugs, knowing they bring death. The eating, too, is my request. Robin doesn't even really want to—she'll be doing it for me. And I'll be alive at that point, so it's not even illegal.

I wish this letter could guarantee that she won't get put through the grinder over this. She doesn't deserve any has-sle. All she's doing is helping me. Helping me to die.

Cate felt a pang in her heart that may have been regret. There was a part of her that thought suicide was a personal right, but why not just do it on your own? Why had David Jenkins involved Alice? And why, for goodness sake, had Alice eaten him? Presumably this act was symbolic, but didn't they realise when they planned it that the police could not overlook such a bizarre perversion, and the media certainly wouldn't? But then, Dr. Gregg had said that Alice could be an egomaniac, and that she thought herself above the law. That must be how she justified it to herself.

Next was a photocopied statement of a police constable.

Statement of: PC Flynn

I responded to an incident that had been called in by a local woman. She said her boyfriend had committed suicide. As it was a Friday and the monthly farmers' market, I had been assigned to street patrol in Lavenham. After receiving the call, I was the first on the scene.

I have only been with the police force for six months, but I have responded to one previous suicide. I knew that my role was to support the paramedics when they turned up, and make general observations.

When I arrived outside the house a woman, who I now know to be Alice Mariani, was sitting on the front step, waiting. She was wearing a dressing gown even though it was nearly lunchtime, and her hair was wet as if she had just showered. The door was open behind her, but I could not see into the hall. Ms. Mariani struck me as very calm, and was eating a cheese sandwich. When she saw me she stood, as if she'd been waiting, and shook my hand. Her hand was wet. I guessed from her demeanour that the 999 call had been a false alarm, and that her boyfriend was okay.

"He's upstairs, in bed," she told me. She was so calm that I thought he would be alive. That he must have fainted and she had panicked.

The bedroom wall was painted white, and splattered with blood. The wooden floor was slippery, and I could see a mop in a bucket further down the hall. On the bed, in a strange crouched position, was a naked man. His head was bowed over, so I couldn't see his face, but his legs were covered in blood and I could see he had some wound to his genitals. I started to speak to him, saying who I was, and approached him to take his pulse. There was none and rigor mortis had set in.

I had to leave the premises at that point as I felt physically sick, and I passed Alice Mariani who sat on the front step. I retched in her garden and she asked if I was all right. I asked her to find a blanket to put over the man. I then radioed my skipper, and was told that further assistance was on the way, along with the paramedics.

As I waited for back-up to arrive, she handed me her boyfriend's suicide note (exhibit 1-a). It was covered in bloody fingerprints.

Cate felt ill just picturing the scene, and so sorry for PC Flynn who had no doubt been enjoying light duties at the farmers' market. How could Alice sit calmly eating a cheese sandwich? And the mention of the mop meant she had cleaned before the officer arrived. Why hadn't she put a sheet over the body?

Cate looked at the next page. The senior officer, Stephen West, who had taken Alice's statement, was someone she knew from an earlier case they had worked on together. She picked up the phone and punched in the numbers.

"Stephen, it's Cate Austin."

"Long time, no see," he said cheerily, "how are things in the prison?"

"I'm out now, Steve. At liberty. My secondment in the prison finished three months ago. I'm based in the Ipswich office now."

"I thought you'd only been in the slammer a few months? Don't prison secondments normally last a couple of years?"

Cate imagined Steve in his messy office, his large feet on the desk, and smiled. "Let's just say I'd served my time. Truth is, Steve, with all that happened there I was glad to move on quickly. And I've been landed another tricky case. I was looking over the witness statements and saw your name. Can I run a few things past you?"

"Who are we talking about?"

"Alice Mariani." She could hear a slight chuckle down the line.

"Might have guessed, you always get the psychos. So shoot."

"It's this question of assisted suicide. I'm trying to write the report, and I'm mulling over what sentence to recommend. I can't find any case histories to base my proposal on. It's such a freakish case."

"Welcome to the real world, love. There's nothing stranger than folk."

Cate knew he was right. But she also knew that all actions had motives, and that all behaviour could be rationalised. However strange Alice may be, she was not beyond help. Cate just needed a bit of direction. "I'm doing a bit of research, trying to look up similar crimes. Do you remember a few years ago there was that guy in Germany who killed that other bloke? The victim wanted to die, and he'd responded to an advert placed on the Internet by the defendant. Armin Meiwes."

"Yeah, that does ring a bell. Course, the Germans are a funny race. Wasn't he known as the Gentleman Cannibal?"

"That's right. And do you know how long he got? Eight years. So I'm thinking Alice is looking at a similar term . . ."

"Nah, you're out of date. That first prison term was upped. The prosecution objected if I remember right and he got convicted for murder. Anyway, Meiwes wasn't like Mariani. He killed that bloke just so he could eat him afterwards. He was a self-confessed cannibal. That's not like her. Jenkins' death was more like euthanasia. He took the drugs and left a suicide note, after all."

"Yes, but then she ate some of his flesh . . ."

"Don't remind me. It's enough to make a bloke weep. She ate Jenkins' penis, said it was a symbolic act. Wouldn't feel symbolic to him, poor fucker."

"Do you know why, Steve? Was she trying to emasculate him, or was it some sexual fetish?"

"God knows. The bloke must've been a masochist. He cut his own todger off, y'know. Probably served it for her on a bloody platter. That's why we couldn't even charge her with wounding, not when he'd done it to himself. So she's not like Meiwes, no way. He froze his victim, then ate him for several meals. And you know he filmed the death, masturbated over it later."

Cate's stomach clenched, and she was grateful for the small mercy that Alice had not done likewise. "Still, this isn't a typical euthanasia case, isn't it? She wouldn't have been prosecuted if it was. Jenkins wasn't dying, didn't have any fatal disease."

"Autopsy said not. He died of a cardiac arrest brought on by the overdose of GHB. And I remember he didn't have a GP, so he can't have been unwell. Digging anything up on him was hard. I even went to London, met his boss, then tried to find out who his doctor was. He wasn't even registered with the local surgery. But he must have been one sick puppy, depressed or whatever. Doesn't that count as an illness?"

"I don't know, Steve." Cate breathed deep, wanting to find the answer in a pause. Nothing came back. "None of it seems right to me. I can't think of this as assisted suicide. It feels more sinister."

"Yeah, well that's just tough, sweetheart, 'cos the charge has already been decided, and she's pleaded guilty. Assisted suicide it is. So you better think of a sentence that matches."

That was Steve, always a straight talker. "I know. Thanks for the pep talk."

"Anytime."

Cate put down the phone and logged on to the Internet. After thinking for a moment, she typed in the search box, 'Internet suicide pact.' She sighed as the screen filled with article after article, faced once again with the extent of weirdness in humanity. Perhaps this wasn't such an unusual case, after all. She looked for cases that were British, so she could see how sentencing had panned out.

There was the boy from Manchester, only fourteen years old, who wanted to commit suicide but couldn't do it himself. Instead, he tricked a friend by starting an Internet relationship posing as a female spy, telling him that he and the fake spy could have sex if he killed him. Another case was that of

Matthew Williams, whose friend Potter wanted to be killed. Williams had slit Potter's throat and then drank his blood. Cate then remembered the case of Suffolk murderer Jason Mitchell, who had tried to eat his victims . . .

But none of the cases were like this one.

After making a few notes Cate turned back to the Crown Prosecution bundle. She had come to Alice's own statement:

Statement of: Alice Mariani Age—Over 18

Smith placed the advert. He came to me. He never even told me his real name. He wanted to protect me. That was our arrangement. I agreed to be with him when he took an overdose, knowing it would be fatal. He took a knife and cut his own skin. Smith wanted to die. It was his free choice. His death is the result of a suicide. I was just with him because he didn't want to be on his own when he died. Who wants to die alone?

I should not be here. This is not a police matter. It is a free country and two consenting adults have free choice. I don't pose a risk to anyone. He wanted to die and I agreed to assist him to do it.

Choosing to live or die is a basic human right.

Cate sniffed through her nose in distaste; talk about romanticising! Having just read PC Flynn's statement, and then Alice's account, she knew which rang truer. No wonder Alice was in St. Therese's, she was unhinged, that was certain. But one sentence resonated. The sentiment that Cate struggled with. She read Alice's words again, testing to see if she believed them: I don't pose a risk.

13

As I regain consciousness, I'm aware of the smell of Dettol and the swishing sound of a mop. I open my eyes, sticky from sleep. I'm in a cell. The walls are bare, the floor is plastic, and the door has a small window. Someone's peering in. It's a man, and when he catches me looking he disappears. Then I see the steel frame of the bed, the curtain on wheels collapsed against the opposite wall. I'm in a hospital, then. Institutions are all the same: hospitals, schools, even airports. That smell of boiled food and bleach, the noise of wheels on plastic, beeping machines and voices through intercoms. Night is never dark, never quiet; always someone is working, someone is awake, doing a job. How am I supposed to sleep? I think that jail would be the same. Except I'd be without power, would have to wait for a long time, striking off the days until I could be free. In hospital there's no release date. I just have to be pronounced well.

I reach for the folded pile of shoddy clothes on the bedside table and wish that I had something decent to wear. I push back the limp white sheet and the heavy blanket to see that I'm wearing a gown, which has risen to my waist, and no knickers. Filthy bastards, they would have seen everything. Quickly, I pull on knickers that, although a day old, are at least decent, and then reach with less enthusiasm for my leggings and t-shirt. I remember now that I wore no bra for Dr. Gregg's visit. The tee shirt is not fully on when, after a single knock, a male nurse comes in with a plate of sausages and chips and a sachet of tomato ketchup. His name badge tells me he is called Shane.

"I'm a vegetarian."

"Then leave the sausage." Shane stares at my top, my breasts loose under the faded cotton, then makes a big show of looking away. "I did knock. You should've said you was getting dressed."

"What day is it?" I'm totally disorientated.

"Wednesday. You came in yesterday afternoon." He places the tray on the bedside table.

"How long do I have to stay here?"

"Until the doctors say you can leave. Dr. Gregg will be round tomorrow morning."

"Tomorrow! What about today?"

"He's already been today. You were asleep so you missed him." He's turning to go.

"So what do I do in the meantime? I need clothes and toiletries."

"You can make a phone call and get a visitor to bring them in. Do your family live nearby?"

I shudder, imagining my mum wandering into this place. My dad scanning the bare walls for something to focus on other than his mad daughter. No, I could never inflict that on them. Then I have another thought. "I need to use the phone. Now."

The nurse has his hand on the door handle, "This isn't a five-star hotel, you know. Good manners go a long way." I scowl at his back as I follow Shane into the corridor.

"Ms. Austin? It's Alice Mariani. I need to see you."

"You're calling from St. Therese's?"

For a moment I wonder how she knows, but obviously the news has reached her. Nothing is private when a court sentence is pending. "Yes. I need a favour. Can you help me?"

She doesn't reply immediately. "That depends. What is it you want?"

I wake to a cold morning.

I'm alone in this hospital room that is really a cell. Through the small glass window on the door I see the glare of a fluorescent light. I can hear the night staff in the community room watching some chat show, they don't bother to control their laughter. The staff laugh more here than in other workplaces. I've never seen staff laugh so hard that tears course their cheeks in shops or supermarkets, but these nurses and social workers, even the auxiliaries who do nothing more than wipe food off the floor or shit off the walls, find laughter easy. It's hysterical, almost, and I wonder if this is how they survive their own incarceration, their own institutionalisation.

I've been at St. Therese's for two nights.

I count in nights, as that's the hardest time, without the distraction of doctors or activities or mealtimes. And although I managed a nap yesterday afternoon, I can't sleep at night. Being alone makes me feel angry. It makes me feel ugly.

I've no books. My top is old and stained and I'm eager for this afternoon, when Cate Austin will bring my clothes, the skincare products that I asked for. But I forgot to ask for a book. If I had one now, anything would do, I could transport myself from here. I could feel at peace.

My headache has returned, and the dizziness forces me to lay down. It must be the environment, pressing down on me until it feels like my skull will crack. If this continues I'll be forced to ask for stronger painkillers and it was hard enough persuading them to give me two Nurofen. I don't want to ask for anything. I won't be beholden to anyone when I'm here against my will.

I'll be in Cate Austin's debt, but who else could I have asked to go to my home and pick up my things? Not my parents. It would be beyond them, to think of their Alice in a madhouse. There's always Lee, who'll be confused by my sudden absence.

We'd planned to meet today, at my house, and I know that Lee will arrive on time, will wait. I could've phoned, I have a mobile number, as well as the number of the barracks in Colchester, but I was afraid. I don't want to say that I am here. I don't want to find out if Lee has read anything of the court hearings in the newspapers. There is only one thing I want to know, that I am loved, and Lee tells me over and over again. I know it's true. Meagre though it is I don't want to destroy that love, when it may be all I have left.

So I chose Cate. I believe that she won't snoop. That she will do nothing more than I have asked.

I trust her, then. I find the revelation a surprise.

A single knock and Shane walks in. "Come on, you," he says, staring at my body, my bare arms. I wish I had a jumper.

I follow Shane down the hallway, past other patients, men and women who pace like tigers, prowling around each other in the corridor that serves as their territory, all of them concentrating on not touching, looking down at their feet. One woman is wearing kitten-heeled red slippers, but she drags them, and they make a sloppy sound with every step, sipping on a carton of squash as she goes. She stops as I walk past and angles her head like I'm an animal in a zoo and she is the other side of the bars. Her teeth are stained purple.

I'm taken to another corridor, and led to a door that says Occupational Therapy. My heart twitches as Shane herds me into the room, where a middle-aged man in a smart shirt sits on a high-backed chair. Around him, in a circle, are five other patients.

One guy is in pyjamas, which hang low on his body. From where I stand I can see his part-naked buttocks. The only other woman in the room has a long flowing skirt and a nervous smile. She must be one of those middle class neurotics who steal compulsively. The man in the smart shirt rises from his chair and comes to me, putting a hand on my shoulder, "Greetings! I'm Frank, and you must be Alice." I release my shoulder. "Come and sit next to me, Alice."

As I sit, I smell nicotine on Frank, who is still smiling at me. The man in pyjamas is now opposite and also staring, his hands thrust into the sagging cotton, cupping his penis. Frank leans over. "Best just ignore him. He's harmless. He won't be here long anyway. The staff'll come and get him in ten minutes to make sure he doesn't shit on the floor." I flinch, and Frank leans further my way. "I'll take care of you, Alice. I always look out for the new ones."

Suddenly the compulsive shoplifter claps her hands weakly. "Right then!" she says, falsely bright, "Shall we make a start?"

I look from her to Frank and back again. Are the lunatics running the asylum? I see then that he has slippers on his feet and the woman wears a name badge. She is the occupational therapist.

"We'll warm up with a game of Murder Wink. Alice, have you played before?"

You've got to be kidding. "Yes, when I was about six."

"Ha ha," she says, good-naturedly. "We play it to create a sense of teamwork. And to have a bit of fun!" She says 'fun' with a leap, trying to believe it. The man in the pyjamas moves his hands more violently, rocking in his chair.

"Now, Frank, you be the detective. Go on! Stand outside the circle!" Like a trained monkey he does, nodding at me, as if to say that it's wise to indulge this madwoman.

"Okay then, everyone close their eyes and if I touch you on the shoulder you're the killer. Your job is to murder wink everyone before Frank detects you. Ha Ha!"

I keep my eyes on the guy in the pyjamas. The therapist touches the other man's shoulder. He has glasses and a moustache and strikes me as rather military in an old-fashioned, fifties film kind of way. Watching him straighten his shirt where she has touched it makes me sad. Then I notice that although his clothes are perfect, his hands are red raw. He doesn't touch the chair, or himself. His hands are suspended above his lap, awkwardly. He winks at me. I look at Frank, who is also watching me, as is the man in the pyjamas. Then I fall off my chair and die slowly on the floor.

"Oh excellent!" says the woman, "Wonderful dying, Alice. I can see we're going to have fun with you."

The game doesn't take long. It's fairly obvious who the murderer is when a nurse removes the pyjamas guy and the therapist has a noisy heart attack in her chair. I take my seat, wondering how much the state pays her to play party games with nutters. I want to yell, do you have any idea how many qualifications I have? Do you know how long it took me to train as a lecturer? Have you even heard of Keats, you miserable creature? I pity her, with her desperate need for approval. She wants us to laugh and clap like eager children. Frank and I exchange a look, and then she makes us play, What time is it, Mr. Wolf?

I can't do it.

I can't stand with my back to Frank and the therapist and the obsessive. I hate having my back to anybody, so I don't turn around properly and after a few failed attempts she says that she will be grandmother instead. But she's too trusting, turns her back for too long, and Frank has touched her shoulder before she has a chance to call, 'Dinnertime.'

After the lesson, Frank walks me back to the ward. I see the woman with red sloppy slippers coming out of a door. "She's in my room!" I say, beginning to speed up. But Frank touches my arm. "Best ignore it. She only goes for the new ones. She'll stop snooping in your room once someone else arrives."

"Why are you here, Frank?" He's saner than the staff. Nothing mad about him.

"No reason," he says.

I linger with him in the corridor, watching the obsessive man attempt to open the doors with elbows alone, and avoid the eyes of the sloppy-slippered woman with blackcurrant-stained teeth. She brushes against me as she skims by.

Shane pokes his head from the patient's lounge, where the staff go to smoke their fags. "Don't go in the television room until the cleaners have been in," he announces, as if it is of little interest. "Pete's done a crap behind the sofa."

"Jesus." I say, disgusted, but Frank just shrugs and crumples his cigarette under his slipper.

"Worse things than shit."

14

Cate lifted the large plant pot in the back garden, just as Alice had instructed her, and found the back door key settled in the soil among woodlice and worms. She opened the lock with a twist and a pull, wondering why Alice had no friends she could have called on for this errand. It was strange being in the house alone. She imagined Alice's eyes upon her and had no urge to linger. The door opened into a utility area with a washing machine and freezer. She walked through, thinking how tidy it was, how white the walls, not a grubby mark anywhere; so clearly a house without children. Cate thought grimly of the sticky prints on her own walls, the unwashed cereal bowls on the kitchen worktop. The utility room led into the large kitchen area, where she had first interviewed Alice. But it was different from before.

The kitchen table was stained with water and as she approached her heels crunched on glass. There was water on the floor, sprigs of green with orange and red. Snapdragons, in full bloom when she first saw them, now wilted and dead. The glass was mostly in large pieces, but smaller slithers crunched under her feet. That beautiful vase! The stunning blue and white glass vase of snapdragons that had been here on her first visit. It's very valuable, Alice had said, irreplaceable. Dr. Gregg had told her that Alice had been hysterical, holding a piece of glass to her own neck. Had she broken her lovely vase? Carefully, she bent, lifting a large broken piece from the floor. But the glass was not thin or fine. It was not Alice's beautiful blue and white vase, but a chunky yellow vase. Oddly, the vase was different but the flowers were the same.

She climbed upstairs, holding onto the mahogany banister. The noise of her shoes on the wood jarred, and Cate thought of Alice's Moroccan slippers, barely making a sound as she moved around, and she wished she'd taken her shoes off downstairs. She didn't want to mark the grain.

Alice had told her what to collect, and Cate had made a list. Now she took it from her pocket, a sheet of jotter paper that looked like a packing list for a weekend away. As the bathroom was across the hall facing her, its door open, she went in.

It was beautiful, straight out of a boutique hotel, with black and white tiles underfoot and a massive bathtub set on silver balls. Georgian, Cate guessed, and original, not some reproduction number, it had probably been here since the house was built, or Alice had made it look that way. The sink, too, looked antique with its square bowl and large gleaming taps. She must have a cleaner to keep it this perfect, Cate thought, as she noted the Chanel bath oil and body lotion, also black and white, lined up on the windowsill. She wondered if Alice had chosen them for their contents or for the packaging. It all looked so artificial, like a show home rather than a place someone actually lived in. Cate thought briefly of her own bathroom with the grainy tub and sticky shower gels from Superdrug, the mismatched face care products and splayed toothbrushes that needed replacing.

In a mirrored cupboard was an electrical toothbrush with a plug-in stand. Did they have shaver sockets at St. Therese's? Also in the cupboard was a toiletries bag, which she filled with the toothbrush and toothpaste, skin cleanser and moisturiser, a Clarins deodorant, and some paracetamol, before she thought better of it, and returned it to the shelf alongside an extravagance of other products: Crème de la Mer, La Prairie, names she knew from magazine adverts but could never afford. How Alice bought them on a lecturer's salary Cate couldn't guess. Maybe they were gifts.

Curious, she dabbed some of the Chanel No.5 on her wrist and threw that in the bag, too. Closing the toiletries bag she struggled with the zip. She couldn't fit anything else in, so she went to collect the weekend bag that Alice had told her was in the bedroom.

The bedroom was neat and light, a bland canvas of white walls and chalk-coloured bedding. The bed was made, scatter cushions in contrasting shades of pale were placed at contrived angles against the headboard. An image came to her, unbidden, of David Jenkins naked and bloody. Dead. Poor PC Flynn. She would have been sick, too, if she'd seen what he did. But the body was long gone, the splatter of blood from the walls whitewashed away.

The only vivid colour was the mahogany chest of drawers, with a makeup bag on top, which Alice had been emphatic she shouldn't forget. She picked it up. Through the fabric she could feel the bulk of lipsticks and brushes, the sharp corner of a compact mirror. On the dressing table was a grey eye shadow, open, with a brush next to it. A purple eye shadow was also out, as was a yellowish face powder. Cate wondered why they'd not been put away, when every other surface was so neat. It looked like Alice had left off doing her makeup in a hurry. And the colours were so dark, so unlike anything she could imagine Alice wearing. She felt there was something she was missing.

Trying to organise her thoughts, Cate went to the large bay window to look out. It was a picture postcard view, across the road to a striking church on a slope, an ornate iron gate at the start of a yellow brick path. Craning her neck, she saw further down the street a butcher's, an old-fashioned tea-shop, a delicatessen. No doubt about it, this was a pretty place. What the neighbours must think about what had happened in this house, heaven only knew.

Bringing her gaze back to the churchyard, she suddenly became aware of someone sitting on a bench by the side wall of the church, looking up at the window, watching her. Cate could just make out dark, spiky hair and a leather coat, an upturned face, eyes fixed on the very window where Cate stood. When she looked straight down, the person quickly got up from the bench, hands in pockets, and sauntered away.

Turning back to the room, Cate spied the weekend bag on top of the wardrobe and managed to lift it down with the aid of a chair. She began to pack another woman's clothes for another kind of life. Alice could never have imagined she would one day be staying at St. Therese's when she bought her Chanel toiletries and face creams.

The wardrobe, built into the wall in painted white pine, was closed. She opened it with both hands and saw things that most women would covet, an ordered selection of smart trousers and dresses, some clothes with labels still attached, all designer brands. They were hung in a regimented pattern: tops first, then skirts, trousers, finally dresses. Colours were put together, revealing a large number of white or beige clothes with fewer items in black or red. The effect was striking but formal. Like Alice's bookshelves, the clothes were aesthetically correct rather than inviting. The most casual item was a new-looking pair of dark jeans, which Cate lifted out, along with a pale blue jumper. Alice could hardly wear linen suits or silk shirts in a psychiatric hospital.

On the floor of the wardrobe, Perspex boxes were stacked in neat rows, each holding a pair of shoes. My God, thought Cate, how the other half live. It's all I can do to find a pair of socks to match and this woman has her whole boudoir in order. Imagine having control of your surroundings like that.

Remembering that Alice would need underwear she went to the mahogany chest, and opened the top drawer. It held just one item: a child's cardigan.

Curious, Cate lifted it out.

It was woollen, and knitted by someone who wasn't very adept. The wool was the colour of lavender, with pearly white buttons. There was a hole where a stitch had been dropped, and the wool was bobbled as if from much wash and wear, but was soft and well loved. The cardigan was old and Cate guessed that it must have been Alice's when she was a child. Folding it back carefully, she closed the drawer, still troubled that something was not as it should be.

15

1981

It was the most beautiful thing Alice had seen, ever. And Mummy had made it for her. "I've been knitting it at night while you were asleep," she told Alice, "it's taken me ages."

Alice touched the beautiful lilac wool, fingered the smooth pearly button. She snuggled it with her face, feeling the softness on her cheek, and closed her eyes. It was perfect.

"Try it on, then!" said her Mummy, "it might be a bit big." But it wasn't. It was perfect. "You can wear that when you start nursery next week. I'll put a name tag in it so it doesn't get lost."

"I'll never lose it," said Alice, throwing her arms around her Mummy's neck and kissing her. "I'll wear it forever."

"Wear it now, Alice. It's going to be chilly outside."

It was cold, too cold to be playing outside, but they went to the park anyway. There was a swing, a roundabout, a red slide and it was theirs alone. The rest of the world was at home, in the warm. Alice wore her lilac cardigan, and over it a navy coat. On each arm she had a reflective orange band to warn traffic, to keep her safe as she walked, hand clasped to her mother's.

Mummy wanted to go home. She had chapped lips, which she ran her tongue over, only making them worse, and cold hands from pushing the swing. But Alice was determined. "Again, Mummy! Push me again!" Her mother's hands cradled her back, over her shoulder blades like wings, pushing her higher, higher.

Alice stretched out her legs, pulled them back, tried to propel herself into the air. She wanted to fly. What if the swing went all the way up and over the bar, would that be flying?

The swing stopped abruptly, mid-air, as her mother grasped the rubber seat, stopped it dead. "Enough now. Let's go home." She lowered it, reaching into the swing to lift Alice, who jumped up. In the confusion mother and daughter were knocked against each other and Alice's head hit Mummy's chin. There was blood. Alice was dropped, and the mother crouched on the ground, hand cupped over her mouth. Red spots on the black tarmac.

"Mummy?" Alice was scared and confused. Was Mummy angry?

"My tongue," her mother said. "You just whacked my jaw up and I've bitten my tongue." She stuck it out. It was pink with red blood blooming around the edge, like a swollen tulip. There were several marks where her teeth cut the muscle. Then Mummy started to cry. Noisy, so very noisy, and the girl wanted it to stop, but the sound and the tears carried on, until she was crying too.

Alice knew it was her fault. She silently prayed Mummy would still love her. Then she remembered that she was wearing her special lilac cardigan, which Mummy knitted, and knew that she did.

Alice was on the bed, curled around a pillow, watching her favourite lunchtime programme. She'd been up all morning, and was starting to feel sleepy. There was jam on her top and her hair was tangled. On the screen a man dressed as a giant dolphin danced with a boy and they sang about life in the ocean.

The front door rapped with the noise it made when the post arrived. Nothing had arrived for them in the morning post, and her mother had said they must stay in, to wait for the lunchtime delivery. She was waiting for something important.

Mummy opened the door, walked to the end of the hall, and Alice followed her. Downstairs was a snare of paper stuck out of door's mouth like teeth. She watched her mother's rapid feet on the stairs, rushing to grab the paper.

Mummy sifted through the pile, discarding white and brown envelopes on the floor, the post for the other people in the house. Finally, she held one in her hands. She walked back upstairs with it, her feet heavy, and returned to the cramped room. She sat on the bed. Alice wondered if it was the special money called a 'Giro' that arrived by post. The Giro meant food in the cupboard, maybe even crisps. Mummy put an arm around her but still stared at the envelope. It was long and thin like a shark's tooth, and her mother held it, as if afraid it would bite. On the TV the giant dolphin told the boy about all the fish that live under water, and what they eat. In blue letters on the screen was the word FOODCHAIN. Mummy began to tear the envelope.

Alice held her breath without knowing why, perhaps to make amends for her mother's over-rapid breathing. The only noise was the singing of the dolphin and the boy. Mummy pulled the paper, and unfolded it slowly. Then she made a sound in her throat, like there was too much water and the girl thought of when she washed her hair in the bath and the water got up her nose. But Mummy's face was dry and sad, like when Alice started at the toddler group and clung to her, not wanting her to leave.

"Is it our Giro, Mummy?" asked Alice, looking at the paper, which had a shield at the top and a funny line of words in a strange language.

Mummy whispered, "It's a summons. The catalogue company. I owe them a lot of money." She turned to her daughter. "I have to go to court."

"Can I come?" said the girl, thinking of Cinderella in her pretty dress and the glass slippers.

"It's only for adults. You'll have to stay here." Mummy folded the paper up, into three, sliding it back in the ripped envelope. Alice touched the sticky jam on her top, and felt her knotted hair. She wanted to go with Mummy.

*

Alice didn't like Mr. Wilding, but he liked Mummy and they had to walk past his door to get to their own. He always seemed to be about to go out just as they went by, his door just opening. She didn't like going into his room, but Mummy said she couldn't go to the court with her. She must wait with Mr. Wilding and be good.

Mr. Wilding told Mummy that she looked pretty in her flowery dress, but Mummy just tugged at the neckline and said it's out of fashion now, but he kept looking anyway.

Mr. Wilding's room was smaller than theirs, and the curtains were never opened properly, but in the dull room she could see piles of boxes.

"Video players," he said, gesturing with a green and gold packet. "I'll give you one for a kiss?" Alice jumped away, but he laughed like it was a joke. He went back to rolling the paper of his cigarette.

When Mummy arrived home she grabbed Alice's hand. "Thank Mr. Wilding for looking after you, Alice."

"She was no bother," he said. "So what happened?"

"I've got to pay all I owe, plus fifty pounds costs, in twenty eight days." Mr. Wilding looked thoughtful, and his red tongue licked his lower lip. "You got that sort of money?"

"Oh yeah," said Mummy, "I'm loaded. Can't you tell?"

"I could help you, Matty. If you want, that is."

Mummy held Alice's hand tight, so she yelped. Mummy shook her head, and she looked worried. Mr. Wilding said, "You just think about it, Matty. For the girl's sake."

Alice was glad when their bedroom door closed behind them, although Mr. Wilding's door made no sound. He was still standing there, in the hall.

That evening he brought round fish and chips, with a sausage in batter for Alice, and when she was going to bed he came back with a bottle of wine. Mummy didn't even have a bottle opener, but he'd thought of that. Alice lay on the bed watching them drink, seeing how Mr. Wilding touched her Mummy on the arm, and rubbed his leg against her, when he spoke. The more Mummy drank the less she seemed to mind.

16

"I brought your things," Cate says, handing over the bag. She can't help staring. Of course, I'm wearing faded, old clothes, so unlike anything she has seen me in before. Just three days ago I was immaculate. The Alice before her is not the Alice in Lavenham. I no longer match my house and I'm not Alice the academic. This is mad Alice. Cate peers at me, searching for signs of my breakdown.

I grab the bag, rush the zip, and pull out indigo jeans and a baby blue cashmere jumper, then seize on the assortment of knickers and bras.

"Thank God you remembered underwear." I disappear behind the curtain screen on wheels.

When I come out she looks relieved, and I know from her face that I am no longer a madwoman. Smart clothes indicate a woman in control of her life. Packaging over content. She watches me comb out my hair, twisting it and pinning a loose chignon at the nape of my neck. So suddenly sophisticated, incongruous in this institution. Nothing mad about me. But she is not so gullible, surely. She has been to my home. She will have seen the broken glass on the floor.

"Have you tried to harm yourself, Alice?" Her eyes search my arms, the thin strip of exposed flesh at my wrist. She must see the red scratches. "Are you suicidal?"

I sit on the bed, delve into the makeup bag she brought me, and begin to apply lip liner. I don't smudge it, despite the boldness of her question. I finish my Cupid's bow. "No. I'm not suicidal. I was just having a bad day on Tuesday. I shouldn't be here. This is all a terrible mistake." I sift through the makeup bag and choose an eye shadow, using the compact mirror to apply a layer of ivory to my eyelid with my ring finger.

She watches me closely. "But Dr. Gregg decided to section you. He said you held broken glass to your neck?"

I continue staring in the mirror, blood in my cheeks like a blush. "Maybe I seemed to be worse than I actually was." I look up, "But you can see, can't you, that I shouldn't be here? I want to go home now."

"Then talk to me," she says, "tell me why you agreed to help David Jenkins commit suicide. Why did you reply to his advert? When we met at the university you said that time is the enemy of love, not death. I want to understand. Maybe then I can help. You said it was an act of love. What did you mean?"

"So many questions, Ms. Austin. I'm not sure I have any answers. After all, I'm not a psychiatrist. But I can tell you this: I wasn't looking for Smith. He found me. When I read his advert it was like a call. I don't know if you can imagine such a thing. A message on a screen, sent by a stranger. A connection that touches something inside another complete stranger."

"Didn't you think the advert could be a prank?"

"He spoke of a journey, of needing a beautiful woman to help him to die." Catching my reflection in the mirror, I think he wouldn't have chosen me as I look now. Eyes bruised from broken sleep, skin sallow and jaded by stale air and crap food. "I've spent a lifetime analysing words. Poets choose every word with care, Ms. Austin, and Smith had done the same with his advert. I knew that he was seeking a special death. The biblical quote told me his journey was a spiritual one. I was willing to help."

"It sounds straightforward. As if you read his advert and the next thing was to arrange a date for the deed."

"It may sound that way, but life is never simple. We hadn't yet met, remember. And we may not have been attracted to each other. The whole thing could have ended there."

*

It's time for you to meet Smith. Where was I? Ah, yes. I was waiting on the platform in the bitter wind.

He stepped off the train at the far end of the platform, the only passenger. We were alone, walking slowly towards each other. I didn't feel the cold anymore, and my jacket hung open. I was hot under the arms and my face burned.

A few yards still separated us when he stopped. We considered each other. He was short, or seemed to be, but then I'm tall for a woman. He wore a long black coat, too thin to be wool, and carried a worn canvas rucksack. I noticed these things because I was scared to look at his face. But then he said,

"Hello, Robin." I liked his voice. Quiet and low, like water over pebbles. A steady voice.

I looked up.

He wasn't like his photo, and I realised he wore different glasses, trendy frameless ones, that made him seem younger. I moved towards him, kissed his cheek which was clean-shaven and scented with basil. He was better than I'd imagined, perfect in his ordinariness. Everything was right: his white shirt, his plain suit, his cheap coat. His small eyes blinking behind the lenses.

Beautiful, but only to me.

I was shy in the car, but he soothed me, describing his journey in level tones, even his hellish commute across London. He admired my Midget, touched the re-stitched leather approvingly. The car was scuffed and unloved when I bought it but I'd made it new again. I would do the same for him. I felt him looking at me, but I kept my eyes on the road, thinking through my actions like a learner driver, calming myself with the mantra of mirror, signal, manoeuvre.

When I yanked on the handbrake he gazed up at my house and whistled softly. "Beautiful."

I was embarrassed.

I couldn't tell him the house was a bribe, that it was bought with blood money. He followed me upstairs, to the spare bedroom, placing his bag on the bed as if he'd done it a hundred times before. "Do you mind if I have a shower? I want to wash the city off my skin."

I showed him the en-suite bathroom, the new towels on the rail, white and fluffy. All white, spa-like in its tranquillity. In the bedroom was a black iron bed, a mahogany chest of drawers. No mess, no clutter. Not even a picture on the wall. No distractions. Its minimalism calmed me.

I went down to the kitchen and fixed drinks. I hadn't asked what he wanted, so I made my favourite, whisky macs, heavy on the ginger with a peaty single malt. I also grabbed some nuts, which had been lingering in the cupboard for a while.

When Smith came down his hair was wet at the ends, making it curl. He had put his shirt back on, but without the tie, and it was open at the neck. He was barefoot and looked relaxed and at home, sipping his drink.

"Islay malt?"

"That's right."

"You're a connoisseur of whisky?"

I shrugged. "I've learned to appreciate it. I prefer to have fewer things, but have the best."

He looked around the room, "So I see."

The whisky warmed through my blood, loosened the skin from my bones and numbed my lips. I was heavy in my armchair, pulled my legs like dead weights under me, and rested my lolling head on the steep shoulder of the chair. Smith stretched out on the sofa, a hand trailing on the floor, as if he was dragging it in water as he was rowed along a river. The bottle was empty of whisky which coursed through our bloodstreams. If we had stretched out our hands we could have touched, but neither of us did. I wondered, abstractly, if we would spend the night like that. I wanted to touch him.

Smith retrieved his hand from the watery carpet, pressed his brow. "Oh God, the room's spinning."

Despite the deadening in my muscles, the room was the same as always to me. Only he made it different. He was like an animal I'd stolen from the zoo, an exotic creature that I didn't know how to care for, one which might bite. I wished I wasn't so drunk, although what else could strangers do, thrown together by one mutual desire but little else? I knew nothing about him. I waited for his touch, closed my eyes, and thought of his hands under the fabric of my clothes, wanting the warmth, the sensation of skin on skin. I wanted to get up, cross the room. I wasn't a child, not a silly schoolgirl, but a practiced lover, with no reason to hesitate.

I opened my eyes, swung my legs free, slid to the floor and crawled towards Smith. His hand was still upturned on his brow, as if to shield his eyes from bright sunlight. I sat on the floor, my head level with his, and touched his dark hair. A curl wrapped my finger like a baby's clasp. He didn't stir. His breathing was deep, punctuated by the sonorous sound of air through too-narrow airways. Fast asleep. Releasing his hair, removing my hand, I left him to spend the night on my sofa and went upstairs, to my own bed.

Miraculously, neither of us had hangovers the following morning. Another reason to invest in top-drawer liquor. It was February, but the sun was high, a Saturday; there was every reason to be happy. I slipped into a floaty dress, too thin for the weather but I felt warmed by Smith's presence. I listened to the sound of him showering, could hear him humming when the water stopped, the sound of his feet on wet tiles. It felt like my birthday and I wanted to celebrate, but I kept my feelings reined in, not sure of their appropriateness. After all, he'd come to me to die.

I looked at myself in the full-length mirror, trying to see through his eyes. I was tall and slender, and the cotton skimmed my breasts and hips. Under the skirt, shorter than I would normally wear, my calves were shapely and pale, nails a pretty coral that accentuate my long toes. Moving up, as a man's gaze might travel, I saw the faint line of my knickers, the lace of my bra. White on white. My neck, slender and long, and then my head, my face, long hair like a wave down my back. How often do we look at our faces and not see what's really there? I tried to consider slowly, as if seeing for the first time, an artist studying his muse before starting a portrait. My eyes, almond shaped, looked grey that morning but are in fact green; the shade varies depending on what colours I wear. My nose, with a delicate tilt at the end, is feminine but I dislike the nostrils which are too small for my features, my sharp cheekbones, my domed forehead.

I possess classical beauty. No moles or freckles, no irregularities or bumps. Just smooth porcelain and rose, pale hair and peridots for eyes. My looks have made it hard for me to be comfortable with women, and harder still to avoid men. If I could have chosen, I'd be plain.

The bathroom door opened. I could hear Smith in the spare room. I imagined him standing over his bag, naked, selecting a shirt. The image was hazy, as I didn't know what his body looked like. Not yet. It was only our first day together.

We met most weekends after that, but we really got to know each other via the Internet. Each evening I would log on, and he would usually be there, waiting. It was our conversations in cyberspace that mattered, more than our real meetings. It was on the screen, instant messaging, that we talked about Smith's final journey:

Robin: Pleasure and pain are two sides of the same coin. You can't have one without the other. Are you up for that?
Smith: I think so. But I want to know more about you. It bothers me that I don't.
Robin: Why?
Smith: I don't know. It's like marrying a stranger. It feels as if the order's wrong. Does that make sense?
Robin: Not really. Would knowing what my favourite flower is make any difference?
Smith: Maybe. I don't want us to be strangers. I want you to be the love of my life.
Robin: Tulips. Smith: Colour?
Robin: White. Or red. You?
Smith: I don't like flowers, they make me sneeze. Hobbies?
Robin: Books, naturally. And art. Both are ways to achieve immortality, that's the appeal. Eternity on a vase.

Smith: I'd like to know about art. I feel like such an ignoramus, some-
      times! I've been to art galleries, but they leave me cold. What am
      I missing?
Robin: Lots. Like diving into a picture, a scene and feeling it, actually liv-
      ing it. Being able to exist in the image without the need to ration-
      alise or reason. Negative capability, Keats called it.
Smith: Will you teach me? To feel without thinking. That's what I need.

It was like the beginning of any relationship, I suppose. But it was always
there, behind everything we talked about or did: Smith's intention to die.
He'd put a message in a bottle, and I'd plucked it from the sea. It was so
improbable, our being together. It was fate.

Cate Austin gives the memory of a smile. "All lovers believe that," she says.
"Until time and experience proves them wrong."

And I could kiss her. "Now you see! The truth about love. You understand!
Who wouldn't choose to preserve that feeling, if they could? If they dare. So
you see, Ms. Austin, if this is the extent of my madness then surely I don't
belong here, in this hospital. You will help to get me released, won't you?
You'll speak with Dr. Gregg?"

She says slowly, "Helping David to die was an act of love?" I'm happy
she understands but I still can't answer her question. It's too soon. She looks
exasperated, like a parent with a disobedient child. I find that I don't mind.

"Okay, maybe you'll answer this one," she says. "Why did Dr. Gregg section you? What happened to make you put the glass to your neck?" Just then
the door opens and Shane enters, ignoring my visitor.

"Tea time, Alice."

Cate looks at the large clock on the wall. It's only four thirty. "Can we have
a few more minutes?"

He shrugs, already turning away. "It's up to you, but her food'll be in the
bin. The cook can't stand stragglers."

These people have no respect.

"I think it's best if I go," she says, "But I'll come back tomorrow."

"And make sure you talk to that quack doctor who got me locked up in
here. Before I lose my temper and show him what real madness looks like."

17

"Okay, so what are the options?" asked Paul, putting his arms behind his head and sinking lower in his chair.

Cate toyed with a pen, opening the file with it and thinking. Supervision was a time to mull through cases, and she was glad her manager was Paul, that she could speak so freely. "Well, if Dr. Gregg recommends it, I can see a judge being attracted by a hospital order. It suggests that Alice acted because she was ill, something that can be cured. A far more palatable idea than the alternative."

"But when you saw her at St. Therese's she was fine? No mental health problems?"

"Not that I could see. She seemed as sane as I am! Which leaves a community order."

"Talk me through that. What would you do with her on a community order?"

"I'd look at her attitude to relationships, for one. Love and this idea of sacrifice seem to be quite twisted in her mind—I thinks it's only by working through that, that we'll know if she'd do it again."

"Christ, Cate, I hardly think she's a risk to the general population. She was lucky to find one nutter who wanted help to die, I don't think they'll be lining up!"

"I hope not, but that doesn't mean she won't try. She's so cold, so unemotional. She says helping Smith to die was an act of love. I want to feel something for her, Paul. Get some kind of connection, but I just can't. It's like talking to a hologram—it looks real enough, but really it's just an image. I just can't seem to get to the real Alice."

Paul shrugged, leaning back in his chair, the supervision notes forgotten on his desk. "So she's a cold fish. Let's cut to the chase, Cate—what are you going to recommend to the judge?"

"Christ knows. I'm still thinking that a prison sentence is the only real option. If I can't make any headway in the next few days I'll just have to conclude that she's unresponsive and wouldn't be suitable for a community order. If she won't open up, what good would that be to a probation officer?"

"But she's talking to you."

"Yes. But I still feel that she's holding back. Like the motive—I still don't have a grasp on why she wanted to help David Jenkins end his life. And if I don't know that, how can I come up with a plan that would satisfy a judge? Unless I can be certain that whoever ends up working this case would be able to make significant headway in ensuring Alice Mariani never re-offends, then I'm just going to have to propose a prison sentence. I won't be able to offer an alternative."

"Well, Cate, it's your call. But don't be too rash—after all her victim did want to die. It's not like she murdered anybody."

18

I'm in the nut house but I'm not a nut. A nut can be cracked but I will not be broken. Think about that psychology experiment in the sixties, the students faking mental illness to get admitted to a psychiatric hospital. Once they were inside they behaved normally and no one noticed. Label someone as mad and that's what they are. Give a dog a bad name and it'll bite you. I'm surprised that I remember such things, lessons that I learned when I was a student myself, years ago now, and in a different discipline, psychology. My mother's subject. Had she lived, had she not had me, it's what she would have studied at university. Maybe I am a chip off the old block, after all. I wonder if my grandmother thinks this, as she reads the morning paper across from her husband, staring at a headline about her dead daughter's daughter. Alice Mariani convicted. She sweetens her black coffee remembering when we met, all those years ago, and wonders if what has happened to Smith has anything to do with her. That had she shown me some love, it may not have happened. I'm inventing this, of course; I've no way of knowing if she thinks of me at all. About the bribe: she bought my silence. So very Catholic, she bought redemption for her sin, and I bought a house where I could be alone, and nice things like my precious blue vase. I call it blood money because there was blood on her hands. My mother's.

After I took the cheque, I never saw my grandmother again. She'd already abandoned her only daughter, it could only have been easier to abandon me. Once you walk away from love and survive, it must be easier the next time. That is one thing I can't do. I'm incapable of leaving someone I love. But those who walk away are survivors. They know what it takes to get over it, to move on. It's a gift.

Wherever my grandmother is, she can hardly have missed reading about me. And if, by some fluke, she hasn't seen the paper or watched the TV news, surely some well-meaning busybody will have asked her. 'That woman on the news, her name is Mariani too. Are you related?' To anyone who knew my mother, how could she deny the thick mane of blonde hair, the green eyes? Living apart does not stop you from looking like your kin, despite your best efforts. Children resemble their parents, one way or another. So taking the surname Mariani, that impulsive decision I made when I was sixteen, has become my final revenge. Forcing my grandmother to think of me, when she would rather forget.

Cate Austin thinks of me, I'm sure. Trying to work me out. She arrives with her notepad, her chewed pen. She's interested in me, I see it in the way her pen stops writing, her eyes watch for too long as she forgets to take notes. She is wondering if she is like me. How different am I really?

All lovers think like that, she told me when I said that meeting Smith felt like fate. She spoke like someone who's loved and lost. She knows something of my fear, but has she ever had a man willing to be her sacrifice? In the same place, what would she do? I'd like to ask what she thinks of my crime, to see if she gives the easy knee-jerk reaction: 'I would never do that! I could never help someone to die, never eat someone's flesh . . .'

But how do you know? Has anyone ever asked you? Have you thought about it? Really? Other people have chosen death as an expression of love. Smith and I are not unique. There are other cases, ones that don't reach the media, in other countries. Who will have heard of me in France, in America? And there was that case that made the news in Germany, Armin Miewes, who killed his lover at his request. After reading about it in the newspaper, I wondered how it had been done. So now, maybe, somebody is reading about me and thinking they could do the same.

Is it so very improbable?

I dream I'm in bed, but not this bed in the hospital. I'm at home. I dream I'm asleep.

From above, as I look down, I see my sleeping body, wound in a white sheet. I turn and toss in the night, and every motion winds the sheet tighter and tighter around me, like a snake constricting. Then I see I'm not alone. Next to me is Smith; or rather, what was once Smith. His body, his shell, the house his soul sub-let, if you believe in such nonsense. It is rotting; I can smell it even in my dream, the stench of decomposing flesh. His mouth is open and I'm drawn closer, into the blackness. Flies buzz round him, the smell makes me want to gag, and still I go deeper and deeper into him, into his body. When I wake, the sheet is pinned around me and a watery light intrudes through the curtains, telling me it is morning.

The doctor will arrive after breakfast and I have my best smile ready. I'm wearing a cashmere jumper and jeans, Chanel No.5 behind my ears and on my wrists. I no longer look mad. My hair is neat. Dr. Gregg looks at me as if I'm someone he doesn't recognise.

"I see someone brought your clothes, Alice. That must be a relief. You certainly look well."

He's at a loss about how to categorise me in these clothes. A different uniform, it confuses him. Just a few days ago I was mad, but today I'm sane. Which is it to be then? I hope his pride won't get in the way of my freedom. He should have started to assess me for a hospital order, started to prepare the way, not have me locked up! He made a mistake in sectioning me but admitting so is within his gift. I hope he's feeling generous.

He lifts a pen from his lapel and clicks the end, smiling pleasantly, inviting me to confide. "You seem much calmer today, Alice."

I decide to remain submissive. "I feel much better, thank you. I don't know what came over me." I hear myself, like some heroine in a Victorian novel, and think of the word swoon. That is what my voice is doing.

"I'm glad." He sounds doubtful, peering at me like I'm something in a petri dish. His glasses are half-circles and his jacket corduroy. He's the very caricature of a trendy physician. I'd laugh if there were not so much at stake.

"But the staff tell me you've been complaining of headaches and dizziness?"

"It's nothing. Just the worry of being here, probably. I want to go home, now," I tell him, biting back the 'please' that nearly escapes my lips. I will not beg. I don't belong here. Freedom is my right.

"I'm sure you do, Alice." Condescending. Using my first name without asking. To him, I'm a child asking for sweeties. I can hear the refusal already. "But although you seem well at the moment I think it would be wise to keep you here a while longer, just to be on the safe side."

"But . . ."

"It's for your own good, Alice. You were in quite a state on Tuesday. Let's see how you progress. The sedative from yesterday will have worn off now. I'll prescribe something else to keep you stable. And some more painkillers for that headache."

He's not talking to me. The speech is for his own benefit, the routine drone of a doctor doling out pills. Prozac or some other serotonin cocktail.

I shall not take them. I won't be tricked into madness, when sanity is all I have.

"Do you remember what happened on Tuesday, Alice?"

I think back, but my memory is a wasteland. I see outline but no details. What sedative did they give me, that I can't catch the day in my mind? I hear broken glass, and I wonder if it was my patience or my sanity that was shattered.

19

On her way to the secure ward Cate asked a passing nurse where she would find Dr. Gregg and was told his office was in the main part of the psychiatric hospital, near the Brain Injury Rehabilitation Unit. After she had thanked him, she headed to the crossroad of signs, scanning for BIRU. She dodged patients on the way, men and women who shuffled along or loped alarmingly, the very picture of madness. Alice wasn't like that and, even after thinking about what Dr. Gregg had said about egomania, she still wasn't convinced that Alice was suicidal. Determined not to make any mistakes with this case, she wanted this decision explained to her. She'd made a mistake once before. She wasn't going to let that happen again. This part of the hospital was open—no one here was held against their will, and Cate found her way to a general staff room, with a coffee machine and several desks. Two nurses and a woman in a flowing skirt with a nervous laugh were chatting while they wrote in files.

Cate knocked on the open door and said, "I'd like to speak with Dr. Gregg, please." One of the nurses took her name and picked up a phone. Cate heard her tell Dr. Gregg that Alice Mariani's probation officer wanted a word.

"He's on his lunch break," the nurse said, replacing the receiver, "but he's happy for you to go in if, you don't mind that he's eating."

Cate was directed along the corridor to a door below a sign that announced, in gilt letters on a black board: DR. CHARLES GREGG, Forensic Psychiatrist. Cate knocked and waited.

"Come in."

Dr. Gregg was seated behind an oversized desk, on which an open packet of crisps and a half-eaten sausage roll had been laid out on a serviette. He looked in his early fifties, silver peppered his brown hair and he wore half-moon glasses, his eyes framed by laughter creases. He stood, wiped his hand on the serviette, and offered it to her, "We meet at last, Ms. Austin."

"Cate," she said, taking the hand briefly.

"Take a pew, Cate. And call me Charles. I hope you don't mind if I carry on?" he gestured to his sausage roll, and Cate shook her head, "If I don't grab something now I'll miss my chance."

The seat was fairly low and placed her on eye level with a framed picture of a smart-looking woman with a helmet of dark hair, who must be his wife. There was also a picture of a dog, a giant St. Bernard slobbering on a ball.

"I'm just on my way to see Alice Mariani. This is my second visit; I came yesterday to bring her belongings."

There was a pause as Charles swallowed. "Yes, I noticed she was looking smarter this morning. You should have seen her on Tuesday. How did she seem to you yesterday?"

"Very well, I think. At first, I thought she looked strained but then, when she'd gotten herself dressed and we started to talk, I couldn't see that she was any different from Monday." Cate hesitated. "As you pointed out, I'm not medically trained."

Charles finished his lunch and leaned forward on his arms. He lowered his head and peered over the half-moons of his glasses, listening.

"So if you could help me out, Charles? I just don't understand why she's here. Do you really think she's a danger to herself?"

"Today she seems calm. But on Tuesday she was far from stable. As I said on the phone, she was raging. That rage could have been projected, or turned on herself, but she was in a fury. Have you ever heard of Brian Blackwell?"

"Sounds familiar. Was he the guy who killed his parents and then went on holiday the next day with his girlfriend?"

"That's right. There was some suggestion his mother abused him—he was seventeen and she still bathed him. After he murdered her, he moved her body to the bathroom. But I digress. I mention him because Blackwell's charge was dropped from murder to manslaughter on the grounds of diminished responsibility. He had a narcissistic personality disorder. That's how lethal the disorder can be. And on Tuesday, I wasn't going to take any chances. Alice was furious and I believed she intended herself harm."

"What about now? She seems as well as before. Does she still need to be here?"

"Staff have reported her as being angry, and several have picked up on her arrogance. The occupational therapist said she joined in with some of the team-building activities, but acted very superior and refused to cooperate with parts of the session. Alice is asking to be released, but when I had her sectioned she was very vulnerable. Let me get my notes." He found the case file in grey cabinet behind him, and read the notes. The file looked battered, and its cover was torn. "The interview went wrong very quickly. I started by asking if her mother had a normal pregnancy and labour. It's a routine question."

"How did she respond?"

"She seemed perplexed, and then told me that she was adopted when she was a child, so didn't know much about the details of her birth."

"Understandable."

"So I moved on to the next section that is standard in psychiatric assessments, and asked about early experiences, starting with school."

"Yes?" Cate leaned forward.

"She said that she was a good pupil, but never very popular, that she always felt different."

"Different in what way?"

"I asked her that. She suggested she was ostracised because of her extraordinary beauty and intellect. Of course, this arrogance fits with my initial diagnosis. It seems she only had one friend, her inferior in many ways, according to her. And then she became agitated and tearful."

"That can't be unusual." Cate herself saw many people in tears and every probation office had a box of tissues on the desk.

"No. But I have previous medical records, from her GP, detailing some work conducted when she was a teenager. Her mother had concerns about Alice's unhealthy relationship with a friend, which was exclusive and probably sexual, and she was eventually referred to a clinical psychologist. I wanted to ask Alice about this, and it was when I pressed this point that she became destructive, throwing things and grabbing for my notes. She was shrieking again and again 'I won't go to prison!'" The torn file had been Sellotaped, but Cate could still see the tear. "She was in a rage, grabbing and breaking anything she could, including the vase."

Something shifted in Cate's brain. Alice was refusing to go to prison. She remembered the broken glass on the floor. Snapdragons. The flowers were the same, but the vase had been swapped from the expensive blue to chunky yellow. She felt she was missing something, but what? She tuned back in to what Dr. Gregg was saying, "We've got a new approved social worker at the hospital, so I called her to Alice's house. She agreed with me that Alice needed sectioning. There was no way she would have come in voluntarily."

Cate glanced at her watch. She was already late for her meeting with Alice. Then a thought came to her, something triggered by what Dr. Gregg had said before. "You said Alice looked a fright on Tuesday. What did you mean?"

"She was wearing grey, baggy trousers, a well-worn t-shirt speckled with paint and, if you'll forgive me, she wasn't wearing a bra. She looked scruffy, and her hair was tangled and greasy. Very different to how she looks now."

"What about her face?" asked Cate.

"She looked awful. Dark shadows under her eyes, a clear sign of sleeplessness, and a yellow pallor. She looked ill."

Cate thought of the purple and grey makeup on the mahogany dresser, in shades she had never seen Alice wear. "And of course she had marks on her arm?"

"Superficial ones, yes."

Finally, it all clicked into place. It was the vase that had been changed, not the flowers. Why would a vase be changed if the flowers were not dead? Like a dawning light, Cate knew what had happened. She spread her right hand, clawing the nails and scratched her lower arms, digging hard until red welts appeared on her skin. "Were her arms marked like this?"

Dr. Gregg was about to protest, but she wouldn't be stopped. Cate could suddenly see very clearly, and the vision was startling; she knew what had happened. She reached into her bag, removed some pewter shadow, peered in the tiny mirror within the case and smeared it under her eyes.

Dr. Gregg was saying, "Cate, you don't need to do this . . ." but she didn't stop. She knew she was right. Ignoring him, she rubbed until her eyes looked bruised and tousled her hair on to her forehead. Cate peered into her pocket mirror, at the dishevelled, hectic face that stared back at her, and marvelled at how easy it could be to lose one's sanity. She showed him the marks on her arms, her chaotic face. "Did she look like this?"

Dr. Gregg stared, his mouth slack. Perhaps he was thinking that she was mad. Then he sat back and carefully closed the file. "If you are right, then I must commend our patient's acting skills." He sighed, "But why would she want to put on an act?"

Cate thought about what Alice said yesterday, about her fear of going to prison. "To get a hospital order rather than a prison sentence. She went too far and you sectioned her, but I think she was leading you to recommend a hospital order. Isn't it possible?"

"Maybe. But there's something else you should know. That psychologist who saw her when she was just sixteen believed that she was exhibiting signs of a personality disorder. He even identified narcissism. She was already ill, all those years ago. Because of her age a firm diagnosis wasn't made, but I think the notes show remarkable foresight. The episode on Tuesday, rather than being skilled acting, may in fact be a manifestation of a long-established case of narcissistic personality disorder. If she's genuinely sick, and we mistake it for acting, she won't get the help she needs. And that could be fatal."

20

I'm sitting on the bed with a tray balanced on my lap. The food is unappetising: pale chips and sticky beans, a child-sized carton of milk. I'm dissecting the beans with a blunt knife when Cate Austin throws the door wide. She has my full attention. Her neck is bunched muscle, her jaw set and her face and hair are a mess. She speaks before I have a chance to swallow.

"Why didn't you tell me you'd been treated for mental illness before, Alice?"

Her voice is fast over an undercurrent of resentment. I dab my lips with the paper napkin and push the tray aside. "I can't eat this rubbish."

"I've just been to see Dr. Gregg." Cate looks hard at me, demanding a reaction. "He told me that you already had a diagnosis, dating back to when you were sixteen. A personality disorder. You lied to me."

"You're wrong, Ms. Austin. I was too young to be diagnosed. I've never said a word that wasn't true."

"I told you that you had a choice, and one of those was to talk to me. I thought we were getting somewhere, that you were beginning to trust me."

I'm silent. She has great expectations.

"I didn't understand until just now why Dr. Gregg sectioned you, so I've just been to talk with him. He believes you've relapsed. That you have narcissistic tendencies."

She pauses. I see that she's uncertain about this diagnosis but it's no surprise to me. I know how other people see me.

"The thing is, Alice, you were fine on Monday. And yesterday, when I visited your home, it was immaculate. There was no sign anywhere of the woman that Dr. Gregg sectioned. Except the black eye shadow on the dresser. The yellow makeup. And another thing—the smashed vase. It wasn't the expensive blue and white one that I saw on the table. It was a cheaper yellow one, but the flowers were the same. Why did you swap the vase, Alice? Is it because you planned to smash it, and didn't want to break your precious art? Is that why the makeup was still out on the dressing table? Had it been applied in a hurry, before the good doctor arrived at your door? I think you put on a little performance so Dr. Gregg would think you'd relapsed. So tell me. Was it a sham?"

"A sham?" I stand, move closer.

She doesn't blink or step away as I thought she would.

"Don't you trust his judgment, Ms. Austin? It would take more than a broken vase and a bit of makeup to hoodwink Dr. Gregg, surely?"

"Stop patronising me, Alice. Just tell me, was it a sham?"

"Do you want me to tell you the status of my mental health, Ms. Austin, when you have already spoken to a professional?"

"I don't believe you're mentally ill." She speaks softly now, and it's me who is angry. She's still standing too close. Finally, she steps back. "But I'm not an expert."

"No. It doesn't matter what you think or what I say. It's the judge who'll decide. And what Dr. Gregg has done will weigh heavily with him. I can't be locked up in prison. I haven't the constitution for it, to live behind bars. I would be a plant in the shade; I would wilt. Whatever else happens, I must have my liberty. They can make me do anything else, clean ditches, work with cripples, whatever . . . but I had to convince him that I can't be locked away in jail!" Cate slowly shakes her head, as if she has had enough of my words. "Look at me, Ms. Austin. Wearing smart clothes, gold studs in my ears, face expertly made up. How could I be mad when I was so professional and educated? But if I'm not 'mad' then I must be something else, another label will be applied. And if that label is 'bad' or 'evil' then what will become of me? I'll be sent to prison, perhaps for years, and I couldn't let that happen. At least in hospital I'll be released when I'm deemed well again."

Cate looks at me, silently considering.

"My distress was real. You still believe I pulled the wool over his eyes with a bit of makeup? I suppose I should be flattered." My anger has gone, and I taste bitter desperation. Honesty makes me vulnerable, and I sit down on the bed that sinks under my weight. "I'm scared, Cate. I want your help. Is there a choice, an option between mad and bad? Can I be reasonable? Plausible? It's a risk but I want to be myself; I want to tell the truth. But I'm scared. I don't want to go to jail."

"I can't make any promises, Alice. I don't know what I'll propose, and sentencing is just a week away. But I know this much: the games have to stop. Can you do that? You must tell me the truth."

I look away, swallowing a sharp taste. "I've never told you anything else. And I hate playing games." She sits next to me, so close I can feel her warmth. It makes me want to weep.

"Then help me to understand, Alice."

"I'm trying to. I've tried to explain." I blink, cursing the tears that are close. I can't hold on to my thoughts. My sanity is slipping from me.

"Tell me about David. About your family. Did they ever meet?"

I see that once again I have no choice. I must talk. I force the words to sound easy.

They met just the once. I couldn't face taking Smith to my parents' home, so I agreed to afternoon tea in the White Swan. It was Easter, and Smith was visiting for the bank holiday weekend. I remember as we walked to the hotel he put his arm around my shoulder. 'I'm quite looking forward to meeting your folks,' he said. Sometimes he forgot that we were transcending normal relationships. Smith meeting my parents was something I would have avoided if I could, but Mum wore me down with her repeated questions. Finally I gave in, warning them that he was very ill so they mustn't interrogate him. We agreed to meet on Good Friday.

I didn't tell him about the conversation I'd had with them, when I told them he was dying. That they assumed he had cancer. But I felt safe, believing my parents too polite to raise such a terrible topic. I just had to keep the meeting brief.

The Swan is called a destination pub in the Sunday magazines. It's a time warp of a place, with the young waiters, students on a gap year from the other side of the world, in white shirts and black trousers, holding silver trays at shoulder height. It's comfortable with its own brand of shabby refinement, populated by Londoners and locals in tweed suits. Exactly the kind of place my mum dreams of visiting but then ruins by being over anxious.

When we arrived my parents were perched on a window seat, still in their coats, looking awkward. They stood up and started to walk over, "Yoo hoo Alice! Over here!" Other people in the hotel turned to look at us.

The sofa sagged under our weight, a long wooden table at our knees, while my parents each took a low chair opposite. Smith was impeccably polite, offering his hand to both my parents. He introduced himself with a fictitious name, as we'd agreed. "I'm Richard."

We ordered tea, and Mum insisted on a tower of cakes as if it was a party. On the top tier was a choux pastry swan filled with vanilla cream, and I remembered that swans mated for life. It was too beautiful to eat.

Mum picked at a custard slice, smiling sadly, and sneaked glances at Smith. I knew she was trying to detect signs of his illness. It pained my parents that my boyfriend was ill, I knew that. But I also knew they were relieved that at least I had a boyfriend.

I suppose it was nerves that made Smith's hand shake, his cup clattering in the saucer as he held it. Dad noticed, too. "Well, Alice, it's been a while since we've seen you," he said, "glad to see you're still in the land of the living." He stopped, realising what he had just said, looked at Smith, "It's just an expression. I wasn't referring to you . . ."

There was an awful smash as Smith dropped the delicate china. It shattered on the stone floor. He looked at me, and I looked at the broken pieces on the floor. A waiter sulkily began to clean up, a tight look of disapproval on his face. Smith's hand was still shaking.

"Dad!" I hissed, and he was looking sorry but still curious. Next to him, my mother's head was slightly cocked as her eyes drowned with sympathy. I wanted to throw my drink in her face. Smith fumbled with a tissue, mopping up spilt tea though the waiter wanted him to stop interfering. Eventually, the broken crockery was cleared away and the waiter disappeared.

Dad pushed his untouched tea away. "I'm sorry, Richard. I didn't mean to speak out of turn."

Mum pulled out a handkerchief from her handbag, which she must have slid between the purse and her lipstick in anticipation of this moment, and blew her nose. "No, he shouldn't have said that." She shot my father a black look. "But it's so tragic. Our daughter is finally happy, and then . . . Is there nothing the doctors can do?"

I was beside myself with rage, but also shame. Why wouldn't they both shut up? But if I was distressed, Smith was worse. His face was drained of colour, both his hands shaking, clasped together between his knees. When he spoke, his voice was cold. "There's nothing the doctors can do. There's no medicine. No cure. It's just a matter of time."

I never knew Smith was such a good actor. He was so convincing, Mum began to blub. Dad cleared his throat and said, "How much time have they said you've got, son?"

I couldn't believe he would ask such a question. If Smith really had been terminally ill the conversation would have been devastating. "About a month, maybe two. These things can never be exact." His voice was warm, and my parents melted, my mother wiping away fresh tears and my father endlessly clearing his throat. I didn't know what to do. Smith was doing such a good job, that I couldn't fail him. I put my arm around him, leaned my head on his shoulder. His body quivered, losing strength, and I seized our excuse for a swift exit. Mum pushed a custard slice away, and the tea went cold in the pot.

Smith and I walked back towards my house. When we reached the brow of the hill he paused and looked across to the church. It was magnificent. Even I, who sees it daily, am not blind to its splendour; it's large and lavish, perfect testimony to the success of the medieval wool trade in this area.

"Let's go in," he said, leading me across the road and through the wooden gate. Perfect shrubs ballooned around us as we faced a fork in the path, and chose the left, which lead to St. Peter and St. Paul, flanked by sentinel daffodils. It's one of the grandest parish churches in the country. The vast interior has cathedral-like proportions, and we stood looking up like tourists. In the silence, Smith squeezed my hand and we gaped at the ornate carvings, the hammer-beam roof, the luminous stained glass windows. We stepped forward, devout in our silence, heads obediently low. Silence was a relief after the horrible meeting with my parents.

"I'm really sorry about my parents. I should have told you that they think you're dying. I never thought they would mention it. I told them you were ill, but I never said it was cancer. They just assumed. My God, you were convincing! Did you do acting at school or something?"

Smith pulled me to him. "No," he replied, into my hair, "I'm not a good actor."

"You could have fooled me." I smiled as I felt his lips on my neck.

We stood listening to the silence, a hush that echoed across the high walls, the glorious fifteenth-century architecture. Smith bowed his head, lips moving in prayer. Our feet knocked on the ancient flagstones, walking on memorials to the beat of our progress. At the end of the wide nave, facing the largest window, we looked up. The crucifixion. Jesus, nailed to a cross, flanked by three people: his mother, John, and Paul.

"No wonder they call it The Passion. Just look at his face," whispered Smith, as if afraid to disturb someone sleeping. Jesus' eyes were closed, and his mouth drawn down, but not in agony. Rather it's the expression of endurance, the serenity of acceptance. Smith said, more to himself than me, "It's easy to be a sacrifice when you know there's a heaven."

As he gazed at the dying man I looked at the figures on either side. Mary had a painful expression across her heavy brow, eyes intent on her son. Her mouth was pulled in a seam. There is nothing more to say, her mouth told me. An open mouth is a sign of defiance: a shout, a scream, a yell of denial. A refusal to accept. But that closed mouth of Mary's, more than her stooping posture, more than her praying hands, spoke of acceptance.

On Jesus' other side was John, his hands clasped and pleading, but his expression was less peaceful, a bewildered heaviness in the lids of his eyes. I wondered how I would be when Smith was dying. If I would be serene and accepting, like the Virgin, or if in the end I would be bewildered by what we had done.

Smith was still gazing at the face of Jesus. "If I knew for certain there was an afterlife I'd be glad to die. I need faith."

We were holding hands; his was clammy so I dropped it, but moved closer to his side. We were two disciples, under the cross, and he was losing faith. "It will be me waiting there, under your cross, watching you endure, and I'll take you with me after. In my heart. The remembered never die."

He turned, cupping one hand to my face. "There's another way for you to keep me with you. Not in your heart, but in your body. The Eucharist. When Catholics take the bread and the wine they take in Jesus, his flesh, his blood. For my flesh is food indeed and my blood is drink indeed. Do you see, Robin? Do you see how important the Transfiguration is?"

I recoiled. I watched his face for meaning, allowed him to seat me in a pew. He knelt at my feet. "God made his word flesh, and that flesh became a sacrifice on the cross. That's what I want. To sacrifice myself to you, but in you to live again." He placed his hands on my shoes, as if he wanted to remove them. "You are my disciple, Robin." Then he looked at me, and I saw suspicion, hardness in his eyes as if I'd betrayed him. "But I have prayed for thee, that thy faith fail not. Promise me you'll be faithful."

I wanted to promise but the words wouldn't come.

We left the church, passing a stall laden with groceries and an honesty box at the front. What kind of church has its own jams and sauces? How about a pack of 'St. Peter & St. Paul cookies?

"This place is such a tourist trap." Smith wasn't listening. "Have you got 50p?" I dug in my handbag, found a pound coin. It fell in the box with a jingle, landing on a mountain of other coins, and Smith chose a postcard from the rack. It was a picture of the crucifixion scene, which we had just studied for so long. Tight-lipped, he slid it into the inside pocket of his coat.

We left the church and I took his hand. He turned to me as if just remembering who I was, looking like he had just awoken from a dream. His face was serene and accepting.

Later that night, just two hours after I had watched him board a train back to London, I logged on to my computer. He was already there, waiting for me. An instant message flashed on the screen:

Smith: Robin? Are you there?
Robin: Yes.
Smith: Have you thought about my request?
Robin: I'm trying to understand.
Smith: Is it really such a shocking idea? I mean, we're already pushing the limits of what others call acceptable.
Robin: But suicide is noble. In other cultures, in other times—look at Japan, think of Romeo and Juliet. Cannibalism isn't.
Smith: You're wrong, Robin. You're thinking with your Imperialist head, your Western prejudices. Kuru, the eating of the dead, is an ancient funeral rite, a mark of respect. It's a way to keep the dead with us. Theophagy can only be practiced by the faithful. By the devout.
Robin: The only people I can think of who eat humans are serial killers: Neilson, that Japanese psychopath, Hannibal Lecter . . .
Smith: Those people were mentally ill, but the instinct is primitive, already in us. Some animals eat their dead young. It's a kind of recycling but on a spiritual level. It's beautiful.
Robin: Like the Eucharist? The bread and the wine?
Smith: Exactly. It's not ugly, it's a sign of devotion. Taking it in, absorbing. That's what I want. To be carried inside you. To live in your body. To feel there was a purpose.
Robin: Help me.
Smith: How?
Robin: Make it normal. Make me understand.
Smith: You've taught me so much about how you see the world, about negative capability. Experience without analysis. But now it's my turn to teach you. I'll tell you a story. Of another land. Of people far, far away who lived a different life.

He told me the story of the cannibals in Papua New Guinea. But it was still hard for me to see. My understanding was only partial. I didn't want to eat him. But he said I must trust him. I must have faith:

Smith: Do you believe, Robin? Have you enough faith?
Robin: It's difficult, but I'm trying.

94

Smith: I'm almost ready. It's nearly time. I can feel it . . .

Robin: I know. We've come so far. Your final journey. A beautiful death. It's what I've always dreamed of, and now that I've found you I know it's possible. I promise to make your final moments perfect.

Smith: But there is something I want. Will you give me what I ask for?

Robin: Anything.

Smith: My dying request?

Robin: Tell me. Make it clear—I want to be sure I understand.

Smith: Will you taste me? My flesh. My blood. I want you to take me in, take me with you. Like Jesus. Do you see? You must know that I can only live on if you agree.

Robin: I want to make you happy. It's all I've ever wanted, to make someone's final moment the best. But I hadn't expected this. It was naïve of me, but I hadn't imagined any blood.

Smith: 'He who eats my flesh and drinks my blood abides in me.' Robin, will you do it? Will you eat me?

"I didn't want to do it."

Cate Austin looks up from her notepad. "You didn't want to help him to die?"

"Of course I did. That was part of the plan. To cease on the perfect note . . . as long as it was his choice." I must make her see this: "I'm not a murderer."

"What is it you didn't want to do, Alice?"

I hesitate. Is it the right time for this? It must come, I know, but is she ready to hear me; is there enough trust? I breathe slowly, "Holy Communion. The cutting . . . the eating."

She watches, and I see the colour rise to her cheeks. I'm surprised when she doesn't pull her punch. "So why did you agree to do it?"

There are movements in the corridors outside. I look at the clock on the wall. It's ten to two. In a few moments the staff will be collecting the patients for their afternoon activities.

"Alice, why did you do it? What motivated you—what possessed you? Why on earth did you agree?"

21

In the unnatural heat of the swimming pool, the children's voices echoed and screeched off the walls like tropical birds calling to each other over the warm water. They flew around, chastised by mothers and lifeguards who feared they'd slip, but the young feet hurried on, splashing on wet tiles, chattering to each other and climbing to the high bough of the fluorescent slide. Their costumes were exotic too, flashes of indigo and violet as they bombed down the slide, landing in a cascade of splash and bubbles as anxious adults watched from the edge, waiting for the resurfacing, the yells of triumph. In the smaller pool, away from the noise and shove, a younger fledgling paddled, equally bright in a turquoise swimsuit. There was a pink flamingo depicted on the front, and she stood like one, unsteady on straight legs, looking around the water with uncertainty. Next to her swam a young woman with long hair like a silver sword down her spine. She too was exotic. At first a bystander would see two girls, think they were sisters, but on closer inspection would realise it was a mother and daughter who were enjoying the heat of the baby pool.

They were predictions of each other; what one looked like as a child, what the other would look like in seventeen years. The mother was just a teenager, hair in a wet ponytail slapping her back as she bobbed around her nervous daughter. But the relationship was made clear by the child's frequent cries of, "Mummy! Watch me!" as she kicked her feet and flapped her orange armbands as if preparing for flight.

The mother dived into the shallow water. For agonising seconds the girl panicked, looking about but not daring to move, desperate to see the blonde head of her lost parent break the surface. She was like an abandoned chick in a nest, and totally helpless.

A waterfall of giggles celebrated the girl's joy at being found, her mother swimming under her, between her legs. The girl was so small that as the mother glided under, she was lifted onto her back, riding a sea horse through shallow shoals. She held on tight as her mother came up for air.

Later, maybe the same day but maybe not, the girl with the pink flamingo swimsuit was at home, lining up her dolls and animals, instructing them on tea party manners. "Say please, Sindy," Alice told her favourite doll, "and I'll do your hair and make you pretty." The doll had matted brown hair, and the girl pulled a plastic comb through the nylon mop.

Alice's home was just one room, and in that room was her whole world. She didn't have a bed, but a special chair folded out each night, and her Mummy threw a sheet over the orange itchy fabric, making it cosy with a pillow and blanket. Sometimes she was too tired to sort out the chair and the girl was glad, because then she could curl up behind her in the bed, warm and safe as she leant her head against her Mummy's back.

It was home, that room.

There was the big bed and the chair, a sink and a small TV with an aerial that Mummy had to wiggle to get a good picture. Their clothes were in a small dresser, on top of which they kept their shampoo and soap, other things they took with them to the shared bathroom down the hall. Alice wasn't allowed to go there alone, not even to do a wee, because Mummy said you never knew who was about. The little cooker in the corner sometimes flamed, so she wasn't allowed to go near that either.

"Really, Matilde. There's not enough room to swing a cat." The smart lady tutted and stared, and Alice thought what she said was funny, imagining a fat ginger tom on a wooden swing going higher and higher and reaching the ceiling. No, there wasn't enough room. The cat would get hurt. Even though the smart lady said this funny thing she didn't smile and Mummy looked sad, so Alice wanted the smart lady to go away but she just stayed, looking around, in her furry coat and shiny black shoes.

"Come here, Alice," she ordered, and Alice obediently stood up, holding her doll in front of her. The lady stared at Alice for a long time, pulling her forward, a tight hand on her top arm until she thought she would wet herself with fear. The lady said to Mummy, "Well, at least she doesn't look like him."

She let go of Alice who scurried back to the corner with her toys.

Alice lifted her doll on to her lap and whispered sternly, "Just be quiet, Sindy, and give me some peace," trying not to look at the smart lady who was making Mummy cry. "You're a naughty doll and I'm going to smack your bottom," Alice said, seeing in the dressing table mirror that the smart lady was now sitting on the edge of the bed, next to Mummy, still with her coat on. It looked funny because the smart lady and Mummy had the same sort of mouth, both of them looked sad, and then the smart lady opened her shiny bag and lifted out a red purse, which opened with a click. She handed Mummy a bit of that coloured paper people keep in purses, and at first Mummy said no, but then she took it and that made her cry harder and the old lady said it doesn't have to be this way, and that she would have a better chance. Then she asked what kind of a life is this for either of you and then Mummy said, shush, she's listening.

Alice combed Sindy's hair and pretended to be deaf.

Mr. Wilding was always knocking at the door, and sometimes Mummy let him in, usually when he had something for them, not just fish and chips or wine. He brought toys, still in plastic and boxes. Dolls and sketching books. Alice loved the presents, but Mummy always looked sorry he'd brought them, even though he said they were a gift.

That evening, after they got back from the park, Mr. Wilding came knocking. Her mother's tongue was still sore from the accident on the swing and she was grumpy. He tried to make her smile. He gave Alice a Barbie doll, and said he'd take Mummy out. He knew a special place. He said it would be fun. He said she should wear her dress, the pretty one with flowers on it. He said to remember some lipstick.

Mummy looked lovely, like Cinderella after the fairy godmother's done her magic, and the lipstick was nice and bright, so why didn't she look happy? She promised Alice she'd be home soon.

When Mr. Wilding saw Mummy he touched her bottom and said she was a good girl. Alice had never heard her being called that before. She didn't know that grown-ups could be good girls, too. Alice stayed in the room, with the TV on for company and her new Barbie. She fell asleep on the big bed, but she woke to the sound of shouting in the hallway.

Mr. Wilding didn't think Mummy was a good girl anymore, he called her other things. Nasty things. Alice held Barbie and lay as still as she could, pretending to be asleep. Mummy smelled funny when she climbed into bed, like smoke but also like the grass when it's just been cut. She cuddled Alice too tight and sang to her, softly. A lullaby that she had sung to Alice all her life:

"Hush, little baby, don't say a word. Mummy's going to buy you a mockingbird . . ."

Alice and Mummy were in the red telephone box down the street and outside it was raining hard. Alice was looking out of the smeared glass, watching the rain make puddles on the pavement, wishing she could go and splash in them, but the door was too heavy for her to open on her own. They'd left without putting on wellies, or even coats. Mummy had just picked up the envelope from the mat downstairs and once she'd opened it she grabbed Alice's hand and they had run to the telephone box. Mummy hadn't even noticed the rain.

Mummy was shouting into the black receiver, pushing silver coins into the box. Alice heard the words, but didn't understand them all. She knew the argument was about adult things and she heard the word 'money' and 'no, I can't go to court again,' so she thought about Kings and Queens and maybe Mummy needed money to go to the Ball.

After the phone call they walked back to the bedsit in the rain and Mummy didn't even say to hurry up. It was as if she didn't notice that Alice was soaked to the skin.

Back at the bedsit Mummy stood in front of Mr. Wilding's door. Alice shuffled her feet and finally Mummy knocked on the door. Usually, he came to them.

Alice stood behind Mummy, but she could see into his room. The boxes had gone, but there were piles of other things, computers and televisions. Mr. Wilding was laid on the bed and on the table in front of him something was spilt, something white. Maybe washing powder. Maybe icing sugar! Alice squeezed in behind her mother and went to the table, dipping a finger in the sugar.

The slap was hard on her wrist. "Leave that, Alice!" Mummy pushed her away, but then she bent down and cleared up the powder, only not with her hands. She kept her back to Alice, but when she turned round the sugar was gone, and she was smiling and the tip of her nose was white. Mr. Wilding was smiling too. It must be a good day after all.

He tried to kiss Mummy but she gave him a shove, "Not while Alice is watching!" He looked at her mother with narrow eyes like the wolf in *Little Red Riding Hood* and Alice knew he wanted to eat her. He said, "Look, Matty, I'll give you another chance. But you better not fuck up this time."

Alice knew it was a naughty word.

Mr. Wilding was like the wolf in the story. His teeth were brown and pointed, and he licked his lips like he was hungry. Only he didn't want to eat Alice. Instead, he looked hungrily at her mother. He brought food, too, though not in a basket, and it wasn't really food but small parcels in white wrappers that her mum took to the toilet. When she came back her eyes were wet like she'd been crying, her face happy at last.

Mummy said thank you to Mr. Wilding like she really meant it, not like the way she said it to the landlord when he gave her more time to pay the rent, or to the woman from the benefits office who they visited to beg for money. Alice had to wear a jumper with holes in when they went there, and it was a stinky place, and Mummy would say we've no money for food, and then point to Alice saying look at her—she's only four. If the lady said no, Mummy would say I don't know how you sleep at night.

Mr. Wilding really was a wolf, even if he didn't have fur. Once, after Mummy had come back from the toilet, and was lying on the bed, her arms crossed over her eyes but her mouth smiling, he leaned over and pretended to kiss her on her shoulder. Mummy pushed him away, laughing, but Alice knew then that she was right. She had seen teeth marks on Mummy's neck.

Even then, young as I was, I knew love was dangerous.

22

Dave Jenkins had only been dead for sixteen days when the management asked for all signs of him to be erased. Krishna Dasi had been longing for a joint all morning but couldn't see a chance of escaping to the fire exit for a crafty smoke anytime soon. He was normally fairly placid, but the day's tension was under his skin like steel plates, and he just couldn't shake free. He knew it wasn't his job to clear Dave's desk but he had agreed anyway. Mr. Filet had wanted it done, and no one else had offered. The poor sod had only just been buried. Caroline, one of the admin staff, had wrinkled her nose as if the very thought of touching his things offended her. Krishna couldn't let one of the women in the office do it. They wouldn't show proper respect for the dead man, he thought, as he placed the cardboard box on the desk. He'd been putting the job off, but as he was feeling lousy with a summer cold, it seemed the best time. He'd sat opposite Dave's desk for seven months but had never noticed what was on it. They'd been mates: sharing a joke or two, going for drinks after work together, usually just to the bar opposite for a swift half on a Friday, and then on to Krishna's place for a smoke and a chat that usually ended up being about religion or the afterlife; Dave was interested in things like that, and Krishna was always up for a debate. Dave would scan Krishna's flat, picking up the small marble figure of the elephant-headed god, Ganesha, or gaze at the picture of the many-armed goddess. Dave's god looked like a man, so he couldn't get his head round the look of Hindu gods. Krishna had tried to explain, that the whole point was that gods are divine. "If God simply looks like a man," Krishna had asked, "wouldn't that suggest that God isn't divine at all, but flawed?"

"I think," said Dave, "that is exactly the point."

To Krishna this had seemed a bleak and uninspiring view of religion. Depressing, even. And he knew that Dave wasn't happy, that he was too introspective. But he'd seemed better the month before he died. In the days just prior, he was almost chirpy. And then the news had come. Mr. Filet had called them all together. Krishna had listened silently as the other staff, the ones who hardly knew Dave, didn't even like him, cleared their throats or dabbed their eyes with tissues. Krishna just felt guilty; he should have seen that his mate was on the verge of suicide. The signs had been there, if he'd only noticed them. Maybe he could have helped him to think of another way to deal with whatever was bothering him. Then he'd wondered if that was why Dave had brought up all those conversations about karma and reincarnation. If only Krishna had known what he'd had in mind, he would've told him that suicide wasn't the answer. How could the soul progress, when the body had been violated?

The newspapers had said that Dave had taken a fatal overdose, that he'd left a suicide note and his girlfriend had been with him until the end. Krishna hadn't even known there was a girlfriend. Dave had never mentioned anyone and there was no photo of her on his desk. Just a leather desk tidy, with Safe Harbour inscribed pencils, and a thin laptop computer, the same as his own. There was also a *Far Side* desk diary, with a cartoon above each month. It was open at June. The month he had died. Time had moved on regardless.

He slid open Dave's desk drawer. It was tidy, unlike his own, but he saw the same calculator, part of an actuary's essential kit.

More pencils, and a silver sharpener. Technically work items, so Krishna left them. He picked up a box of Nurofen, and a jotter, which he flipped open. Lists of some kind, in Dave's cramped scrawl, so he put that in the box, too. There was an unopened pack of extra strong mints, which Dave had often sucked, always politely offering Krishna one even though in seven months he'd never accepted. Where would all these belongings be sent? Dave had lived alone. His mother had died a long time ago, in a car accident when he was just a boy, and his father passed away last Christmas. Dave had taken compassionate leave to organise the funeral. His father had suffered from Alzheimer's and had been in a nursing home. Dave said that when the end came it was a relief, but he'd looked tired, and Krishna saw his hands shaking. He'd noticed Dave was overdoing it on the cannabis, but told himself it was none of his business. Everyone makes their own choices in life, and Krishna didn't believe in interfering. People must choose their own path and live by the outcome.

Krishna opened another drawer and saw a stack of paper, the two files Dave had been working on and a train ticket to Colchester dating back to February. His hand hovered with the used ticket above the bin, then he put it in the box, just in case. Along with the ticket was a postcard. There was no address, no message; maybe it had been bought for the sake of the picture, rather than to send. The picture was of the crucified Jesus. Either side of the cross were two people, a man and a woman, looking up. The man was weeping, but the woman—Mary?—was calm. Dave was a lapsed Catholic, but in the few months before his death he said he'd found his faith again, so that must be why he'd kept the postcard in his desk. Also in the drawer was a rosary, which Krishna lifted, feeling the beads with his fingers. Catholicism seemed such a hard religion to him. So concerned with guilt and sin that it could weigh you down.

There was one more thing in the drawer. An envelope, addressed: Robin & Smith. Sounds like a comedy duo, he thought.

The flap was open, and he peered tentatively in, seeing a pile of printed-out emails, on top of which was a yellow post-it note. The telephone number was written in Krishna's own handwriting. It was the number for the guy who sold drugs, and he remembered only too well giving it to Dave, who wanted a way to get dope, that was all. Krishna wondered if Dave had used too much; excessive cannabis use could make anyone paranoid and depressed and Dave had already had enough going on in his life to bring him down, what with his dad's death. He peeled the post-it from the paper and screwed it into a tight ball, shoving it in his pocket, wishing he had never given Dave the number.

Krishna didn't read the emails; he respected Dave's privacy too much for that and besides there were some things it was best not to know. He pushed the papers back into the envelope and placed it in the box.

Now the desk held nothing to show for Dave's life, nothing personal. Anybody could have worked there: pencils, paperclips, it just held the usual stuff of office life. At least on his own desk he had a picture of his dad in ivory and gold and his mum, dressed in cherry red, her ears heavy with yellow-gold earrings. The photo had been taken at his sister's wedding, some five years ago now, and still no baby. Being a man he was under slightly less pressure to settle down just yet, but loneliness was a heavy price to pay for independence. He also had a picture of Deva, his bull terrier. Dogs could be depended upon. Blowing his nose, he turned on Dave's computer and waited for Mark from IT to arrive.

Mark, a keen twenty-something with a blonde quiff, seemed to know all the women in the department, and Krishna watched as he took a moment to chat with each of them, a finger hooked in his dark jeans. Then he came to Krishna, still smiling pleasantly. "Alright, mate? Sorry to hear about Dave.

Must be a bit of a shock. It won't take me long to tidy up the computer, then I'll be out of your way."

Mark logged on to Dave's computer using his system password, and brought the screen to life. The company logo on the screen saver, identical to his own, was of two men in profile shaking hands, one on a boat, one on the quayside. The tagline said, 'Safe Harbour Insurance. You're in good hands.'

Krishna watched as Mark saved various files onto a disk with speedy efficiency, recognising file names and client headers. He saw the icon for the office manual, a generic file that held such information as how much money could be claimed for out-of-hours meals, maternity benefits and also the policies of the company, including equal opportunities. Are we equal, though, he wondered. He'd certainly never felt it, and knew that any mistake he made would be taken more seriously than those made by his white colleagues. As one of the few black people working for Safe Harbour he was regarded with a certain amount of suspicion. It wasn't just after 9/11 either, though since then he'd been mistaken for a Muslim on several occasions. At university he'd always been on the edge of the group. That was when he started smoking dope, to relax, but also because it was what the other students did. He wanted to fit in. That was the problem, his parents thought. Why he'd never met a nice Hindu girl and settled down. Any phone call ended with them telling him he was too British. He felt like he couldn't win.

"Nearly done, mate," said Mark, not looking up from the screen. Then, in surprise, "Hello. What's this?" Krishna looked over his shoulder, where the curser flashed over a file named Robin & Smith.

"Sound familiar to you? Is it a client?" When Krishna remained silent, thinking of the envelope in the box, he said, "I'll open it up, and then we'll decide whether to save or ditch it." He double clicked and the file opened. Mark had moved aside and busied himself with some paperwork.

It took just moments for Krishna to realise that this file was only two lines long:

I HAVEN'T KEPT A JOURNAL BEFORE, SO YOU'LL HAVE TO BEAR WITH ME. WRITING'S NOT EXACTLY MY STRONG POINT BUT I WANT YOU TO UNDERSTAND.

Krishna must have made a noise because Mark looked up from his papers. "Everything alright, mate?"

"Yeah, it's just an unfinished report. Nothing important. Delete it."

And, turning back to the keyboard, with a single press of a button, Mark deleted the file.

Krishna sat back at his desk, trying not to think of what he had just done. He ignored Mark tapping on the keyboard across from him, picked up his pencil, and immersed himself in numbers.

A female voice roused him. "Can I get you a coffee?" Caroline from Accounts was standing over Mark, batting her eyelashes at him.

"Cheers, Caz. Milk and two, please."

Caroline glanced over at Krishna, and for a surprised second he thought she was also going to offer to get him a drink. She had done her best to ignore him since he had declined to join her on a trip to the cinema a few weeks ago. She held up a small, brown package. "This was in the post for you. Whoever sent it forgot to use stamps, so it's been sitting at the sorting office, waiting to be picked up. I hope it wasn't urgent."

She threw it on the desk and he saw that the package was marked Private and Confidential. The seal looked as though it had been undone, and then re-sealed as it was uneven and coming loose at the ends. After peeling back the flap, he reached in and felt the shape, something like a pack of gum. Pulling it out he saw it wasn't gum but a computer memory stick. Wrapped around the stick was a letter, folded in two. Opening it, he saw familiar handwriting. He looked up, expecting Caroline and Mark to be staring at him but she had gone and Mark was still tapping away, oblivious to the fact that Krishna had just received a letter from a dead man.

16th June

Krish,

I know you'll look after this. It's important. Sometimes things don't work out as we planned, as you and I both know. After all, we deal in improbabilities. By the time you get this I'll be long gone, but I want to travel light. Keep this safe for me.

   I hope to see you again, either here or in another life.

                                                                                            Dave

Krishna slid the USB stick into his computer. If he'd been stunned to read the letter, he was even more freaked out now. He felt like a ghost had touched him, had seen him telling Mark to delete the file on the computer. The title that flashed up on his screen was Robin & Smith.

"There. All finished. I'll be out of your way now," said Mark.

"Thanks."

"No probs, mate. When the police get here, can you tell them I've got all the files on a USB for them?"

"Police?" Krishna said, cautiously.

"Yeah. They're coming to take the computer, check out the workstation. It's routine, apparently, with a suspicious death. I guess they'll want to interview you."

Krishna felt heat rise under his collar. He removed the memory stick from his laptop, and picked up the envelope from the box. He tucked them both into his jacket pocket along with the screwed-up yellow post-it note with the drug dealer's number.

Detective Inspector Stephen West looked Krishna over, a swift appraisal and dismissal. Krishna felt tense, his shoulders stiffened under his shirt.

"So, you knew him well?" demanded the detective.

Krishna was unable to meet the glowering gaze. "Not that well. We just worked together."

The man was regarding Krishna as if he were stupid. "Worked in the same office, just yards across from each other, five days a week? You knew him well, all right. Friends?"

"Not friends, exactly," said Krishna, then, feeling the end of the stick in his pocket, "I mean, I liked him. We got on. We went for drinks after work, that kind of thing. We had a laugh; he was a good bloke."

The detective looked as if he never had a laugh. Shifting in his seat, Krishna thought of the stick in his jacket, the diary that he had not yet read. He wished Dave had been more explicit in his letter. Had he meant Krishna to give the USB stick to the police? The fact that he couldn't ask Dave was an unexpected weight to him. He hadn't realised how much Dave's regular presence across the desk each day was part of his life. Maybe he should just hand over the stick, the envelope containing the emails, and be done with it. But he couldn't. He didn't know what was in the file entitled Robin & Smith, but what if it referred to Krishna using drugs, giving Dave the dealer's number? With his own criminal record for drugs, he just couldn't risk that.

The detective was standing over him like it was his fault Dave was dead. Like he could have prevented it. Dave had sent the diary to Krishna for a reason. He had trusted him. And Krishna did not trust DCI West.

"So, what are you looking for?" asked Krishna, cautiously.

"For evidence, lad. Anything to shed some light on this fruitcake's motive. It's a strange one, that's a fact. Not like any suicide I've worked on before."

"But it was suicide?" Krishna asked, still struggling to get his head around it. "Drug overdose."

Krishna thought of the screwed up note in his jacket. Was this his fault?

West brought his face to Krishna's level, both hands on the desk, "Between you, me and the gatepost, there's something about this whole case that stinks. The girlfriend is saying he wanted to die, but why involve her? I mean, what was to stop him offing himself on his tod, like any regular nut who wanted to do himself in? Why would he want to die? Did he seem depressed to you?"

"No." Krishna lied with conviction. He'd known Dave wasn't sleeping; it's hard to hide fatigue when you work opposite someone. But he hadn't thought Dave would kill himself. That last month he had been more cheerful than he had been for a long time.

"And," continued the detective, with quiet intensity, "what kind of sicko actually wants to be eaten?"

Krishna swallowed hard. He'd heard some rumours about this, from office gossip, but deliberately avoided newspaper and TV reports. "She ate him?"

"Not all of him," said West, straightening up. He shoved his hand in his pocket and scratched his testicles. "What I'm saying is, if some sadist wants his girlfriend to watch him die for some twisted kick, I ain't gonna weep over it. In fact, it's none of my business. I just wish he'd found a way that didn't waste so much police time." Then his face straightened, and his eyes narrowed. "But if this woman didn't just watch. If he didn't want to die, well, that's murder. And that is my business."

23

It's a cold day, biting, but Krishna doesn't notice. He has too much on his mind, and has to think about making his way from Ipswich station to the Crown Court. He's on a mission. Since the day it arrived on his desk Krishna has kept the USB close, usually in his jacket pocket, except when he's at home, when he puts it on the shelf next to the elephant god, and tries to understand what Dave wanted him to do with it. He's read the diary, but only once. It wasn't easy reading. It's a burden, this knowledge. He hadn't known what to do with it, so in the end he did nothing. But he has been a fool; he sees that now. Today a woman will be before a judge for sentencing. Holding onto the memory stick hadn't kept him neutral. He was still affecting the outcome of the case, just by doing nothing. He'd been too worried about how he might be implicated to see the bigger picture. He can't keep the stick to himself any longer. Today he will hand it over. Whether to Alice or to the police, he still isn't sure. All he knows is, when he gets the train back to London later today, he'll no longer have the black stick of plastic in his jacket pocket. And that will be a relief. Krishna walks through the doors at Ipswich Crown Court feeling like a criminal, waiting for the detection machine to beep as he passes through, watched by the stocky security guy, who despite the threat of snow is in a short-sleeved shirt. Krishna feels himself under familiar scrutiny. "Name?" the guard asks, lifting a pen to the list of defendants. The last time he was in a court his name was on that list, for drug possession. His palms sweat at the memory.

"You won't have my name. I'm not a defendant. I just want to watch."

The guard's assumption that he's one of the accused doesn't surprise him. White faces and plumy accents surround him. The fact that he's an actuary means nothing when people judge by the colour of his skin. In this place, what else could a black man be but a criminal? Unlike at the magistrates court where he had been tried, professionals outnumber the criminals here. Fewer cases, but more serious, so they have larger legal teams. It isn't hard to tell which side of the law folks were on: serious people in smart suits and carrying briefcases stand in the hallway while on the benches across the hall sits a man in a cheap-looking double-breasted jacket and jeans, twisting a tie around his fingers, occasionally looking up as if waiting for a call. Next to him is a younger man, maybe only nineteen, hunched over and holding a baseball cap between his knees. He looks up at Krishna and scowls.

Krishna feels distinctly uncomfortable. "Where do I go to watch?" he asks the security guard, who points a brawny arm to the sign that says Public Viewing Gallery above an arrow indicating a wide staircase. He mumbles thanks, struggles past the solicitors and their clerks, with their armfuls of files and cups of dispenser-machine coffee. As he walks, he accidentally knocks a woman's arm, sending her coffee cup tumbling, the coffee splattering her jacket. "Oh! I'm so sorry."

"Shit! You should watch where you're going." She looks at her jacket, holding the paper cup away from her as the stain darkens the blue fabric.

Krishna rummages in his pockets. "Here," he hands her a clean hanky, taking away the half-spilt cup of coffee to enable her to wipe herself down.

"Shit," she says again, "that's all I need. I'm in court in a few minutes."

She's flustered, her cheeks are flushed. She hands back the wet hanky, and stalks off down the corridor. Krishna watches her go, still holding the remains of her coffee.

The viewing gallery is a large balcony overhanging the main courtroom below. It is rather grand, with a wooden balustrade, oversized benches and desks. The gallery has three rows of wooden benches, with backs at ninety-degree angles. Whoever designed this place didn't want observers to get too comfortable. Krishna is alone and he relaxes slightly, choosing the bench nearest the balustrade. Even at his height he can only just see over to the room below. Peering down, he grits his teeth together. He'd vowed never to enter a court building again but he's curious and wants to hear how his colleague, his friend, died. It's the one thing the diary didn't reveal. Now he wants the truth.

In the room below a few people are chatting. He can see the backs of their heads and the long black gown of one man who is holding a clipboard. He's surprised to hear laughter, and thinks it disrespectful, given why they are here. It has come from a striking woman, blonde hair pinned into a bun high on her head, wearing a smart cream suit that sets her apart from the others who wear sombre colours. She looks professional and groomed, a slick of scarlet on her lips and pearls on her ears. He guesses she's someone important, maybe a barrister. The kind of woman he tries to avoid: self-assured, conscious of their beauty. He's known women like that, and it always ends badly.

Behind Krishna an elderly couple in matching beige macs shuffle in. The woman has that pinched look his mother gets when she has a migraine. The man supports her elbow, but he looks no better. His face bears the bloody marks of a clumsy shave. If observing trials is what they do for kicks, Krishna thought, they'd have been wiser to stay home in front of the television and watch *Murder on the Orient Express.*

A rush of people arrive, jostling over the bench behind him, open notebooks and mobile phones on cords round their necks or attached to belts. Reporters here for the show. A discreet figure is seated in the corner, unobtrusive despite a severe haircut and bulky leather jacket. A military look. From their intent and fixed expression, this is someone else with a great interest in the case.

In the courtroom below Krishna spies the back of the woman's head, the one whose drink he'd spilled. She finds a place at a desk, and shuffles papers. She glances at the striking woman with the blonde hair, who is watching her intently. He doesn't know if they're on the same side. Before he can see any more, a loud buzzer trills and the man in the black cloak says, "All rise."

The reporters, used to these theatricals, are already on their feet. The elderly couple leans on the railings and, as they peer over, the striking woman in the cream suit nods at them, smiling confidently. The old man bows his head in acknowledgment, but she turns away. They aren't here out of mere curiosity, they know the woman in cream. Then Krishna realises that the woman in cream isn't a barrister after all. She's the defendant. She's Alice Mariani. She is Robin.

A man wearing a large poacher's coat plonks himself down next to Krishna. He sits back with a gusty exhale of air, removing his misted glasses and polishing them on the jacket. Then he leans over to Krishna, who fights the urge to back away. The man has ruddy cheeks and is out of breath. "Have they started yet?"

"Not yet," Krishna confirms, staring straight ahead. From the corner of his eye he sees his neighbour's sausage-like fingers unzip his coat and slide under the flap, fumbling. He pulls out a sheaf of A5 flyers and slides one onto Krishna's lap, then turns and hands them to the reporters. He reaches in front of Krishna, forcing him to lean back, and passes a flyer to the right. The old woman looks at the offered paper as if it's a foreign object but her husband snatches one and reads it. From behind him, across his shoulder, comes a square hand, and Krishna sees that it is the person from the corner, with the military cropped hair. "I'll have one of those, mate, if you don't mind." The man next to him is delighted to oblige.

The sound of the buzzer makes the man freeze then fumble to return his papers inside his jacket. In the courtroom below, two of the group have put on short white wigs and a woman has taken her place in front of a long wooden desk below the throne-like chair underneath a coat of arms with a Latin motto. The antiquated lessons from his Birmingham grammar days prove useful, as Krishna is able to translate the Latin: left and right. The promise to balance up both sides of the argument. What a lofty ambition.

A section of wooden panelling behind the chair opens and the judge steps forward like a character in a play, complete with long white wig and red cloak. He surveys the scene at his feet and then, taking his time, peers up at the public gallery. He slowly takes his seat, settling himself before saying, "Court, please sit."

The woman at his feet remains standing, a plain creature with a centre parting and mousy hair. She turns to addresses the judge. "Your Honour, this is the case of Alice Mariani, who has pleaded guilty to assisted suicide. Would you like the Crown Prosecution Service to recount the details?"

The prosecutor is already on his feet, adjusting his wig. "Your Honour, at a previous hearing Alice Mariani pleaded guilty to assisting David Jenkins to die on June 16th last year. David Jenkins had a cardiac arrest after ingesting a fatal dose of Gamma Hydroxybutyric acid, street name GHB. Mariani waited until Jenkins was dead before contacting the police. On their arrival she produced the suicide note."

Feeling the fug of a headache beginning at the top of his neck, Krishna looks at his lap where he has the flyer handed to him by his neighbour. It reads:

The Hemlock Trust: Fighting for the Right to Die

The Hemlock Trust is an organisation that believes every individual has the right to choose his or her own death, that it is the most basic of all rights. We are supporting the case of Alice Mariani, who assisted her boyfriend with his suicide. We do not believe she should be prosecuted.

Morally, she is innocent.

Assisted suicide is lawful in some countries, and even where illegal it is rarely prosecuted. We believe that an example is being made of Alice Mariani, whose only crime was to follow her boyfriend's wishes in not calling the ambulance after he took a fatal overdose.

If you wish to support our campaign to free her from a criminal conviction please contact Roy . . .

Then a telephone number and email address.

Krishna steals a sideways look at the man on his left, who is taking notes in a dog-eared jotter, and guesses that he is Roy. Stretching his neck to each side to relieve the tension, Krishna tunes in again to what is being said in the courtroom below.

"As Your Honour will recall, the case was adjourned for sentence and you requested a pre-sentence report to be completed by the probation service," says the clerk.

"Indeed I did," the judge acknowledges, "and I haven't seen it yet."

"Yes, sir. That's because there has been a delay. We have a representative from probation service. Would you like her to address you?"

"I would."

The whole court looks to a place in the room, below the balcony, which Krishna can't see from his seated position. He hears the tapping of heels on the wooden floor and there she is, standing at the front, facing the judge: the woman whose coffee he spilled. There is a determined set to her shoulders but he can see she is tense. Her hand is a fist at her side. The rest of the court watches her with a mixture of unfriendly curiosity or disdain. She smoothes the front of her jacket, touching the stained area self-consciously.

"Good Morning, Your Honour," she begins, a slight catch in her throat. "My name is Cate Austin and I am the probation officer responsible for writing the pre-sentence report on Alice Mariani."

She was writing the report on Alice. Krishna now knows why he had bumped into her in the corridor. Karma was at work.

Alice Mariani sits straighter in her seat, the old man to Krishna's right leans over the balustrade so far that Krishna is worried he'll fall. Behind them reporters crane their necks for a view and there is the sound of pencil on paper.

"Your Honour, I would like to request a further adjournment, as I was unable to complete a full report for today's hearing." One of the reporters said a disappointed, 'fuck.' The old woman turns to whisper something to her husband.

The judge sighs impatiently. "And why is that, Ms. Austin?"

"Because, Your Honour, last Tuesday the defendant was sectioned under the Mental Health Act. She has since been detained at St. Therese's secure unit. This change in circumstance means that I need more time to consider this new element in the case. I would request an adjournment of a further two weeks."

The pencils scratch rapidly and Krishna can feel the reporters' collective excitement that the woman in the dock is a lunatic. What a juicy story this is going to make. To his side the old woman leans towards her husband, holding a hand to her mouth.

"Indeed," says the judge, rubbing one hand on his chin and peering down at the clerk who is scribbling madly. "Do we have the psychiatrist's report?"

The clerk stands, proffers a clutch of papers. "We have a letter from Dr. Gregg, Your Honour."

The judge takes the letter and, seemingly unaware of all the people watching him, reads it slowly, then he sits back and looks at Cate Austin. Krishna can almost hear her exhale when he finally speaks, addressing the man in the black coat and white wig sitting nearest the defendant. "It seems that Dr. Gregg would also like more time. Mr. Thomas, any comments regarding an adjournment?"

"As Your Honour has heard, my client is currently in a secure hospital and is keen to be released. However, if a further adjournment is required for the probation service to consider her for the possibility of a community penalty, then she would of course comply with any interviews." He nods at Cate Austin, as if to secure allegiance, but she does not respond.

"Very well," says the judge. "Two weeks. We'll adjourn until February 9th. And on that date, Ms. Austin, I want a completed report with a clear recommendation. Do you understand?"

"Yes, Your Honour."

"Now, the subject of bail. Any directions, Mr. Thomas?"

Again, the defence barrister jumps up. "Yes, Your Honour. I have spoken with Dr. Gregg who confirms that my client has settled well in the last week and is now on appropriate medication. He's in agreement with our request for her release back into the community, provided that she continues to take her medication and sees him for out-patient appointments."

"Conditional bail, then? Does the Crown Prosecution Service have any objections?"

"No, Your Honour."

"Alice Mariani, you will be conditionally bailed back to your home address for two weeks. You must continue to take your medication, and attend all appointments with your psychiatrist and your probation officer. Is that clear?" Then the judge rises and everyone mirrors him, standing to attention as he disappears behind the hidden door.

Krishna moves quickly to get past the reporters, down the stairs and into the corridor. He's made his decision and there's no time to hang around.

He thought Alice would be rushing from the courthouse, but she is standing in the middle of the large hallway, surrounded by the black gowns of ushers and her legal team. Her blonde hair is like a star in a dark sky. No doubt about it, Alice Mariani should be on TV, not in court. She glances over at him briefly, but then looks away. He's a stranger to her. She has no idea how well he knows her.

Leaning against the wall, he wonders what he should do now. Seven months of procrastinating, and now that he's finally made a decision he can't see beyond the crowd. He watches the old couple struggle down the stairs and approach Alice, sees the woman place her gnarled hand on the cream sleeve, and the way Alice throws it off. They must be her parents then, despite their dull appearance. But he's too late. The woman he really wants to see is gone. Krishna thinks of Dave and sadness aches his chest. He has let his friend down.

Just then the door to the ladies' toilet opens and Cate Austin walks out. She shakes her hands dry and makes her way past him towards Alice, joining the small crowd around the film star figure. He's not too late after all.

Krishna watches and waits. Eventually, Alice crosses to where the security officer guards the door, and leaves. Reporters, yelling at her and asking for comment, surround her as the security officer ushers her out the door and into the waiting taxi. The scrum of reporters watch as Alice Mariani is driven away. Cate Austin walks away. This is his chance.

She walks quickly, heels clicking on the pavement, her brown hair loosening on her neck. Sensing his closeness, or hearing his steps, she glances behind. A few more yards and she stops. Her voice is confident and steady, but her eyes dart around him.

"You can stop following me now or I'll call the police." Krishna gasps at the mention of police. "I just wanted a word . . ."

"I refuse to speak with any reporters. So you can leave me alone." She turns back around and Krishna has to hurry to catch her. "I'm not a journalist. I worked with Dave. He was my friend." Cate stops so suddenly that Krishna almost catches her heels.

"Then I'm sorry for your loss, Mr. . . .?"

"Dasi. Krishna Dasi."

"Mr. Dasi." Her voice hardens as she recognises him, "It was you who spilled coffee on me! You really shouldn't be following me like this. I don't believe there's anything I can say to you."

"Please," he says, feeling every letter of the word in his throat, "I can't speak with anyone else. I want to speak with you. I have something—something from Dave. And I think it's you I'm meant to give it to." He slides the memory stick from his pocket, holding it out like a gift. "I'm sure it is."

"What is it?"

"Dave's journal. Everything . . . it's all there." He feels the heat on his cheeks. He wants to say more. As her index finger touches the plastic, he blabs his planned monologue. "I didn't know what Dave wanted me to do with it, even after I'd read it, but then I thought, shit, I can't keep this to myself. It's too big . . ." He's desperate, he knows that, hears his own voice an octave higher than normal as he rushes to explain how David sent it to him, posting it on the day he died, with no stamps on the envelope, in a rural post-box in Suffolk where the collection was only daily. From Suffolk to London, then via the collection office to Krishna's desk. When it arrived David had been dead for sixteen days, the funeral already over. "And this," he hands her a sheet of paper, "is the letter that came with it."

Krishna has kept the USB stick and letter for seven months, waiting for a sign, some indication of whom he should hand them to. With the same certainty that he believes in karma, he knows that Cate Austin is the one.

24

"We know it happens behind closed doors, and we think euthanasia should be sanctioned in this country, as it is in Switzerland."

"And how did you come to be involved in the Hemlock Trust?"

Roy paused, wiped the sweat from his lip. "My wife had a terminal brain tumour. We fought it for months. Chemotherapy, radiotherapy. She was exhausted. After the third cycle of treatment the doctors said there was nothing more they could do."

"So she took her own life?" the interviewer asked, sympathetically.

"No," said Roy, suddenly forceful. "She died a protracted and painful death. But after watching her die, I knew it was wrong. And I knew there was another way. That's when I set up the Hemlock Trust."

Cate watched the man struggle to finish the interview, the tears for his dead wife budding behind his glasses, then pressed the off button on the TV remote control. She wasn't sure she'd done the right thing, taking the memory stick from Krishna Dasi, but he had been so certain that she hadn't felt able to say no. He was grieving for David, she could see that, his brown eyes full of concern as he handed it over. It's important, he had said, I think there are some things in the diary that make the whole situation look different. He wouldn't explain what he meant, he just said it was pretty heavy, that it freaked him out. Then he had looked at her and said, but I guess you're used to stuff like this.

She took the handwritten note from her bag, and smoothed it onto her lap, bringing it close to her face to read the small, cramped handwriting:

16th June

Krish,

I know you'll look after this. It's important. Sometimes things don't work out as we planned, as you and I both know. After all, we deal in improbabilities. By the time you get this I'll be long gone, but I want to travel light. Keep it safe.

I hope to see you again, either here or in another life.

Dave

Cate felt uneasy, reading a dead man's final letter. But it confirmed that he had chosen to die, and soon—'by the time you get this I'll be long gone.' That travelling metaphor again, just as he'd used in his Internet advert, talking of the journey of a lifetime. She hoped he got the death he wanted, though God knows it wasn't what most people would choose. But maybe the diary would explain it. Alice hadn't been able to tell her why David had wanted to die, and that was the question that bothered Cate most. She put the letter to one side.

Cate slid the USB into place. There was just one file on the memory stick, entitled Robin & Smith. She double-clicked.

This is my diary, the only one I've ever written so bear with me, okay? I'll just write it in the only way I know how. Numbers are the only way I can make sense of things.

One is a great number. There's a history to one, a single digit that holds an infinite number of fractions, of parts. Some people love it because it is the start of things. To me, it's great because it's so definite. Anything less than one represents uncertainty. In statistics one is 100%. Anything less, say 95%, is 0.95. I collect ones, a list in my head, like I used to collect stamps, only that kind of collection doesn't mean anything. Stamps just end up hidden in a cupboard under the stairs, only interacting with dust particles or passing mice. My new collection reflects events that will happen, real lives. I work with one. In fact, everything from nought to one, but one is my favourite. I try to live my life by it. It makes it easier. The number one is like a dependable shirt, comfortable and familiar.

Only God is immortal, but it simply never enters the average bloke's head that he could die on any given day. He gets up, has breakfast, kisses the wife and kids goodbye, drives to work, comes home, sleeps, and starts all over again. He believes that waking up tomorrow and the day after is a given, a certainty of one. I guess human beings are designed that way.

On the way to work one morning he passes an accident, an ambulance's flashing lights, and remembers he's mortal. 'The certainty of life is not one. It's a lot less, slow down!' Sober thoughts flash up on the windscreen of his mind, all the possibilities of that journey, the motorbike that swerves before him, the car that brakes too suddenly to make the slip road. But he looks at the time, and the traffic jam, thinks about the next meeting and wonders why the incompetent woman in front can't just move to the inside lane rather than insisting on driving at just seventy miles per hour in the fast lane. Is she trying to make a point? The wipers in his mind wipe away the knowledge of death. Back to the certainty of one.

Most people who die move from one to nought in a blink.

One is the only number that can be both male and female. It can also represent God.

Krish, you know our job is to make things safe, to help people take chances. After all, who'd buy a house if they couldn't insure it against fire or flood? Who'd want to drive without insurance? It's what we do. Work out how likely that flood, that fire, is and give a figure, an equation that allows you to protect yourself against it and give you peace of mind, if you have the money. I guess it's always about money, though I don't think of it in pounds and pence. I think in primes and decimal places, fractions and percentages. We work with actuarial risk, the risk factor that's fixed, determined by a group; a woman will get cheaper car insurance on the basis of her group, not her individual skill. We all belong to groups: gender, race, age, class . . . and any probability can only apply to a group, never to an individual. So, there could be a 99% chance that you won't crash that car, but today just might be the one.

My own statistics, based on my group—white, male, educated, class A2—were good. Excellent, in fact. No money worries, a lower chance of divorce, of illness, of being the victim of crime. But as I said, who knows who that one in a hundred is. Or, in my case, one in several million.

I didn't know it could be that way, that one moment could divide your life in two like a split lip. Before that moment, that realisation that I was the oddity, the statistical improbability, life was predictable. It was how I liked it; maybe a bit routine, some would call it boring, but there's a comfort in structure. But the doctor's words cut through me, tearing my life apart, I saw that I'd been a fool, living in a fantasy world built on nothing but a quicksand of numbers. I'd been chosen to die, and the reason was beyond me. Like Jesus, I felt forsaken.

Krish, let me tell you my story. I just need to know that someone, at least, gets the message.

Mirrors are the worst. My vision splits between the glass and my image, confused over the focal distance. I know that this can only get worse, as my brain sends twisted messages to my roving retinas.

I'm a marked man. But moving between being one of us, and one of them, didn't feel any different. I didn't even know! How many others are there, the one in a million of us that haven't yet discovered they are already one of them? One of the walking dead.

In my case it's my brain that is poisoned. Deep, hidden in the tissue. Are you reading this, full of pity for me? Well, ask yourself one question, Krish: would you know if you had a ticking time bomb in your heart, your lungs? And if you did find out, who would you rather pressed the button? Fate? God? Or you?

It's my brain. And it's my finger on that button. When I look in the mirror I think, is this it? Is the sum total of my life what I see every day? This desk, this computer, these clothes. Is this what I am? Is this all I am? Questions I wouldn't have asked myself before. I'm not reflective in that way. The numbers, probabilities, eventualities are about someone else's life. When I hold the calculator, work the percentage, I'm in control.

This time I'm the statistic. And the control is somewhere else, in a message my brain is sending my body, turning my own cells against me like a conquering army, colonising as they move through, turning allies to enemies. Turning normal protein molecules into deadly ones. All I have is time. All I can do is wait for my body to fail, and my brain to forget. It's no choice. It's no life. No one chooses to be a martyr.

Cate stopped reading. So, David Jenkins had been ill after all. He said there was a time bomb in his head, he talked about the terminally ill, as being one of them. But she'd asked Alice about this, and she'd been adamant he was well. Neither Alice nor the police had any idea that he had a terminal illness. And what exactly was the illness?

If he was ill why hadn't he made it known, got it out in the open? It made more sense of his decision to die, lessened Alice's culpability. He must have had a reason for keeping it from her. Surely Alice had some notion he was sick? She must have asked him why he wanted to die. She must find out, but carefully, so that Alice has no idea about Cate having the diary. So that Alice wouldn't know Cate's secret.

She knew she had to hand the memory stick over to the police, but that could wait until she has seen Alice tomorrow.

25

The suitcase was pale blue vinyl, with a picture of Winnie the Pooh on the front. It was a boxy shape, with a thick handle. Just a small case, yet Mummy was trying to put everything in it. Even Alice could see that nothing else would fit, yet still Mummy tried stuffing in another top, another book. "Mummy?" Alice asked, but her mother didn't respond. She just carried on pulling things from the wardrobe, trying to cram them in the case. The wardrobe was nearly empty, like a wooden shell or a boat with space for hiding. Except it was the wrong way up for a boat and there was no water. Water was like the swimming pool and Alice liked to think of that, of her mother swimming through her legs like a mermaid. But they hadn't been swimming for ages, not since Mr. Wilding became Mummy's friend.

On the floor of the upturned boat were her armbands, flat and airless, and under them her turquoise swimsuit, the one with the flamingo on the front. She liked the picture of the pink bird, but wondered why it stood on only one leg. What if it toppled over? She grabbed the swimsuit, hid it behind her back, not that her mother noticed as she was trying to do up the zip on the case, make the teeth close together like a dog's bite. Alice didn't want the case to close. Wherever she was going there was only one case, and she didn't want to go alone. She would not leave Mummy.

Alice pushed the swimsuit to the back of the wardrobe, into the darkest corner, where her mother wouldn't look. If she left it there, then she would have to come back. Mummy wouldn't let her go without it. Would she?

Mummy hugged her tight, really tight so she couldn't breathe, and said, "What's the point? Oh, what's the point, Alice? There's nowhere for us to go anyway."

Mummy lied. The next day she left Alice forever.

Alice woke up and Mummy was gone.

The night before, Alice had stayed up late. They drank hot chocolate, and Mummy painted Alice's nails and her own, even their toenails! Alice could still smell the scent of the nail polish in the air, and she looked at her pretty pink nails, wondering where Mummy was.

Their bedsit door was wide open. Mummy told her off if she didn't shut it. She picked up Barbie and went to the door. She felt hungry so it must be time for breakfast. She was so cold she put her cardigan on over her nightshirt. Her special cardigan, the lilac one with the pearl button. The one Mummy knitted.

She couldn't find Mummy—she wasn't in the bathroom. Alice tried Mr. Wilding's door. It was unlocked and the room was a mess. The table was broken and there was glass on the floor. The boxes had all gone, but there was other stuff on the floor, bits of rubbish. Then she saw a sandwich on a plate. She was hungry so she walked gingerly towards it. "Careful! Don't step on the glass," she said to Barbie. It was a cheese sandwich, and she offered some to Barbie, then took a bite herself. She saw a foot. She knew it was Mummy's foot because of the sparkly pink toenails.

"Mummy!" she was pleased, but also surprised because Mummy was sleeping on the floor by the side of the bed, next to the wall. And she was not wearing any clothes.

Alice took off her special cardigan and carefully laid it over Mummy. It was too small to cover all of her, but Alice smoothed it over her arm and shoulder.

Alice snuggled against her. Mummy was so warm, but she must be asleep because she didn't move. Alice finished her sandwich, stroking Mummy's hair with her free hand. "Wake up," she said, but Mummy didn't move. She was too tired. So Alice sang to her:

'Hush, little baby, don't say a word.' Mummy's going to buy you a mockingbird . . .

Alice yawned. She was tired too. Safe, next to her Mummy. Snug. She closed her eyes and slept.

Later, much later. They were found. Other people arrived.

Alice was strapped into a car seat by a woman she didn't know. Mummy was still in the house, still lying on the floor, but the woman carried on clicking Alice into place, giving her a tight smile. Next to her, on the seat, was her blue Winnie the Pooh suitcase and a black bag with the things that her mother couldn't squeeze into the case. There were other people, too, men in the green uniforms who came in the ambulance with its screaming siren. The woman opened the car door and got into the driver's seat. As she did so, a man in green uniform ran from the house, to the car, and tapped on the window. "You'd best take this," he said to the driver, poor kid, she's only wearing a nightie." The man handed her the lilac cardigan.

The woman put a key in the ignition and Alice panicked, erupting into tears like a split heart, shouting, "Wait for Mummy! My Mummy!" The woman turned round, reached to pat the girl's leg. Alice couldn't move. She was strapped in. Just then she heard the front door to her home open, and a metal bed was lifted out. On it was a bundle of sheets. No, it was a ghost. And then Alice saw a foot and pretty pink polish on toes so white.

But the woman was turning the key that started the engine, and the car was moving. Alice was still shouting, but Mummy couldn't hear her, she was too far under the sheets.

As the car pulled away the girl kept shouting. No one answered.

Alice had lain with her dead mother for nearly four hours until they were discovered.

When the landlord found them, calling on a routine visit to collect rent, he saw the mother and daughter entwined on the floor of their neighbour's bedsit. Matilde Mariani was naked, and her daughter was clinging to her like a baby monkey. He said that coaxing the child away from the corpse had been the hardest thing he ever had to do.

The postmortem exam found a high level of narcotics in Matilde's blood stream. They called it an accidental death. Mr. Wilding was nowhere to be found.

The social worker, who subsequently took Alice to her new home, concluded that she had not accepted her mother's death. She said that after the initial outburst in the car Alice displayed an 'irregular, detached demeanour,' and speculated that she would require help to recover, including age-appropriate grief counselling if she was to come to terms with it.

Help never came. Not for me.

26

I'm home. Released. Bailed. All of these words. But mostly, I'm free. As I open my front door the neighbour's cat appears, looking at me with widened eyes as if demanding where I'd been. I stand in the cold air, and the cat comes to me. He pulls away when I stroke his black fur, only relaxing after my hand has massaged his sharp spine several times. But it's too cold to stay outside for long, and I have much to do inside.

Like Goldilocks, I sit in each of the chairs, hurrying between them, unable to rest. I open my cupboards, touch the cold tins and crinkling bags of pasta. A feast after ten days of meals on a tray. I hardly know where to begin. I go to my bookshelves and touch the worn fabric spines, the smooth leather covers. I clean up the broken glass, the dead flowers. I'm like a child in a sweet shop, running from room to room. Oh, my bed! I'd forgotten how soft the mattress was. I open the drawer where I keep my most prized possession. My lilac cardigan, almost as old as I am. It's still there, still soft under my fingers. What we forget in such a short time. Ah, a bath all to myself. No one will come peering in to check that I haven't scored my wrists with a razor. I won't have to navigate a dayroom of drugged patients pretending to play Scrabble, or digest a meal without fresh vegetables.

I make myself some toast, with butter and jam. It's the best thing I've tasted, ever. I'm happy to be home. And then someone rings the doorbell.

"I want to know what's going on, Alice!"

The door is barely open when my father pushes me aside and walks into the hall. His face is grey with fatigue and he looks old. There's dried blood on his chin, where he nicked himself with a razor. His eyes are the only lively thing, young with anger, narrowed and piercing in that face of lines and weariness. I feel a stab of pity that I've done this to him.

He didn't speak to me in the courthouse, and I can see all the words are held in his chest, which he pushes out slightly, his hands deep in the pockets of his old trench coat. "What have you been up to, girl?"

I arrange my face to hide my disquiet and gesture with my square of toast. "Eating?"

"Don't be clever," he scowls, "it may work with your mother, but you don't fool me. Why didn't you tell us you were in a mental hospital?"

I'm less sure of myself, but carry on with the charade, as I can see no other way. "I didn't want to worry you." He comes close. He hasn't brushed his teeth this morning and his face is a mess.

"And don't you think not knowing where you'd got to was worrying? I even called the college to see if they knew where you were. You've been sacked, haven't you?"

"University," I correct. I turn my back and return to the kitchen, my father close on my heels. It's a struggle to swallow the last of the toast and when I do it scratches my throat. I need a drink and can feel a headache starting at the top of my spine. I want him to sit down, but think he'll refuse if I ask. His arms are across his chest, moving up and down with his rapid breathing. I sit at the table, pushing the plate with the remaining toast to one side but taking a sip of tea. He stares at me.

"Well?"

"I haven't lost my job, I've just been suspended. Until after the court case."

"Why didn't you tell us, Alice?"

"I didn't want to worry you. I'll be reinstated soon enough."

"I didn't mean about the job, I meant about David. That is his name, isn't it, David Jenkins? Not Richard. In the newspaper it never said anything about him having terminal cancer."

I can't even look at him.

He reaches into his pocket and removes a crumpled piece of paper. I recognise it at once, of course. I've seen it before. It's the Hemlock Society flyer, designed by a do-gooder by the name of Roy who has made me his cause. My father is not willing to be my champion. He looks at me as though I wound him, "What the hell have you done, Alice? Your mother is worried sick."

My head snaps up, searching his face, "How much does she know?"

"I've been hiding the papers, though what she heard in court today was bad enough. God only knows what she makes of it all. I've no idea."

"Of course not," I say, bitterly. "That would mean you'd actually have to communicate."

He takes a step forward, his fist tight. "Don't you try to put the blame on me and your mother. We've done our best for you, God knows. And this is how you repay us?"

Something inside me snaps. "Repay you? I didn't realise I was in your debt! Is that how it works when you adopt a child? Buy me now, I'll pay later?"

Dad sits heavily on the pine bench opposite me. He runs a hand over his scarred chin. "I didn't mean that, but since you said it, maybe it's true. Only we're the ones who are paying. We took you in, Alice. We knew you'd had a hard start, but we tried our best to be a family. You're not like us, Alice. You're clever, I know that. But this . . . A man died, Alice, here in your house. The newspaper . . . they said something else . . . that he castrated himself and you . . . God, it's so disgusting . . ."

I interrupt, not wanting him to say it. "How much does Mum know?"

"More than she lets on, that's certain. Some of her friends won't come round anymore. And that Betty from across the way? She's always popping in on some excuse or other. All this publicity seems to attract the wrong kind of people. Your mum didn't deserve this."

"She's not my mother!" The words are out before I can stop them.

Dad stands up, wringing his hands as if they're wet. "She's all the mother you've ever had, girl. And she loves you. You think on that while you're tearing her world apart."

I don't get up to see him out.

Two Nurofen and a glass of water. I sit and breathe, waiting for the dizziness to pass. I still haven't unpacked my bag when I hear the knocking. I recognise the sound, the slow, steady pace. I open the door, and Lee stands there like hope. I am held, caught up in Lee's familiar smell of salt water and fresh air, the battered leather jacket on my cheek. I long for a warm shower, to rid myself of the institutional stench of cabbage and bleach, the courtroom tang of penance. But Lee doesn't know of my inner turmoil, and I receive the kiss gratefully. From the strength of the hold, Lee must have thought I had gone for good.

My God, it's so good to be home, even if the relief is temporary. In fourteen days I'll be sentenced. Being locked up once against my will is surely enough. What could they hope to gain by doing it again? I'll be a good girl now.

Lee knows nothing about Smith's death in this house. Lee never bothers with reading the papers or watching the news, but with other things, like the best technique for butterfly stroke, the fixing of a slow puncture on an RAF dingy, and now it's simply a warm mouth and hands running over skin that hold interest. What does it matter what happens in the world outside?

Lee has brought me tulips, large red petals, elegant proud heads, and long green stems. They're my welcome home gift, and as I search those puppy-dog eyes I see understanding. I wonder if I'm wrong, that maybe Lee does know where I've been.

"I want you to know, Alice, that I don't mind. Whatever you did. That I'll cope."

I look at Lee carefully. "Aren't you going to ask where I've been?"

"No. I'm going to wait until you tell me."

"How can you be so patient?"

Lee manages a half-smile. "I've learnt to be patient. Sometimes I thought I'd leave you for good, but it just never worked out that way. So now I just wait, for the time to be right. You're an attractive woman. I mean, just look at you. You always were out of my league. You're beautiful. So I can't really be surprised that you've got someone else. I don't blame you, either. I'm just glad to have some place in your life. If I have to share you, then I'll accept that."

Does Lee know about Smith? I'm surprised when I see tears in those brown eyes. A survival equipment fitter should be made of stronger stuff.

"I was here last week, and I saw the car. The Volkswagen. I saw someone at the window, and it wasn't you. I saw brown hair, not blonde. The thing is Alice, I'm not good at saying this, but I love you. Really. And I'm willing to hang on, hoping that at some point it'll just be me. That I'll be your only lover."

Last Thursday Cate Austin was here, collecting my things. Her car is a Volkswagen. I start to laugh. I laugh so much that my face is wet with tears. "There's no other lover for me, not since last summer. It's only you now."

The relief is so great it registers in those eyes, and Lee is like a child who just found a way home, holding me tight. I am kissed, my face, my lips.

"I love you Alice. I can't believe how much I love you." This is something I've heard seldom in my life. It's a treasure. I will keep it safe.

Although I've known Lee all my life, there are still surprises, like a child's game of pass-the-parcel. With each layer I unwrap I think I've reached the prize, only to discover yet another bright wrapping. I didn't expect this return, this respite. This love, so undemanding. So seemingly unconditional. But all things have conditions and I would be a fool to believe that it would withstand my confession. Love never lasts; I know this. It must be trapped, at the perfect moment, if it's to remain unsullied. Lee loves me, but I can't trust that it will always be so. And although I love Lee, it's not enough. It's not the love I felt for Smith. It's not the kind of love that inspires poetry.

The stillness of the middle hours is a harsh landscape and it's always in the silent part of the night that we are stripped bare of our pretensions and confidence, taken back to our basest insecurities. Seeing Lee's head on my pillow, cupped hands resting on clean sheets, I taste what it is to have a normal relationship. Part of me yearns for it; shared bills, holidays—children, maybe. It's a mirage, a pretence of what my life could be. Yet when Lee looks at me, when our bodies join, I believe it.

The night is dangerous for me. It's an infidelity to the past, to Smith's sacred plan, too much a cosy illusion of love.

At the very least, Lee gives me this.

27

1981

Alice had another mother who was older and didn't cry so much but didn't laugh so much, either. She made Alice wear different clothes. The special lilac cardigan had disappeared and she wouldn't help Alice look for it. She bought her other things to wear: dresses with lace and bows at the back. And Alice mustn't climb trees, mustn't stroke strange dogs. New rules for a new life.

The new mother tried to tell Alice why she had a different mummy. Alice was learning Bible stories, which she read to her every night. No more *Cinderella* or *Little Red Riding Hood*.

"It's like Jesus," New Mummy said. "He had two daddies: God, who was his real father, but also Joseph, who raised him like his own son. Who was there for him every day."

"So I'm like Jesus?" Alice was thinking of other parts of the story, the bits she didn't like, with the soldiers killing the babies after the Three Wise Men spoke to Herod.

"Yes—well, no—but you do have two mummies. The one who had you in her tummy, who's in heaven. And me. And I love you as much as if you came from my tummy." It was getting confusing and New Mummy was getting teary. Still Alice couldn't quite grasp the idea. "So my real Mummy, she's like God?"

But New Mummy started to set out the dolls' china tea set. "Let's have a tea party, Alice. Which of your dollies would you like to invite?"

Alice arranged her teddies and Barbie in a line, still thinking of her real Mummy who was like God. Who she couldn't see, but whom she felt every minute, watching her. Especially when she prayed.

When Alice was five she started school.

She wore a stiff shirt and stood in a playground, counting seconds until she returned to the dusty classroom where the chalk scratched the board and made her shudder. Until she must sit in the plastic chair with a hole in the back, through which the boy behind poked her with a sharp pencil, breaking the lead on her new white shirt, gurgling that dreaded word into her ear. Over and over, that same word, 'posh' which she didn't really understand, just that it was what New Mummy called other people, and what Real Mummy had called nice places. I used to live somewhere posh, Mummy would say, in a beautiful home for the perfect family. Then she'd laughed like it was a joke, which Alice hadn't understood. Some jokes were just for grownups.

The boy said 'posh' like it was a bad word, making Alice feel ashamed without even knowing why. She looked down at the thick, hard cuffs of her new shirt, the red tie on the desk like a dragon's tongue. She wouldn't cry. She bit her lip until it bloomed.

In the cold playground she watched other children kick balls and skip ropes and tangle elastic with new shoes, and wondered if that was why they wouldn't let her play. But she didn't feel posh, like the new clothes, like the big house in the photo. She felt cold.

Another girl stood on the edge of the playground. They were solitary together. Her tie wasn't a sharp tongue but a floppy thing, and her shirt was baggy on her narrow shoulders, no longer the white of new clothes. Everything about her looked used.

The poor girl smiled, an uncertain crooked thing, and Alice dared a smile back. Are you my friend? She wanted to ask in this place where everyone shouted and everyone wore the same colours and everyone was a child, but no one was like her. Where no one liked her. Are you my friend?

And the girl still smiled. A miracle. They stood together, faced the other children, shoulders touching.

"I'm Alice," she whispered, shy with her gift.

The other girl coughed suddenly into her thin hand. She turned to Alice. "My name is Lee."

Alice had a friend. Had someone to smile with. Their teacher, Miss Giddyhoo, was a kind lady, teaching her last class before she retired. She explained that this meant she wouldn't work anymore, but would have more time for gardening. She dabbed a pink hanky to her eyes as if gardening was a sad thing. Miss Giddyhoo knew that Lee was Alice's friend, that the boy behind her wasn't, and made them change places. Soon it was not a pencil in Alice's back, but Lee's nudging foot, the shoe abandoned on the floor, secret whispers from behind as they chatted through the days and weeks to Miss Giddyhoo's gardening leave.

Lee was allowed to come to Alice's home after school, and New Mummy preferred that. "I like you where I can see you," she told Alice, "besides, it gives Lee's mother a break." Lee had three brothers, two of them babies.

"Twins," Lee stuck out her tongue, "both as horrible as each other."

They laughed at that, and Alice wished Lee could come and live with them forever. Or that she had a brother or sister, so she would never have to be alone. She told New Mummy this, who rubbed her flat stomach sadly and said, "I'm afraid that won't happen." Then she started to clean the kitchen.

"Can't we play something else, Alice?" Lee pushed out her lower lip.

"No. We're playing my game."

"It's boring!" Lee looked ready to cry but she wouldn't leave. Lee knew what to do. It was a game they'd played many times. She lay back on the bed. "Not the bed," said Alice, "on the floor," she whispered, knowing New Mummy was downstairs. She didn't want her coming up to see what they were up to.

Still sighing, Lee dropped to the floor, as stiff as a plank, "It's cold," she complained, but Alice was soon next to her, her head on Lee's flat chest. Her arm was over her waist and Lee said, "Mmm. Better," snuggling her face into Alice's hair.

Alice told her, "You've got to lie still, remember. Only I can move."

Lee closed her eyes, lying straight, and Alice placed a leg over her leg, stomach against waist. Lee was firm and bony, and that was good. It made the memory come back easier. Alice felt the heat under her, and listened to Lee's heart, wishing her friend understood the game. Lee was weary, she sighed; she was only still when Alice kissed her. Her cheek was soft with warm skin, like dough.

It was cold outside, and the floor was drafty but they remained, the two girls, as the weak sun died behind the clouds and the smell of steaming vegetables rose from the kitchen below. Lee's stomach grumbled and Alice nipped her, hard.

"Ow!"

"Well, be quiet then."

Alice closed her eyes, but she didn't smell the food, she didn't feel the cold. She remembered the smell of clean skin. Of fresh nail polish and old carpet. She smelt cheese ripening in the sun and bread crusts. She remembered love.

Alice knew that no one else noticed Lee, with hair the colour of dishwater and big brown eyes like a pathetic puppy. Alice liked that Lee was so invisible. It meant Lee was all hers. That she wouldn't leave.

"I had a heart murmur when I was a baby," Lee whispered proudly, "it didn't beat right," like it was a wonderful secret. Alice looked at her thin chest as if she could see through the second-hand clothes to Lee's heart. As if she could see what hadn't worked properly.

At night, when Alice was in bed, she listened to her own heart, its strong beat in her ears, going quicker if she thought about it too hard, until she got scared that she might faint, like a jogger who had run too far. She wondered if her heart didn't work properly and that was why it hurt so much.

New Mummy tried to hug her, but Alice pulled back from her thin, sharp body. Real Mummy had always been soft, but Alice couldn't say this. Who would she say it to? She had a different home, a different family. But her heart, caged in her chest, was still the same.

28

Cate Austin is here. I prefer her seeing me in my own home. Like a cat, I can adapt, but only within limits. At St. Therese's I was a singular, exotic flower amid rubble, but here I'm dominant. It's better this way. I know she hopes to find the crack in the glass; she needs to make a breakthrough if her report is to have substance. She understands the weight of the questions she asks, but carries on asking, picking over old scabs to see if they bleed. She wants to know if I'm so very different from her.

"Alice, are you clear on why the case was adjourned?"

I hate it when she talks to me like this, as if I'm a fool. "More time was needed to see if the drugs can keep me stable since, apparently, I wasn't stable a few weeks ago. If I can't cope in the community, a hospital order will have to be considered, and that takes time to assess."

"Well, that's one reason. But, I needed more time too, Alice."

"You're still not sure what to propose?"

"I'm still not sure I've heard what I need to know."

She bites her lip, and I wonder what it is she expects me to say.

"I saw your parents at the courthouse. They looked pretty frail, up in the public gallery. It must be very hard for them. How do they cope with knowing their daughter helped someone to die?"

"I explained it to them, as much as I could," I say, as if it was a simple thing to be explained. "I did it the day after Smith died. I'd been bailed from the police station. I hadn't been charged yet. The police hadn't a clue what to do with me, so I was released and asked to return in a week. I knew I had to talk to my parents before someone else did."

"Did you tell them the truth?"

"The truth," I reply carefully, "is always a matter of interpretation."

As I've already said, I didn't want my parents to find out from gossip or the local papers about Smith's death, and I knew it was just a matter of time before word got out. After all, nothing much happens in Suffolk, so Smith's death was bound to cause a stir. I was worried about Mum and Dad. I didn't want to hurt them. It's not that I was ashamed, but I knew they wouldn't understand. How could they? Their lives are so ordinary.

I always visit my parents one evening a week, just for an hour. Dad is usually in the front room, watching TV or reading the daily paper, and Mum will be in the kitchen, bleaching an already immaculate surface or polishing the teak table in the tiny dining room. When I arrive we always go up to my old bedroom, and she sits by the window to smoke. Dad doesn't approve, so she has to lean out of the window like a disobedient teenager. If she forgets and smoke seeps into the room, she wafts it like mad and sprays some of the floral air freshener she keeps under my bed. It's a tiny bed, smaller than a single, and Dad made it with a built-in shelf underneath. He's handy like that, as you'd expect for a woodwork teacher. He's good with wood, but not so good with people, and when I was at school I was ashamed by how easily the kids bullied him. He should have been a carpenter by rights, working alone in a workshop, but he didn't have the motivation. Preferred the security of a pension.

In my parents' house we stick to our own rooms. It was always like that even when I was living with them. For all the dining table is polished daily it's never used except at Christmas, and when I lived there Mum would bring up breakfast and tea to my bedroom on a tray, after giving Dad an identical one. She never ate much, just leaned against the windowsill talking. I think she was happiest then. I know it was hard for her when I left, with no one to talk to. With Dad at work all day what has she to do but clean? Not just our home, but other people's, too. She's good at it, of course.

So when I visited them on the day of Smith's death, the stench of the police station still on my clothes, my mother insisted on making up my tray, mashed potatoes with a vegetarian cutlet, and a bowl of ice cream, and we sat in my room. Though the blood was no longer on my hands its memory lingered in my senses and I couldn't eat. I watched her smoking, thinking for the millionth time that she was too skinny and I really should say something. I knew I should have gone straight home: Smith had only been dead for nine hours, and I'd spent most of that time in a cell. I needed to go home and shower, but I couldn't bear returning to that empty house. Not yet.

"Why don't you move back here for a few days, love?" Smoke was in the room, but she wasn't reaching under my bed for the air freshener. That's how I knew that she'd heard about Smith's death.

"I'm okay, Mum."

"But are you sure you should be alone right now?"

"I like to be alone. There's a lot I need to do at home. Just until everything's been cleared up . . ."

She looks hopeful, "Cleared up? A mistake . . . ?" I found out later that Smith's death had been reported on the evening news. I'd been named as his girlfriend, and it was said that I was helping the police with their enquiries.

"Yes. A big mistake." I tell her.

I couldn't say anymore, because the stench of blood was stuck in my throat and I had this pain around my chest like I might cry. I don't cry in front of anyone.

"You know, we always tried our best for you. We only wanted you to be happy. After everything you went through, when you were a little girl . . ."

"I know, Mum. Please, don't." I hate it when she gets upset. She looked so frail sitting there, trying to fight back tears. When did she get so old? Of course, she was always old. I realised that when I started primary school and she was the only mother with grey hair. Some kids would ask if she was my gran, and I would say yes. It was easier than explaining.

My parents were lucky. I don't think they let older couples adopt so easily now. My mother was in her late forties when they got me. That's older than I am now, and I know I don't have the energy to cope with a young child. But then, not everyone would want a four-year-old. It's not like getting a baby, is it? A child that age already has a personality, it's not like a blank sheet you can stamp your mark on. And the mark on my personality was death.

I always knew they weren't my real parents. The social worker told them it was better that way; no big shock when I was sixteen, no sudden realisation if I ever needed a blood transfusion and neither of them matched, nothing dramatic like that. I knew I was adopted and it was fine. It didn't matter. I was wanted, and that's what counts. Isn't it?

Sometimes I wish I was more like them, that we were closer, but then we never argue, and how many families can say that? It was clear from early on that I was heading somewhere they'd never been. 'Always got her head in a book,' my mother would boast, to anyone who'd listen, 'she'll be off for university, that one.'

She was so proud of me, but she didn't count on me leaving home to study and never coming back. She didn't realise that books would become my life, an existence she couldn't comprehend. Still, we get along. It's more than many mothers and daughters can say.

"So what did you tell her?" Cate asks. Her pen makes a careful note on the page and I want to knock her arm, to smudge the ink.

"Well, as I said, I realised she knew something. Probably that he'd died. Of course, I'd told them that he was dying of cancer. I hoped that was enough, that I wouldn't have to say much at all. Then mum asked something I hadn't expected, something that made me kick myself for my short-sightedness when we had all met that day at The White Swan."

"Alice, on the news this evening it said the man who . . . passed away . . . it said his name was David. Not Richard. We—your Dad and me—are a bit confused."

I thought quickly. "David is his given name, but he prefers to be called Richard." I corrected myself, "preferred."

Mum shook her head, "Such a terrible thing. A young man like that. He looked so poorly. I hope you told them. I hope you told the police about the cancer. You did explain, didn't you?"

What could I say but yes?

"There is another question I'd like to ask, Alice." Cate looks less sure of herself, and her colour is high. She looks at the writing on her jotter, and I see that she has prepared this question. This must be important.

"Alice, did you at any time get an inkling of why David Jenkins wanted to die? If the cancer was a hoax you made up for your parents, why do you think he really wanted to kill himself?"

"That, is something I never asked him."

"Most people would have asked."

"Exactly," I say. "Inferior love demands reason."

Cate Austin's pen is poised in mid-air, "So not asking was a demonstration of your superior love?" I nod. "Including the eating of his flesh?"

I've been expecting this question. "Of course, it repulsed me, too. It wasn't my choice, Ms. Austin. It was his. But death and suffering can make people behave differently. So can love. We were making a sacrifice together. He needed me to do as he asked."

I see that she is incapable of such rationale. Her mouth is curled in distaste, despite the level note she has forced into her voice. "Why do you think he wanted you to eat him?"

"Ours is not to reason why. My devotion was absolute. I was merely his disciple. I simply agreed to do as he asked."

She is fixated with the cannibalism. She can't see clearly. And this woman is going to judge me.

"It was a strange thing to do, Alice. Some would say deranged."

"Some would say it was an act of faith." I lean forward, hands clasped in front of me on the table, and realise I must educate her. My voice is one of authority; I must enlighten her or she will never understand. "One of Keats' poems tells the tale of a woman, Isabella, who has fallen deeply in love with a man whom her brothers consider to be unworthy of her. Seeing that she will not be dissuaded from her affections, the brothers take him into the forest and kill him, burying him in a shallow grave. But such is the strength of his love, that he visits the woman, in ghost form. He tells her where he is buried. The woman goes to the forest and digs up her dead lover. She can't bear to leave him. Bereft, she cuts off his head and puts it in a pot, over which she grows a basil plant. The plant thrives and the woman will not be without her pot, which is always in her arms. It's a story showing extreme behaviour, some would say madness, but also of great love."

She looks at me, student to teacher. I see that she has failed to understand.

"The problem is, Alice, that what you have just recounted is a story. Fiction. What happened to David isn't a fable, it's reality. This isn't an academic exercise, it's the real world. And in the real world, unlike in literature, people don't eat their lover's penis in the name of love."

29

"You're a bit late bringing Amelia home, Tim. I hope she's eaten?"

"Fish fingers and chips."

Relieved not to have to start cooking, Cate collected the remnants of her own meagre tea—a cheese sandwich—and put the plate in the sink. Tim hovered behind her, checking his mobile and pressing buttons to send a text.

"Sally wants me to ask you about Beth's christening."

Cate smiled mockingly. "Not asking me to be godmother are you? Only you know how unreliable they can be at giving good blessings."

"Very droll, Cate. No, we think it's best if you don't come."

Cate thought of the godmother that wasn't invited, wasn't she the one who cursed the baby? Tim was distracted, still fiddling with his mobile.

"This christening's a big deal to Sally—to us—and we'd like Amelia to look pretty—it'd be good to see her in a dress for a change rather than those jeans she always wears. Sally wondered if you'd got anything suitable?"

"Well if you don't like the way I dress our daughter, Tim, you know what you can do. Why don't *you* get her a dress?"

"Come on, Cate. Don't be difficult—it's a simple enough request. You know the kind of thing we mean."

"Not really. You see, I haven't ever been to a christening. Your first daughter wasn't christened—I seem to remember you thought it was hypocritical."

"Yeah, well, it's important to Sally."

He shuffled his feet, picking one of Amelia's juggling balls from the worktop and toying with it. "So why are you being so arsey with me? Why did I have to bring Amelia home an hour before my time was up?"

She switched the hot tap on full. Soapsuds rose on her arms. "I want Amelia rested before school."

"You're being unreasonable."

"What was that?" She turned, soap dripping on the floor, and Tim held up his hands.

"Whoa! All I'm saying is you're not making it easy for me to be involved in Amelia's life . . ."

"How dare you Tim!" she hissed, coming closer to be heard over the pouring water, "I didn't want to be a single mother! You left me, remember? So just put your coat on and go back to that perfect home you share with the woman who you fucked when you were still living with me, okay? Just piss off!"

Clumsy with a hasty need to distract her heart Cate brought David Jenkins' diary up on the screen, opening a notepad by her side. She hoped that the diary would give her answers, even if Alice refused. This diary would help her to understand, to get it right. Even if her personal life was a mess, she could still get it right as a professional.

11th January

(Though why should I care about the date, the year? It's my last January. My last year. Numbers are irrelevant now.)

Straight up, I'm happy to die. Well, perhaps that's wrong. I'm happy to choose the hour of my death. There. That's it. After all, it's a privilege isn't it? Today I read about a guy who travelled across Europe just for that—to die. Now the police are questioning his wife, and the poor bloke was practically a vegetable. He couldn't even feed himself or wipe his arse. He had one of those colostomy bags. What kind of life is that? He had to go abroad to die. And they say it's a free country! It got me thinking about Robin. I mean, I wouldn't want to put her in any position, you know, with the police. What we are doing is illegal—not that it matters. You can't arrest someone who's dead. But if someone helped, well, then they can cop it. Literally. But that's something she has to deal with. It'll be too late by then.

My advert wasn't so unusual. I'm not the only one. Just do a little research and you'll see. In Japan the government is worried about the rise in Internet suicides. Last year, ninety-one people killed themselves after hooking up with people on the Web, and arranging suicide pacts. This year the figure looks likely to double. What about that case in Wales a few years back, all those kids with everything to live for? I read about a woman who hired a man to kill her. She wanted to die, but was nervous about doing it herself so she paid him to shoot her, to catch her off-guard. It was how she wanted to go. But the man welched on the deal, ran off with the money, so she reported him to the police. He was convicted for breaching a contract! You couldn't make it up, could you?

Robin and I may be an oddity, but we're not the only ones. We deserve to be understood.

There is one thing that links us, those who get help to die. Most have "poor health." Such a nothing expression. What does it mean? Prone to coughs and colds? A bit spotty and fat? Does it include mental health? Whatever the definition, I fit it. I'm in "poor health." It's a club I was enrolled in without my consent. I'm a member without paying any subscription.

I found myself confused today in the supermarket. I couldn't remember what I needed, whether it was cornflakes or toilet rolls, and I got into a panic. I lurched between the two aisles, hoping that just seeing the product would kick-start my brain into remembering, but the data was lost. In the end I bought the cereal and a large pack of toilet rolls and a bottle of whisky. When I got home I saw what I was missing, but realised the real loss had been in my head. Short-term memory is one of the earliest casualties. So, in defiance or out of sheer stupidity, I drowned my brain with alcohol, punishing it for letting me forget.

It was just a few days into the new year when I found out I was dying. The doctor had telephoned me at home, so I knew it had to be bad news. I arrived at his surgery to find him staring out of the window, his back to me. When he turned around he couldn't look me in the eye.

I'd gotten to know him quite well over the previous five months, since I'd started to suffer from occasional bouts of dizziness and shaking. What had first been put down to overwork and the need for three square meals a day, developed into lack of balance, so bad that once I collapsed on the tube. After that I started to get more forgetful, and I had blinding headaches. Dr. Froy referred me to a neurologist who did an MRI scan. I was told it might be Meniere's disease or simply bad migraines. Dr. Froy had the scan results, and judging by the tension in the room it wasn't good news. I just wanted an answer. A diagnosis would be a relief, at least that was what I thought.

"Would you like a seat?" he had said, not taking one himself.

I felt a dull ache at the top of my spine. I knew I was ill, I just needed to know what with.

"Mr. Jenkins, have you heard of Creutzfeldt-Jakob disease?"

I was non-plussed. "CJD?" he said.

It sounded familiar. "You mean mad cow disease?" I had a vague memory from my childhood of John Gummer, the Tory health minister, force-feeding hamburgers to his daughter after BSE ravished the countryside. All those piles of dead animals, the news reports on the television each night.

He scratched his head. "It's extremely rare. Only one in several million people gets it."

"So am I the lucky one?"

He cleared his throat and gave a brief nod. "I'm afraid so."

I knew it wasn't good news but seduced by the claims of modern medicine, I still believed that a diagnosis equalled a cure.

"Have you ever had a blood transfusion, Mr. Jenkins?"

"No. Why?"

"That's one way you may have caught it. The other is through eating contaminated offal products. Probably years ago. This illness has a very long incubation period."

There was a silence then, as I considered the slow-growing illness, the symptoms that had got steadily worse.

"Is that why I've been dizzy?"

"Yes. Symptoms include hallucinations, loss of memory and jerking. Similar symptoms to those associated with Alzheimer's disease."

Alzheimer's. My father had that. It was a bastard of an illness, robbing me of my dad long before his body gave up. "So what's the treatment?"

The doctor finally took his seat. At last he looked at me directly. "There is no cure, at present."

I felt my jaw give way, words like marbles in my mouth, "There must be something you can do?"

He looked down at the pen he was fingering, cleared his throat, but remained silent.

"How long?" I asked.

"Usually patients live for twelve months from the onset of symptoms."

Twelve months. I had first complained of a headache in July. I had six months left. Science had let me down. I had to pray that God wouldn't.

Cate's eyes were the only thing moving as she scanned what she had just read. So that was the illness—Creutzfeldt-Jakob disease. CJD—mad cow disease, as Cate thought of it—yes, she too remembered the piles of carcasses in fields, and some of the farmers who refused to have their animals culled. Had Smith really wanted to be slaughtered just like a wretched animal?

She looked at the picture of her daughter Amelia on her desk, feeling the swelling around her heart. What a choice: to face death in a matter of weeks or months, or to choose your own end. Maybe she would have done it, too, choosing the moment herself rather than waiting for the end to find her. Symptoms of dizziness, memory loss—how awful. What a truly awful way to die. She steeled herself to read on:

15th February

Since my father died in December I'd thought about what to do with his bungalow, a 1970s two-bedroom place with a square of lawn at the front and patio at the back. I'd thought about selling it but hadn't got around to having it valued, putting it on the market. Now there was no time and no point in paying rent on my flat when the bungalow stood empty so that weekend I moved in. It took three trips to the skip to get rid of dad's stuff, but my belongings hardly filled the place. One bedroom was an empty box, and the lounge looked spartan. I was used to a small flat, and now I had a whole house. Moving to the bungalow added another forty minutes to my journey to work, but it gave me a fresh start.

I didn't bother registering myself with the local doctors. There was no medicine they could give me. It was a few days after the move that I put the advert on the web. Then I met Robin.

She stood on the railway platform, wearing a white wool jacket, the collar high on her neck, staring into the middle distance like some actress in a film. I knew straight away it was her. I'd expected a drama queen. After all, she spends her time with fiction and she was preparing to star in the story of her life.

In the eighties there was this urban myth going around that I keep thinking about. Maybe you've already heard it? It's about a young widow who decides to take a cruise, an opportunity for her to start to heal after the death of her husband. She isn't rich, and it's cost all her savings, but as she sits on the breezy deck she knows it was worth every penny. There's a man on the cruise, handsome and smartly dressed, who takes an interest in her. They eat together in the evenings and walk around the boat each day. They talk. He's a widower too, and they get on well. As the cruise progresses and the boat reaches warmer water the man and woman sleep together. He's a good lover, and the woman begins to believe she's been rescued. The man says he loves her, that he wants to be with her forever.

On the boat's final stop they walk around a Caribbean island, but when the time comes to head back to the boat the man is nowhere to be found. Assuming that he's gone ahead of her the woman rejoins the cruise and the boat begins to pull away from shore. When it's far from the harbour the woman sees the man on the land, waving at her and smiling. He is waving goodbye. Before she has a chance to cry out she feels a tap on her shoulder. It's one of the porters. 'The gentleman asked me to give you this.'

It's a package, beautifully wrapped in gold paper and she thinks it must be jewellery, maybe a ring. But inside the paper is a small wooden coffin. Inside the coffin is a note, which reads: I have AIDS. RIP.

Although this story must be fiction I've heard of people deliberately infecting others, or threatening to stab them with a contaminated needle. Only last week a woman was imprisoned for infecting her lover, without warning him that she was HIV positive.

I suppose I'm thinking about that tale because in the Eighties everyone was paranoid about AIDS, and everyone was terrified they'd be infected like the woman on the boat. But now I sympathise with the man on the shore. Who wants to be in his shoes? Who could bear to suffer alone? It's supremely selfish, but I long to be with someone else who's dying, to talk with them. But how? There are no volunteers. Not usually anyway. I don't want to be alone when I die.

We meet at weekends and I'm careful to protect her. I protect Robin from my sickness, hiding the signs of it.

We don't sleep together; sex is something we are saving for the hour of my death. I try not to think of the lovers she must have had before me. I tell myself it's an advantage; she'll guide me.

My body is losing its fight with my brain. No amount of positivity or herbal potions will help. I'm learning about death. I'm reading about other people who faced death how they found the strength. The Bible shows me the way, that epic study of death. I thought of Jesus, looked to his example first, but then I looked back at the Old Testament. There's the woman who, after a siege by the King of Syria, tells of how her neighbour said, 'Give thy son, that we may eat him today and we will eat my son tomorrow.' So they boiled the son and ate him, and the next day the woman said, 'Give Thy son, that we may eat him,' but the neighbour refused . . .

And Jesus, asking his disciples to eat the bread, the flesh—to drink the bloody wine. Krish, do you think only unnatural people are cannibals? You believe in reincarnation. Can you see how it's a way of living on, of cheating death?

Normal people do abnormal things. Even after I'd placed my advert on the Internet, seeking a woman to help me die, my life was ordinary. Even now, when I've found the right woman, when I've decided that I want her to eat part of me, life carries on as before: I shower and hate the water too cold, I still moan about the amount of crap on the TV, I still get pissed off when I run out of milk in the mornings and can't have my coffee. Normality, despite everything.

Some things have changed. My kitchen cupboards, normally stocked full, a sure sign of my need for order, that obsessive gene in my DNA, are less organised, and I haven't replaced the lines of baked beans and peas and dried pasta. I don't think about food while I read about death and cannibalism. Instead I hunger for emptiness, for stories. I'm starving myself with words. It's all part of the preparation . . .

3rd March

Sacrifice. (n)

1. The act of giving up something valued for the sake of something else more important or worthy. 2. The slaughter of an animal or person or the surrender of a possession to a deity. 3. Offer to kill as a sacrifice [from the Latin sacrificium]

By reading, by searching, I've discovered a group of us sacrificial men. Jesus, of course. Suicide bombers would be in, and many, many more.

I've read the story of The Mignonette, a boat crippled some 1,200 miles from the Cape leaving the crew with no food or water for twenty days. Though surrounded by seawater they believed that drinking even a small amount of it would kill them, and threw rainwater and turtle meat that had been 'contaminated' overboard. The youngest of the four crewmen, just seventeen, couldn't resist the water when his lips were black with thirst. Already dehydrated, he got violently sick, and this marked him out as the weakest of the crew; the strong will always prey on the weak. The captain spoke of drawing lots. The man who drew the shortest straw would be sacrificed for the survival of the others. Whether this process of selection actually took place is disputed.

On the twentieth day the captain found the boy, who looked up from where he lay, weak and sick, saying, 'What, me?' in recognition of what was to come. He struggled and cried but while another sailor held the boy down, the captain slashed his jugular artery with a knife, catching the blood. After the boy had slowly bled to death the three men drank his blood then feasted on his vital organs.

When they finally arrived on land, the men claimed they'd done nothing wrong, that the boy had died for a greater good. The captain even complained when his knife was taken away as evidence, as he wanted it as a 'keepsake' of what had happened.

Sometimes I'm the boy, sometimes I'm the captain. Sometimes I'm the sacrifice, the body ready to be butchered, the boy who has drawn the short straw, but other times I think that I hold the knife. I'm in control. I'm choosing. In asking her to eat me I'm fulfilling a finer destiny for Robin, a clearer end for myself. I give myself up freely, in the belief that I will live on afterwards.

The boy didn't volunteer but that doesn't make his sacrifice less noble. Even Jesus doubted his martyrdom, stumbling three times under the weight of the cross. That's why I have to keep Robin's destiny hidden from her. It's for her own good.

I found something out that changed everything.

There are remote tribes where, at least before the 1950s when white missionaries forced their own beliefs on them, it was part of the ancient funeral rites to eat the dead. But the tribes became sick. Those who ate the dead and prepared the body for the feast, cut the skin and drained the blood, developed symptoms: palsy and memory loss, aggression and confusion. In short, they had CJD. Then the missionaries came and taught them a different cannibalism, with wafers and wine. All of this, it got me thinking, and I start to wonder if my brain is impaired. I'm sick, carrying the damaged prions with diseased messages, but is my brain so affected that I can think of passing this on to Robin, of letting her eat my flesh, and it doesn't seem horrible? Instead I see a circular, poetic justice, like the karma that you told me about.

To live on through her, until she dies. Why is it a comfort to me? I've been emailing Robin. I told her about a place where funeral fires are built high into the sky, smoke lifting up to the hot sun as leaves of falling ash touch the ground like a blessing. Strange men, red paint on their brown limbs, dancing to the rapid beat of a skin drum, as the women sway and sing and raise their hands.

I told her about the cut in the soft flesh of the belly, the taking away of the sweetmeats inside. The women, who sing as they slice, boil and season, using vines and flowers and grain in their cooking. Who drink the blood and eat the meat. What remained was burnt, a gift to the gods. It doesn't happen anymore. It's only a dream, but it's mine.

I told her of the love, the deep respect, the mourners had for the dead. How by eating the dead they carried strength in their stomachs, in their blood. I told her that this was my choice.

The immortality of sustaining her, of living within her body.

I want her to eat me.
She needs to practice. I'm thinking about how.

Cate stopped reading. She understood now, why David Jenkins had kept his illness a secret . . . *she will follow me* . . . he wanted to infect Alice. Because, if she had known he had CJD, she never would have agreed to eat him. What a twisted ploy . . . Christ, what a sick bastard. Could Alice have had no idea? Surely Smith must have looked ill? Surely she would have wanted to know why he had asked to be eaten?

She felt sick, and breathed deep to calm her stomach, listened carefully to the silence in her home, glad that Amelia was fast asleep, as if dreams could safeguard her from the perversions written in the diary. She longed for sleep herself, or at least not to think about what she was reading.

When she first read about Jenkins' terminal illness she felt sorry for him, and began to understand why he had wanted to die, to choose his own end. But now, reading that he wanted to take Alice with him, she wondered how someone could consider such a thing. Cate didn't believe in Evil. She'd worked with enough criminals to know that even the most heinous acts are rooted in dysfunction, be it abuse, bereavement, or addiction of some kind. Evil, however, was a fixed, permanent state and easy rhetoric for those who didn't want to acknowledge their shared responsibility in the crimes around them. Cate knew that David Jenkins wasn't evil, but his rationale, his decision to infect Alice, was so calculating, so horribly detached, that it was a very close imitation.

The right place for this memory stick was with the police. But first she must finish reading. She had to finish what she'd started:

1st April

My brain is playing a joke on me.
I can feel my recall losing ground, struggling for a good grip, but there's a dusty filing cabinet that's left in the dark corner of my brain, undisturbed, so what happened in the past can be retrieved. It's only new data that's flimsy.
I'm obsessed with my own death.
I romanticise it, like the writers and artists Robin talks about. I'm also obsessed with other people's endings. Untimely suffering, tragic coincidences are my fixation. Now, instead of seeing the world through insurance facts and variables, the risk of a car crash or divorce, I look for the improbable, the freakish deaths. I want to read about shipwrecked boats where

sailors threw passengers overboard into the icy sea, an orgy of murderous self-protection, a death-cull that took hours. I'm surprised that such stories aren't more common. I read about men forced to eat human flesh to survive, who are then driven mad with gluttony.

When I visit Robin I insist that we go to the sea, just over an hour from Lavenham. She doesn't like the coast, but I don't care. The sea is a greybrown sludge. I watch for most of an hour. The boats make me think of travel, of being somewhere else. Of escaping myself and my destiny. I cast my fears into the North Sea, and tell myself that Robin is my ticket. She is also my destination.

Krish, us actuaries think in numbers. Well, here are a few for you: in 1970, when figures first started, there were 21 deaths from sporadic CJD. In 2002 there were 67. This year there are already 80 cases in the UK. Me being one of them. 10% of patients have symptoms usually associated with Alzheimer's. In younger people the average age for onset is 28, but it can happen at any age. And my favourite fact: Creutzfeldt-Jakob disease has been prolific in a tribe in Papua New Guinea.

Statistics are a great comfort. It's only human to want to belong in the majority. When it comes to misfortunes, we escape by being in the norm. How many passengers at airports, hands clammy and heartbeats rapid, tell themselves that they are more likely to be killed crossing the road than flying in an airplane? Exactly! We don't want to be exceptional, or stand out, and we believe our ordinariness is a charm. When something happens, like 9/11, it shakes this belief and we suddenly see that those on the edge of the statistics, the unlucky minority, are just like us. Suddenly a world of terrible possibilities opens up and we're afraid to use the tube, step on a city bus.

Did you know, Krish, that in America the chance of being killed by a terrorist bomb is 1 in 2,200,000? In short, you have more chance of winning the lottery, which is a comfort, because everyone knows they'll never win the lottery, they could never be that lucky. So if that is more likely than being blown up, they must be safe. It's logic of a sort.

But what about other deaths, other ways?

The chances of being hit by lightning are 1 in 600,000. The chances of being killed in a fire are 1 in 70,900. Still feel safe?

You and I both know that one of the first laws of an actuary's work is that human beings have a distorted view of risk. They don't see the whole picture. Our perceptions are twisted by stories in the media, by films, by our own personalities and experiences. So, despite the unlikely odds, we still worry about being raped or murdered. We hear a sound in the night and think of burglars, not mice. We're programmed to imagine bad things happening to us, as opposed to good things, even if the good are more likely. It's a kind of protective pessimism: if we worry about the worst happening, it may miss our door.

Likewise, people who are blessed, who are lucky, worry that their good fortune will 'run out', as if there is just one quota of happiness and they are using up their store and are destined for imminent tragedy. We believe in fate. Insurance companies exploit this, and I've always hated those adverts for life insurance, the bereft wife with her child, thinking back to when her husband told her insurance was a waste of money. The message is clear: protect yourself with anxiety. If you don't worry, it will happen to you. Don't walk under a ladder, don't let a black cat cross your path. Be lucky.

Even before my luck ran out, I didn't feel safe. But my fears, fire and lightning and train crashes, were more likely. Despite all my neuroses and obsessive tics, I never thought a disease had already found a home in my brain, maybe a decade ago. It was something I'd vaguely heard about but, like everyone else, I thought it was something that happened to other people. I couldn't even spell it. The chances of being diagnosed with Creutzfeldt-Jakob disease are 1 in 12,000,000. In disease terms, I've won the lottery several times over.

I thought about telling Robin. In many ways it'd make it easier. She's never shown any signs of doubt about helping me die, but any niggling worries would soon go if she knew I had a terminal illness.

Terminal, like an airport or train station. A final destination. To terminate: to end, to cease. My illness is my final stop. I shall be getting out there.

But any thoughts I might have about telling her disappear when I'm in her home. You should see it, Krish. It's like a show home! It's so clean, so white. The surfaces sparkle. Nothing in the fridge is dripping or stained, as if the cartons and wrappers have been wiped and cleaned, like a show fridge. 'This food is for display only. Please don't attempt to eat it.' How can I tell Robin that I carry disease? It'd be like bringing a sick rat into her clean home. She'd shrink back, she wouldn't be able to touch me. I understand her cleanliness; it's an obsessiveness I recognise. I can't bear the idea that she'd refuse to kiss me. I could reassure her, tell her that CJD is almost impossible to catch. Kissing and sex are not the way it travels but she wouldn't be reassured, not totally. The idea would be in her head.

I'm not a fool. My illness would clear Robin of blame for her part in my death. It'd give a reason for my suicide and remove any suggestion that my death wasn't euthanasia. If they discover the CJD, that is, which is unlikely. Even during autopsy, CJD is a hard thing to determine.

It requires the removal of the brain, a special process that they're unlikely to do. My medical records are with my old doctor; finding them would take a great deal of tracking down, when I no longer live in that area. The only written knowledge of my illness is this diary.

It's why I'll send this to you, Krish. I need someone to know the whole truth, and to understand what I'm doing.

The only person I need to persuade right now is Robin. There's a deal to be made, and I don't think she'll find the price is too high. The sums, the numbers all equal the result. I've balanced both sides of the equation, and she has her own reasons, no doubt, for agreeing to help me. All she needs is faith.

But first she must prove that she can do it.

2nd May

I'll die next month. I've settled on June 16th. I chose the day specially. It was the day of my parent's car crash. The day I started to believe in God.

I needed to book annual leave for the Friday because we've decided on midnight. Krish, thank you for agreeing to cover for me. I told you I was taking a trip to Brighton. A mini-break. All Mr. Filet needs to do is sign my leave card. This is a detail, I know, but I don't want anyone to notice I'm gone until it's too late. If I simply didn't turn up to work on Friday you'd call the bungalow, or get HR to do it, and when they found no answer someone might suggest alerting the police. Unreliability isn't in my nature. It's easier to plan my absence and when I don't turn up on Monday morning it will be too late.

Robin and I have talked about it. We've agreed that she'll call the police, but only when I'm dead. She'll have to be patient and wait until there's no chance of resuscitation. She'll have my suicide note, ready to hand over. I hope they won't interview her, take her to some scummy cell, but I guess there are procedures to follow. She's told me not to worry, that she'll be fine. She tells me to think only of the moment, the instant of my death. She tells me it'll be amazing.

I wrote my suicide note at work today. I like to be prepared. I was just finishing it when you decided to go to the machine for coffee and came to my side of the desk, to put the paper cup in front of me. I was conscious of the notepaper, the pen in my hand. You probably didn't even notice but I bundled the letter into the drawer. Then you did something that surprised me. You put a hand on my shoulder and asked if I was okay.

You'd never touched me before, and your hand was warm. You removed the hand but not your gaze and I saw that you really cared. It embarrassed me, and I told you I was fine, but you didn't believe me, did you?

Then you did something for me, gave me the dealer's phone number. I needed it, Krish—I need cannabis to steady me. I know you didn't want to hand the number over, that you're worried about it but eventually you agreed. Thanks for that.

Cate looked away from the words on the screen, and rubbed her eyes. So the suicide note was written a month before David actually died. He was certainly organised. Her head hurt and jelly-like shapes were floating across her vision.

The diary was a testimony to his depravity, and Cate now felt that Alice was the victim. The disease may even now be growing inside her, slowly taking root. She had a right to know what she had risked in eating David, what he had subjected her to. Alice had a right to know why he had asked her to eat him. But first Cate had someone else she needed to speak with, someone who might be able to help.

30

1993

She was lying on the floor, naked and very still. Just as she should be. But Alice watched Lee, and thought that it would never be quite right. Lee fidgeted too much and moaned she was cold. This wasn't working for either girl. The feeling Alice chased was a ghost memory, quickly gone after one sweet taste. All she wanted was to experience it again, that feeling of love, but each time she tried it slipped further away. Was she forgetting? It was twelve years ago and she had only been four. Sometimes she had to screw her face up, really concentrate, to get the feeling back. If she forgot what her real mother looked like, the smell of that room, the taste of the sandwich, she would be lost. She knew that. Lee tried her best, but just didn't get it. And she'd become shy with her body, her sixteenth year had brought puppy fat and breasts and she needed soft words and caresses when Alice would have preferred to be silent. Alice sighed; it would have to do. She dropped onto the floor, next to her friend, and slid a hand across her waist, thicker than it was, skin was no longer clear. She was spotty. Poor Lee, no wonder the other girls at school ignored her. Alice felt a wave of protectiveness for her friend who never seems to notice what others said, who lay naked just for her. Wearing only the fresh nail varnish that Alice had carefully painted onto her toenails.

Alice put her head to her friend's soft chest, and listened to her heart which quickened as she tightened her grip around her waist, and Lee turned her head, wanting a kiss. Alice could feel her warm mouth on her hair and whispered, "Lie still!" Lee always ruined it by moving.

In the bedroom they lay, thinking only of love, and they didn't hear the soft tread of Alice's mother coming upstairs with a pile of washing.

Mrs. Dunn paused, and wondered for the hundredth time what it was they did in there, so silently. She worried about things, things she's heard about on the TV, like drugs. Like solvent abuse, apparently just sniffing a pot of nail polish can kill instantly. *Do you know what your teenager is up to?* The headline demanded that morning, making her flinch. Her daughter was so contained, so aloof, that she knew she would not know. The room always smelt of nail polish after Lee had visited. If they were sniffing solvents in there . . .

She couldn't discuss this with Alice. She hadn't the words. But if she should happen upon them, if she had an innocent reason to go into the bedroom and found them in the act . . .

Telling herself that this was what any good mother would do, she made her way up the stairs, silently avoiding the steps that would groan under her weight, stopping when she was outside Alice's door, her hand raised in the air by the handle. She listened at the door, fingers touching the aluminium blade of the handle, daring herself to push it down. Finally, she opened the door.

She didn't find them, as she expected, bent over a pot of candy pink nail varnish, inhaling fumes. Instead, she found them on the floor. Lee was naked, on her back, and alongside her was Alice, holding her tight. She was sucking her breast.

Alice was excelling at her studies, absorbing facts and ideas at a marvellous rate. She was hungry for knowledge, for understanding, and it was clear she would go far. Her decision to remain at school to take A levels was welcomed by all her teachers: we wish her well with her continuing education. That's what her form tutor said in last year's report card. But Alice didn't excel at everything; she failed at the break times, at lunchtime. She failed at interaction with others. In the sixth form block, the other young women avoided her. Lee was no longer at the school so Alice was always alone between lessons. She often sat in the library, surrounded by a barricade of books.

She didn't care about not having friends. It was their loss, their error, if they couldn't see what a good friend she would be. She held her nose in the air and looked down on them and they hated her for it. She taught herself to rise above such pettiness. She resolved not to desire friendships, and she still had Lee. Why would she need more than one friend?

Lee worked as a lifeguard at the local swimming pool, and talked of joining the Forces. She'd worked hard at getting in shape and valued strength and fitness. Lee wasn't like Alice, she couldn't immerse herself in learning. She preferred practical subjects, using her hands.

Alice used her brain, her mind. Of all her three A levels, Alice was best at English. The teacher encouraged her, told her she should think about studying it at degree level; he said she had a knack for interpretation. The interpretation of words and details. She had a literary eye. And then she discovered Keats. They were studying *Ode on a Grecian Urn*:

> More happy love! More happy, happy love!
> For ever warm and still to be enjoy'd,
> For ever panting, and for ever young;
> All breathing human passion far above . . .

Alice understood immediately how the figures on the urn were immortal. Understood straight away how a frozen image could transcend the inferior, too-human passions. She thought of her mother, of that single image that had haunted her down the years; her immortal Mummy, frozen in time on the bedsit floor, forever beautiful, eternally loved.

Alice had found a way to be understood. The Romantics gave her a world in which her feelings made sense. The relief was immeasurable.

Between poetry and Lee there was little choice. The ethereal over the physical.

Lee was heavier now, weighed down by swimmers' shoulders, muscular thighs and smelling of chlorine. Alice no longer asked her to strip, and anyway she wouldn't feel safe since her mother found them. Nothing was said, but her mother stopped coming to her room. She wouldn't say anything to her father, Alice was sure.

Alice knew she wasn't a lesbian. Her desire transcended gender. What she wanted from Lee wasn't sexual. Her need for Lee's body, for the stillness of her flesh, was spiritual. But how could she explain that to her mother? She would never understand. Instead, Alice would bide her time until she could escape. And Keats was showing her the way.

Alice was in the doctor's waiting room, but she wasn't sick. Her mother, who brought her there, was in with the doctor. The waiting room was full and two children fought over the dirty dolls' house in the corner. Alice assumed her mother had asked her to come along because she wanted moral support. She'd been tearful all morning, and bleached the floor twice before they left home. Maybe she needed more anti-depressants. Alice yawned and waited.

When her mother appeared she looked older, her eyes weary and her forehead wrinkled with worry, but then Alice sometimes forgot that she was an elderly woman. Her smile was thin and her hands were clasped around themselves as she said in a whisper, "Come with me, Alice. The doctor wants to see us together."

Alice's heart thumped, in spite of her controlled teenage nonchalance, all chalky foundation and red lips and feet encased in Doc Martens, her heart had no disguise. It hurt to think her mother was unwell.

The doctor's door was open, under a large sign announcing 'Room K.' Eleven rooms; so many sick people. Her mother stood aside and Alice took the chair pointed out to her by the man behind the desk.

It wasn't their usual doctor. This man was older, with a bushy beard and tiny dark eyes. He wore a brown cord jacket with leather patches, and looked nothing like the other GPs, who wore smart shirts with ties, or bow ties. This doctor looked like a hippy.

"Now then, Miss Dunn. Or may I call you Alice?"

Alice mumbled yes, but she was surprised. When had a doctor wanted to call her by her name? She looked to her mother, who had taken the opposite seat and was studying the floor, maybe thinking how dirty it was. Her mother looked so pale and faded. She must be dying, thought Alice, a sharp grip squeezing her heart. That was why this doctor wanted to call her by name. She braced herself for bad news.

"And you must call me Dr. Murray," he smiled, as if he'd just told a clever joke, then placed his hands flat on the desk, a magician showing he had nothing up his sleeves. "Alice, I'm not a medical doctor but a clinical psychologist. Your mum has referred you because she has concerns about you."

Her mother was still staring down at the carpet. Dr. Murray smiled at Alice, as if these concerns were good things. Alice glowered under her white foundation, realising that she was the reason they were here. Her mother had referred *her*! Her mother wasn't sick at all.

"Now, Alice, I explained to your mum that at sixteen you're not strictly speaking a child anymore, so any assistance I can give must be with your full consent." He paused, smiling, inviting trust. "So your mum will leave us in a little while, and you and I will have a chat. But first I want you to hear from her why she is so worried. Mrs. Dunn?"

Alice watched her mother struggle with words, which eventually came out defiantly and accompanied by sniffs.

"You've always been so withdrawn, Alice. You've never had any friends to speak of. Except for Lee, of course. I just thought you were shy. But then, after I found you both . . ."

"You told him, didn't you?" Hot anger burst in her chest.

"Alice, what else could I do? It's not natural . . ." She started to cry.

Dr. Murray pushed a box of tissues across the desk, saying in a kind but firm tone, "Now, Mrs. Dunn, I've already said that homosexuality is not a sign of psychological disturbance. All sixteen-year-olds have issues around their sexuality."

The penny dropped on what he was saying. It is all Alice could do to keep her voice level. "I'm not gay! Is that what she told you?"

"You're bound to feel ambivalent about it, Alice, especially when your mother clearly struggles with . . ."

"No, Dr. Murray! This has nothing to do with my mother. I'm not a lesbian. I don't find any woman even slightly fanciable."

"But your mother said that she found you and your friend—"

Alice erupted, "Especially not Lee—she's spotty and fat!"

Her mother had stopped blowing her nose. Dr. Murray cocked his head in curiosity. "Oh? But Lee is your best friend?"

"She's not a friend. She's a leech I can't shake off."

"So do you have any friends?" He was interested, and so was her mother.

Alice pushed out her lower lip and looked at them both like they were idiots. "I don't need any friends. I have poetry."

"Poetry? You like reading?"

Alice's mouth becomes a sneer. "No, I don't like reading. I live in images. I can achieve a state of sensation without the need for reason." She looked over to her mother. "I would hardly expect her to understand that."

31

Smith: I want to see you.

Robin: When? This weekend?

Smith: Yes. We should start planning out the details. June 16th isn't far off.

Robin: We still haven't discussed how you want to die.

Smith: Poison. A slow, lingering death. I want to savour every moment.

Robin: What type of poison? Paracetamol?

Smith: Something else. Something that brings pleasure. Don't you have any students who use drugs?

Robin: What do you think?? But getting them to supply me would be too risky. Whatever we use you should buy it.

Smith: You answered my ad—I thought you liked playing with risk?

Robin: I'd like to keep my job.

Smith: Point taken. But I don't know any drug dealers. Although I've got a good mate who uses a lot of dope. He works across from me, so I could speak to him tomorrow. The dealer he uses must sell harder stuff, too. I'll get his number.

Robin: I just had a thought. I do have a student who has failed a couple of essays. A total druggie. Maybe he would be interested in an exchange? One grade for one hit.

Smith: I thought you said it was too risky?

Robin: Not when he has something to lose. Without my help he'll have to drop out. But I could make him an offer. He gets his pass, and everyone's happy.

Smith: Let me ask my friend first. If he can't help, then you can ask your student.

This was how Smith and I planned; messages on our computer screens, one sentence communication that helped us prepare. Smith wanted to die of a drugs overdose, and his friend from work gave him the number for a drug dealer, but the mobile went unanswered every time he tried it. We were both getting impatient. It was time to try it my way.

I waited in the lecture hall, watching the students fan out into the corridor. I waited until the hall hummed only with noisy air conditioning, the sound of no words. Still, I waited. Alex was slumped in his usual place, near the back of the hall. Despite being drugged to the eyeballs, he always made it to lectures. This told me a great deal. It told me that he didn't want to drop out, despite all signs that he was going to fail anyway. It gave me the advantage.

Alex was too stoned to have learned anything that day. There was no notepad on the desk, no pen. His pupils were wide as saucers, his body caved in a stupor. Awoken from his doze he looked up and scowled.

I opened a bottle of water and placed it in front of him. "Drink it. It's dangerous to become dehydrated."

But water was not the medicine that would cure him. He was spaced out and his pupils were dark; he needed a stronger fix.

His face was waxy, unreal, and his clothes were loose. He was a marionette, limply waiting for life to be pulled into him by a puppeteer. By me.

"Alex, why do you still persist in coming here? Why attend my class when you can't possibly gain anything from it?"

He frowned in the effort of thinking. His hands were like newborn puppies, jerky energy but uncoordinated as they scrambled for the water bottle, fumbling with the cap. "My parents would freak if I dropped out."

"But attendance alone won't earn you a degree."

Despite whatever drugs coursed through his blood, he reacted. His mouth drooped before the expression was masked as he swigged the water. Some ran down his chin.

"I want you to be honest with me, Alex. What drugs are you on?"

His body sank back into the chair, his hands momentarily still in his lap. He was about to protest but hadn't the energy. Instead, he gave in. As I had anticipated.

"Speed. Coke. Anything I can get. Why, what are you selling?" His lip curled and I saw his brown teeth.

"You're throwing away your education. Are drugs worth that?"

He was bored and agitated. "You better believe it, mate. Speed gives you this incredible high, the most amazing up. But coke! Wow, that's the best. It's like this soaring energy. Like being King of the World."

"But you're failing your degree. Essays handed in late, poorly written. Not to mention the cost to your parents."

He looked up sharply, "What are you, a fucking counsellor? What's it got to do with you?"

"Nothing. Absolutely nothing." Here I paused, then said evenly, "Unless you're interested in a proposition."

"A proposition?" He tried to focus on my mouth but his eyelids were heavy. "What proposition?"

"I want you to get me some drugs, Alex."

He half laughed, but his voice came out a drawl. "You must think I'm fucking mental if you reckon I'd do that. I don't want to be had up for dealing."

His scruples amused me, "Teach me about drugs. What would you take if you wanted to be relaxed? Really relaxed, so you were anaesthetised from pain. So you felt that anything that might happen to you was just a dream."

Alex chuckled, his face suddenly lit with good humour. In that moment I could see the appeal of this young man in the student bar, in the student digs. He was at ease, knowing his expertise, taking a viva on his best subject: narcotics.

"Gees would be the drug of choice for that situation." "Gees?"

"GHB. Gamma Hydroxybutyric acid." He looked at me with disgust for my ignorance. "You'd know it as a date rape drug."

"I thought that was Rohypnol?"

"GHB is better, 'cos it's a liquid so it's easier to slip into someone's drink and then they're away with the fairies. You can literally do anything to 'em and they can't remember a thing about it." Alex checked himself. "Not that that's my bag, y'get me? Only sick fuckers do that. I just use it for the sleep it gives. Man, it's deep! Oblivion." He drawled, enunciating every vowel, as if he was on the edge of it. He smirked, cocky. "Course, you have to be careful with the dosage. Just two teaspoons and you'd OD. More kids end up in A&E after taking GHB than Ecstasy."

"What with?"

"Worse case, heart attack. A little bit see, just a few drops on the tongue, and you're the life and soul of the party. A few drops more and you're in a coma, a few more and your breathing's fucked so your heart gives. But I've got a high tolerance. 'Sides, I know when to stop. I don't let myself get too careless. I only buy two vials at a time, max, and each one is only half a teaspoon, so I could never overdose, even if I wanted to."

"Alex, I want to be clear about this: I don't want you wasting my time here at the university. I am going to do something very unorthodox, something I would never do normally, but I believe you are an exceptional young man. I believe you have talent, and I'm going to help you to use it. I'm offering you a deal. But we need to keep this between ourselves." I allowed there to be a pause, for us both to register what I was saying. The air conditioning hummed, our only witness. "This must be our secret."

Alex narrowed his eyes, interest fighting with mistrust. "What deal?"

"If you give me your two vials of Gee, then I'll change this year's final grade. You will no longer fail or have to retake this year. I'll give you a 2.1 for the course you have taken with me, and persuade my colleagues not to fail you outright on the other courses."

"Can you do that?"

He was suspicious but alert. I thought of my dusty colleague who took the Medieval Literature course and knew that persuading him would be no effort. "I can promise you a good enough grade to get you into next year. But you must complete your half of the deal."

"What are you gonna do with the drugs?"

"I will safely dispose of them. In exchange you will get a pass, and no need for Mummy and Daddy to discover what a fuck-up their darling boy has become. I'm offering you a lifeline. A solid grade to end this academic year should give you the motivation to get the help you need over the summer, and come back ready to start clean in year two. That is the deal. Two vials of GHB in exchange for a pass."

Later, I sent an instant message to Smith:

Robin: I did it! I have what we need. We can practice now.
Smith: What do you have?
Robin: The perfect drug. One that brings deep, easy sleep . . . I was told, on expert authority, that it's blissful.
Smith: So this weekend we'll test it. You know, just a little, to make sure it's the right one.
Robin: I was told it could lead to death easily. Heart attack.
Smith: I just need to be certain, to try it out first. I want to minimise the risk of anything going wrong in June.
Robin: Ever the actuary!
Smith: Something like that.
Robin: Okay. This weekend then. A trial run. I'll think of something special . . .
Smith: I'm looking forward to being relaxed, I'm so tense at the moment. What do you do when you can't sleep?
Robin: Take a bath. Drink warm milk.
Smith: Doesn't work for me . . .

Robin: What's up?

Smith: Feeling low . . . depressed . . . it happens.

Robin: John K would call it 'melancholy.' Isn't that a beautiful word?

Smith: How would he recommend snapping out of it?

Robin: He wouldn't. He believed all emotions, even painful ones, should be explored, and revelled in. 'Glut thy sorrow.'

Smith: Why? Was he a sadist?

Robin: Of sorts. He saw that experiencing melancholy gives a greater appreciation of the other side of the coin: happiness, passion, love. All emotion is intensified.

Smith: Ah, love! Do we love?

Robin: Do we? Do we passion?

Smith: Are you toying with me?

Robin: Never. I love you.

Smith: More than ever before?

Robin: More than. Much. Sleep, now, my love. We will be together soon enough.

I couldn't sleep, I was so excited. You can imagine, can't you? How wonderfully thrilling it was to be so close to the time when I would feel that love, that sweet warmth that comes with the perfect moment?

Outside the night was fading, and the sun would soon rise. It would be a hot day, the weatherman said, especially for May. A beautiful day was dawning and we were going to practice. It was a test for both of us.

Without bothering to dress I went to the spare room where Smith was sleeping. The curtains were open, and the windows, so I could hear the rising call of birds. Smith was shrouded in a white sheet, his eyes closed although his breathing told me that he, too, was awake. I lay down next to him, my weight pinning the sheet tight to his side. "We don't need to sleep."

He opened his eyes, blinking as he tried to focus and I passed him his glasses from the bedside table. "We could do something else."

"Okay," he said, sounding excited as he looked at my naked body, "is this what you were thinking of?" His hand slid towards me, grabbing my left breast. I pushed him away gently: petting was not what I had in mind, and we'd agreed to wait until June 16th to have full sex. To make his death more special.

"It's a surprise," I told him. "Just come downstairs in fifteen minutes. Don't bother getting dressed."

It had to be outside, because of the sunrise. Also, it was more practical. I'd put newspaper down over the grass like a blanket of words. In my garden was a bench, on which I'd laid out everything I needed, neatly angled like a surgeon's trolley. I'd put a white sheet over the bench, not wanting to spoil the surprise.

Smith appeared at the open door from the breakfast room, and I called softly. My neighbours couldn't see us but if their windows were open any noise would travel.

"Come here. Don't be shy."

He came to me, naked except for his glasses. I was also naked; I'm comfortable in my skin and didn't feel exposed. I went to my makeshift table, lifting the sheet so I could see the things on the bench. I chose the smallest item, but a potent one: the first vial of GHB.

When he was close to me, our bare bodies touching, I removed the plastic stopper from the tiny vial.

"Stick out your tongue," I said.

He laughed, then became serious. "Do you know how much to use?"

"No questions," I said, "just trust me." I dropped two tears onto his tongue, watching his face as he absorbed the drug into his system. It was amazingly quick. His shoulders relaxed and his smiled broadens. But I'd not finished yet. "Lie down."

He looked at the newspaper.

"Lie down," I repeated and, relaxed by the potent drug, he did. I lifted the sheet on the bench once more, this time choosing the lightest object, a black sash of silk. I knelt at his head, lifting his glasses away. "You don't need to bother with the blindfold," he joked, "I can't see a thing without my glasses." Still, I wound the silk around his head, easing his head forward as I tied a knot at the back. He was pale and naked, black silk and thin bones, red smiling mouth laughing from the intoxication of the drugs. It was perfect.

Without telling him what I intended to do, I returned to my bench, lifting the sheet fully off now that he was blind. I picked up the rope.

I admired the scene, marvelling at my ability to step away from my handiwork even when in its thrall. The rope was blue and narrow, deceptive in its strength. It was last used when I moved in, to hoist my mahogany chest through the sash window of the bedroom. Smith was smiling, laughing at some private joke, no longer bothered by his nakedness, knees bent and arms stretched wide. I took one of his arms, running my hand down the length of it, making him giggle some more. Smiling, I circled his wrist with the rope.

Smith chuckled as though I'd told a great joke as I pulled the rope, secure but not tight. I didn't want to mark his wrists. I straddled him, and his free hand groped for my breast, kneading the flesh and pulling me lower, his mouth rooting for my nipple. I bent over, allowing his wet tongue, his grasping hand to grip my breast, as I looped the rope over once more, and pulled one hand up above his head, joining it with the other. Smith was lost in his ecstasy, sucking and writhing under me, as I concentrated on binding his wrists together. I held his chin, eased my breast away from his insatiable tongue. He thought I was playing and reached up, biting my nipple in his eagerness, but I wasn't interested in those games.

I had something else in mind.

I was forced to be rough with him. I slapped him, once, across the face. He stopped laughing but his smile told me that he was enjoying it.

I lifted myself from his body, glancing at his erect penis. So vulnerable. "Robin, come back to me . . ." I began to wish I'd thought of a gag.

I went to the bench, picked up a second rope, pausing to look at what remained, a veritable bag of tricks that made my breath catch in anticipation. I arrived at his feet, his ankles. When he felt the rope touch his foot he yelled, no longer laughing. I remembered Alex telling me how two drops of Gee made you the life and soul of the party but any more made you lethargic and affected the heart. Smith was becoming tense. He needed to calm down. Into his open mouth I dropped two more tears from the vial, telling him to be quiet. We didn't want to disturb the neighbours. I pulled the rope tighter, and Smith's legs were dead weights. The drug worked quickly, a miracle. It should be available on the National Health Service.

When the knot was tight I stood and admired the bound and blind man. With his arms above his head, ribs jutted sharp as knives and hipbones creating a cove for his abdomen, with the gentle line of brown hair from navel to pubis he looked like Jesus on the cross.

I knelt at his head, stroking his cheek. His breathing was shallow but even, like a relaxing cat and I knew that beneath the blindfold his eyes were closed. I leaned my head on his chest, listening to his speeded heart, the rise and fall of his life.

"My Lord," I whispered, my eyes wet as I felt the truth of the words. "Just one more step now. Have faith. I have one more surprise."

Just two things remained on the bench and I lifted the first, feeling the wooden handle in my palm. The thick blade caught a ray of early sun. It was a small knife, but it would do.

It was intricate work. Precision was important. I didn't want to make a mess. It would be hard to explain.

I lifted the knife, pointing the sharp blade towards him. I touched the steel to his penis, now only half erect, and slid the blade under, to the soft testis where I pressed. The tip of the blade described a throbbing vein in his scrotum.

He took a sharp breath.

32

I removed the blade from Smith's scrotum and slid it under the lip of the nail polish pot, loosening the dried rim, waiting for the release of red. Once loose I twisted the top off, revealing scarlet nail polish. Then, with the brush, I tested the red polish, painting a shiny drop on my fingernail. I went to where Smith was enjoying a peaceful daze, his bound body moving only slightly as he breathed, touched his flesh with my hand and stroked his body with the brush. I finger-painted shapes on his arms, his stomach, a moon and sun. I opened a second pot and painted the shapes I imagined on the cannibals as they danced under the lunar light, sated with human flesh. I paid special attention to his penis, drawing sun-like rays across his testicles.

"Do you remember," I whispered, "the story you told me of the tribe in Papua New Guinea? This is our funeral rite, our Kuru."

When my artwork was complete I adored the surrendered Jesus, marked with ancient ritual in red like blood. I knelt at his feet like Mary at the foot of the cross and worshiped him. By the time the nail polish was dry the sun was up. I untied Smith, as one would unswaddle a baby. I helped him into the house, and to the bedroom. He'd had only four drops of the drug but was disorientated, heavy. I laid him on the bed. Some still-wet nail polish made a bright smear on the white sheets, but I didn't mind. The test had been a success.

An hour later I was seated on a wooden high-backed chair next to the bed, perched like a schoolgirl in a lesson, watching him. The colour had gone from his face, leaving white flesh taut over bones, shiny on his chin and cheeks. One arm was collapsed across the bed, the other close to his chest where he rested a sports-bottle of water. His head, propped by two pillows, was partly covered by a wet flannel, like a red flag across his brow. His eyes were closed.

Unbidden, the image returned. The memory I wanted to live in: I saw Mummy's pale body, her cooling hand on her gentle stomach, the curling cheese sandwich on the plate. I remembered the softness of my lilac cardigan, how I placed it so carefully on her shoulder. I remembered kissing her, my head on her chest, my lips on her nipple like I was just a baby, and then her cold cheek. Smith's drugged body released the memory of my mother. Two became one. I finally had that love, I was once again with Mummy and she was mine, just as she had been when I held her for those final hours. The outside world was forgotten, and her body was still warm. She didn't belong to Mr. Wilding then, or to the drugs. She belonged to me. I had that love again, thanks to Smith.

He was beautiful, like a marble figure in a crypt, the red marks telling stories, the smell of the polish taking me back. Like art, no longer flesh.

"I feel so tired," he said, lifting his fingers slightly, dropping them to illustrate his lack of energy. He had no will to do anything but sleep. The drug had worked beautifully. My heart danced like a circus horse, knowing that we had created a perfect moment, a tableaux of love. Like all tableaux, all images, it had been beautiful to the eye. I worried about his scattered clothes, the jaunty angle of the chair. I itched to dust and polish, but forced myself to sit. I didn't want to waste the moment, only to think afterwards that I squandered precious minutes because of my concern to set the scene. I didn't want to miss the point. "It's like being drunk," he slurred, "the room is spinning."

The window was open, and outside I heard a car passing, a woman calling to a child to mind the road. In my heart I held on to the feeling that Mummy was with me. I held on to love. "Tell me your real name," he said, suddenly.

My racing heart lurched, missed a beat at the unexpected demand. "But we agreed. No details." All the weekends that he had visited me I was careful to grab the post from the mat before he saw any envelope; I was meticulous in obliterating any signs of my name from my home.

"Please. I want to know." He was weary, his voice quiet and slow.

"You do know. It's Robin."

"I don't want to die without knowing your real name."

How could I refuse? I would have done anything for him, anything at all, after what he had given me. "It's Alice."

"Alice," he repeated, "in Wonderland," and then he laughed, a straining wheeze that sounded painful and dissolved into a string of coughs, as he expelled the excessive air from his lungs.

"Can you help me to the toilet?"

I supported him as we slowly shuffled down the hall to the bathroom, his hands on my shoulders, and then helped lower him onto the toilet. Sick and pale, his naked body disgusted me. I thought of an old man at the nursing home where I worked as a teenager, who would sit on the edge of his bed every morning, saggy testicles hanging low as he ate his cereal. The degradation of age. Smith, even in his prime, had been brought to this same state by the imminence of death. It wasn't the epic demise of a hero, he was no Hector, and this wasn't the scene I wanted in my mind, especially as he opened his bowels with me still in the room. I made a hasty retreat, but he called me back, "Fetch a bucket! I'm going to be sick."

I held the bucket under his head and, mercifully, he wasn't sick, but the smell of faeces made me gag. I prayed he didn't ask me to wipe him. I thought of Keats nursing his brother Tom, and steeled myself. I mustn't be squeamish. I must remember the greater good we are achieving, and stop being pathetic about trivial details.

Once Smith was back in bed I felt easier. He closed his eyes and quietened, which was a relief. It was minutes, only minutes, before I realised that his breathing was shallow. I placed my head on his chest and listened for his heart. It was faint and slow. My own heart stepped up, over-compensating, and I shook his shoulders.

"Smith?" Oh God, I had given him too much. "Smith!" I slapped him, hard, around the face. His eyelids opened slightly and I saw the whites of his eyes, his head rolled away from me. I shook him violently, calling and shouting, knowing that it wasn't right, not the way we planned it. He couldn't die yet—June 16th was the agreed date.

He gasped, he gagged, and spewed his last meal all over my lap. "Alice?" he whimpered, an animal in pain.

"I wish you wouldn't call me that . . . I thought you'd gone." I sounded furious, surprising myself.

"What if I change my mind?" He struggled to speak, and the sentence took an age to form. A tear slid down his cheek. "I don't think I can do it. I don't want to die."

33

It still surprises me how I panicked when I thought Smith had overdosed. I've always been calm in the face of death. Both times I had witnessed it. Death didn't scare me. My fear was growing old.

After Mummy died my second meeting with Death came when I was sixteen. I took my final GCSE exam on the last Friday in June, and walked out of the school gates knowing I'd never return to that school, not even for my exam results, which they would post on to me. In September I would start my A levels at the local sixth form college, but before then nine weeks stretched ahead of me, a blank sheet. I didn't know what to do with myself.

Time is only a luxury for a minority, those with funds and activities to keep themselves amused. I had neither and I was quickly despondent and agitated. I hung around the house mainly reading in my bedroom but occasionally disturbing Dad's peace by demanding to watch the TV, or traipsing through Mum's kitchen and raiding the cupboards, spilling fruit juice on the floor so she had to use even more bleach and kitchen scrub to keep the place immaculate. Although they wouldn't ever say it, I was under their feet, disturbing the tentative balance of the house.

School holidays meant my father was also at home. The downside of him being a teacher was all that extra time for family life. All those weeks to kill. Eventually, annoyed by having to watch the Open University programmes I liked when speedway was on the other side, Dad asked, "Why don't you get yourself a job?"

I looked at him, mouth agape. I didn't think of myself as a worker. But Dad persisted, "It'll do you good. When I was your age I was working a full day as a carpenter's apprentice and then biking to technical college every evening to study. It wasn't handed to me on a plate, y'know, my education. I had to work hard to get where I am." He said it defiantly, knowing that his status as a woodwork teacher impressed no one. "It's about time you started earning your own money."

This dig was a reference to my recent insistence that the pocket money they gave me each week was in no way enough. Just one lipstick and it was gone, no change for anything else. And what about going out?

Lee had left school for good, and was working as a lifeguard at the local swimming pools. It wasn't well paid but considering she only had two GCSEs to her name (design & technology and physical education, both grade C) it would have to do. Anyway she loved the water, and when she swam she was no longer awkward or odd. No one taunted her when she was at the pool, the kids stopped running when she blew her whistle and the mums were grateful for her presence. She liked to feel useful. She never admitted it but I knew she dreamed of saving somebody from drowning. Maybe it came from being the only girl in a large family of boys, that urge to protect, I don't know. Lee was happy and didn't mind smelling of chlorine or that her hair went frizzy from the humidity. She'd just cut it all off and it suited her. At the weekends she wanted to go to the cinema and Pizza Hut, but I couldn't keep letting her foot my bill. Or rather, I could, but really I shouldn't. She made me feel beholden to her as it was, with those puppyish glances and that pained expression. It was like having a lovesick boyfriend who didn't get that he'd been dumped but who proved useful when you were at a loose end. Dad was right, I should get a job.

Working in a shop didn't appeal to me. I just couldn't bear to put on a phoney smile and sell to people I didn't like, things they didn't need. So I took a job in a nursing home for old people.

The nursing home was close, just a ten-minute walk away, and I got the night shift which suited me just fine. It was better pay and meant less work, as the old biddies were tucked up in bed, or should have been, although one woman, Beattie, who had dementia, often disturbed me, asking when it was time for the wedding. She was all beady eyes and saggy skin, and in her white nightdress she looked like a ghost, legs like sticks. She really got on my nerves but as long as I made sure she took her pills she slept heavily enough.

Beattie hadn't been pestering me that night and I was glad. The home was silent and I laid out the trays for the morning's breakfast, following the instructions on the printed sheet taped to the kitchen cupboard door. Most of the residents shared rooms so the trays were a squeeze, what with prunes, cornflakes, juice and toast. I arranged the bread, brown or white or both, on the plate, all set for toasting. I put dry cereal in the bowls, ready for the milk. It was how I was told to do it, though now I think about it, it was unhygienic leaving the food out all night. By seven the next morning the cornflakes can't have been very crunchy, but maybe that was a good thing considering most of the residents wore dentures.

After setting out the breakfasts, I doled out the medication which was labelled with the names of the recipients. I had to open each bottle or jar and put a plastic cup on each tray, also with the names on the side. Most residents had a shot of Gaviscon, and there were red or pink or white tablets for everyone. No one was left out. I was sixteen and didn't know what any of the pills were for. I was in a position of trust which I was too young to shoulder. I hope things are different now; no teenager should be able to dish out drugs like I did.

It was about half ten by the time I'd finished setting up the trays and that was my duties done. All I had to do then was be there, which was why the job was such a cushy number for me. I settled in the square hold of an arm-chair and pulled *The Bell Jar* from my rucksack. Eventually I dropped off. Technically it was a waking duty but I always managed to fall asleep, curled like a cat between wings of yellow Draylon. By my side was a travel clock, with the alarm set for a quarter to seven, and I normally slept through until then so I put the clock in my pocket. It was only tiny and I wanted it close enough to wake me.

I was disturbed very soon by shuffling feet on the corridor carpet. Sleep in conditions like that is never very deep, and I quickly realised that the looming figure was Beattie, no doubt about to pester me about some imaginary wedding she thought she was going to. I thought I'd give her another pill, but then I saw that she was holding something and whatever was in her hand was dropping to the floor. I got up, and walked towards her, but she seemed surprised to see me and her hand went flat on the wall.

I saw then what it was. I smelt it.

I didn't want to touch her, but I couldn't let her daub shit on the walls, so I pushed her back, man-handling her towards her bedroom. I was disgusted, and wanted her out of my sight. In her bedroom the curtains were still drawn with the lights off and I kept them that way, not wishing to see the excreta. The smell assaulted my nostrils. If I saw it I would feel obliged to do something about it but if I waited until morning it would be someone else's job. So, taking Beattie under her arms I hoisted her into bed and told her, firmly, to stay there. I shook her and she jerked back, damn her, starting to get up again and what with the smell and the fatigue and her fighting me I lost my temper. I hit her around the head. Not hard, just to make her sit back on the bed.

How was I to know her head would be so wobbly on her neck that the blow would sound like an axe felling wood? Her head hit the pillow hard, her eyes tight shut, and I thought it was a good sign. I wouldn't need to medicate her after all.

I hurried to the kitchen, washed my hands until they were red and wondered how successfully I could ignore the mess in the hall and lounge. I decided it was best if I remained in the kitchen which thankfully had one low chair. With my coat folded like a pillow I managed to get comfortable enough to doze, and I didn't leave the kitchen all night.

The alarm woke me and I tried not to think about the dried faeces on the wall. I poured milk and toasted bread, carefully scraping margarine and marmalade until all the breakfast trays were ready. I began my deliveries, bypassing the hall, deciding to leave Beattie until last.

The men tended to be up, sitting on their beds or on chairs. The women usually waited for their trays in bed, enjoying this parody of hotel living. The ones who had more money, and therefore their own rooms, took the trays as if this being waited on was their due, eyeing the plastic medicine cups with restrained glee.

Finally, there was just Beattie's tray left, with cornflakes, one slice of white with marge and three prunes (it always amused me that the number was stipulated. What would happen if I put an extra one in the bowl? In Beattie's case, maybe I should put one less). But as it turned out, it didn't matter.

She'd been dead for some time and rigor mortis had set in. We were supposed to do regular checks through the night though no one said how often and I can't have been the only one who didn't bother.

She was on her side, in the same position I'd left her, curled like a baby. I put the tray on the bedside cabinet and sat in the space within the curve, looking at her. My feelings from the night before washed away, and I was only concerned with her face. The knotted tension, the folds of skin, the beady eyes, were all gone and she looked about twenty years younger. In fact, seeing her that way, I knew what she had looked like as a child. I was calm when I touched her. The cold skin yielded to my fingers despite the firmness underneath. Her cheek was smooth. I kissed her. I don't know why, it just felt right. I touched her face, her cheek, and closed my eyes to think of the other time, when the woman had been the most loved, when the body I curled against had been Mummy's.

That was my second encounter with death and it hadn't been horrible. It had been fine. I knew death was something I could be happy with. For me it held no fear, only beauty. The promise of something better, removed from the slow wasting of daily life.

Maybe it started then, at sixteen, my desire to assist the dying. Maybe younger when I was just four, when I clung to Mummy in those precious minutes before the world intruded. But I didn't invent Death's beauty. This new-found philosophy was reflected back again and again in poems and novels. The final moments of life can be lovely. If you're young or in love they can be perfect. Romeo and Juliet may be a tragedy, but it's also a love story. Who wouldn't choose the path of immortality over infirmity and dementia?

Mummy is always young and always beautiful. She is with me. Always.

34

I'll be sentenced in just three days. I dread it and long for it at the same time. I want it to be over. My days are a blank page and Lee is happy to fill them. I don't ask her when she's returning to Germany and she doesn't ask me about my plans. Together we drift.

"Oh, Alice," she says, "It's like a cathedral." She stands under the impressive roof of the church, looking up like a tourist in New York gazing at skyscrapers. "How did a tiny village get to have something like this?"

"It's because of the wool trade. Lavenham was a big deal in Tudor times."

The details of this place are so familiar to me. You can't go for a drink without reading on the top of the menu about this Tudor village with its roots in the manufacturing of cloth, wool, and yarn. The whole area is defined by architecture and symbols of that time, mini-factories dominated the area when Henry VIII was on the throne. Perhaps I take this history for granted because Lee is impressed, squinting up at the carved roses on the eaves. "It's like *The Da Vinci Code*. Maybe Dan Brown should have come here rather than traipsing up to Scotland."

"Well, you know what Americans are like for the Highlands." I look up all the same, piggybacking on her enjoyment of deciphering the codes. The last time I was here was with Smith.

We walk through to the silent chapel where candles are lit, and a thin visitors' book is open. Curious, I go over and read:

For my son, John, who is on duty in Afghanistan. Bring him home safe.

Pray for our neighbour Reg, sick with bowel cancer. Thinking of the WPC who died in Ipswich last week while doing her job, stabbed by a drunken teenager.

I flick back the pages revealing pain and illness, so much bad luck. If lighting a candle and asking a few nuns to pray could work, they'd need a much larger volume.

"What's that?" Lee peers over my shoulder, and I stand aside so she can see. She peels the pages, more slowly than I had, then puts her hand in her back pocket for a coin which she drops in the box. She chooses a thin white candle. Touching its wick to a flame, she lights it and places it on the rack. I wait to see if she will lift the pen, if she's going to write a message. She doesn't.

I'm itching to know. "Who's the candle for?"

She pauses, and for a second I think she is praying. When she looks at me her eyes are like sorrowful pools. "For you."

"Me? I'm not ill."

"You've been having a lot of headaches recently. I think you're really stressed, and it's my job to look after you." She takes my arm and leads us out of the chapel. Lee knows about Smith, she must know. How could I ever have thought otherwise?

Later, back at my home, we lie together in bed. Lee asks, "Why don't you have any photos around?"

"I don't like clutter."

"But, not even a picture of your family." She is silent for a moment, but her eyes flicker with active thought. "Your mother was always so kind to me."

"She liked you."

"How would she feel is she saw us together now?"

I look at Lee's cropped hair sticking out randomly from the shape of the pillow, her face free from make up or any other artifice. She works hard for a living and she loves me. It would be everything my mother would want for me, if only Lee were a man. "I think she'd throw a fit. Probably refer me to a shrink, like last time."

"Well, she couldn't do it any worse than my own folks did. When I first came out my old man said I wasn't to set foot in the house again. But he came round, Alice. It just took time. You can't deny what you are. You can't hide your nature."

"I'm not like you, Lee. You know who you are. What you are."

"What are you then, Alice?" Her voice rises to uncharacteristic volume. She props herself up on one arm, and with the other she reaches for me, her fingers form a bangle around my wrist. "Poor Alice. So clever, yet you can't see what's staring you in the face."

I pull my arm free. "Don't Lee."

"Why won't you ever talk about it, Alice?" she asks, collapsing back down onto the mattress, looking up to me. "Why do you never talk about your real mum?"

Suddenly I'm melancholy. I can't speak for a long time. When the words do come they surprise me. It's not something I ever talked about. "I was four when I lost her. She was only twenty-one, she had her whole future ahead of her, if the world had been just a little bit kind. She deserved a better life than she got."

Lee kisses my shoulder. She knows more than anyone that this is hard for me to talk about. "She could have achieved so much, if it wasn't for me. Having me ruined everything for her."

"It wasn't your fault, Alice. None of it was your fault."

I kiss her, stopping both our mouths from saying anything we could regret. She pulls away, serious. "Tell me something you've never told anyone else."

I try to pull back, but she won't release me. "Let me in, Alice. Tell me a secret."

I tell Lee this:

"When I was twelve I was invited to another girl's sleepover party. I didn't often get invited to parties, but this was a girl from the church youth group so she probably had to invite everyone out of Christian duty. I was determined to go but when I arrived I was miserable. I watched everyone else laughing, their teeth stained red with cherryade, feeling more alone than if I'd been in my bedroom. As we settled down in our sleeping bags some of the girls began to tell ghost stories.

I hated it and wanted them to stop. I wanted to go home. Then the girl whose party it was, a morose thing with mousy hair whose name I don't remember, began to tell the story of a woman, in her isolated cottage at night, doing a jigsaw puzzle. The woman slowly places piece by piece into the puzzle until she realises that the picture she is creating is of her own room, and the figure in the picture is herself. Cautiously, she puts in the final piece of the picture that shows a man outside the window brandishing an axe. The final noise she hears is breaking glass.

I cried and cried. I wouldn't stop until Dad came to collect me. I was never invited to a sleepover party again.

There. That's my secret. I'm scared of the axe man at the window."

Lee kisses me as tenderly as if I was a child. "No," she says, "you're scared of finding the final piece to the puzzle."

Lee's weight is on me, along me, the tight muscle of her thigh tense on my hip. Her fingers move inside me. She is expert at my body, opening me wide, eyes never leaving mine, as her sweat salts my mouth. "Make some noise," she says. A sound in my throat like air rising, her hands, her thrust urging me on. "Keep going," she says, and I do, I do. She bites my shoulder, and my mouth gapes, then the noise comes, my sound, and she replies, a yell and call from animal urges, and I'm with her, not in my head, but in my flesh, with her hands, while she is rising and pushing and I know, I know . . . and I'm rising, above, with her, with her, and the noise is there, and there, and there, and her weight, and eyes, and hands, I fall, and fall, and fall.

We are still. But not silent. And she smiles. I smile back, our bodies bound together like poetry.

I can feel myself slipping into Lee's world, into her hopes. She wants me, wants to be with me, and I'm getting used to that. There's warmth between us, and skin, only that. And I think that I was wrong. It was never Smith, after all. It was Lee. She was always waiting. Isn't orgasm a sort of death? *To cease upon the midnight with no pain* . . .

I had a choice, between Smith and Lee. Two lovers, offering different things. I chose Smith. But all along the person I really wanted was Mummy.

35

Alice was seventeen when she decided to find her father. She had lost Mummy
but she had at least known her. Loved her. The gap, the aching hole in her heart,
she put down to the absence of her father. Who was he? Where was he? How
old? Hell, he could even be dead. She knew nothing about him. She had no one
to condemn or reject, to try to forgive. Nothing but a space. She felt the absence
in her soul. She sat before her mirror and examined her heritage, the genetic
evidence of the past: the ash blonde hair, she knew, was like Mummy's. The eyes
too, green like a cat. And Mummy's mouth, pink and full, a perfect cupid's bow.
She remembered that. She remembered the smart lady in the bedsit, offering
Mummy the money. Making her cry. Alice had inherited her grandmother's
mouth. But what else? She was tall—Mummy had been average height, she
supposed, or even shorter. Next to Mr. Wilding she looked tiny. Alice smoothed
her fingertips over her forehead—domed and smooth, a rounded profile.
Romanesque. Mummy had lacked that, had a shallow forehead, a sharper chin.
So, this must be her father's legacy. His contribution to her gene pool.

She allowed her head to fall into her upturned hands and wondered what
her father may or may not be like. The blank on her birth certificate was
filled with shadow, a ghost that she tried to conjure like a medium. Please, oh
please, reveal yourself.

She stared hard at her reflection until her features distorted and she saw a
man, staring back at her. The face mutated, grotesque, and she blinked with
a start. She'd stared too long and scared herself. The man was gone—it was
just her own face, so familiar, staring back.

She longed to see her father, however horrible he looked. Since the
appointment with Dr. Murray her adoptive mother had been pleading with

her to go back for 'therapy.' Alice didn't need therapy, she needed the truth. Or so she believed.

She knew she'd another family somewhere. She knew she was adopted because Mummy was dead. She could never forget that. It was the image she held in her heart, the scene that filled the hole. When she wasn't thinking of Mummy the hole gaped.

But there was a man, out there in the world, who shared her blood. Every child had a father. She began to fantasise that he held the key to her happiness. Maybe her father had no idea that she was adopted. Maybe he knew and was searching, unable to trace her. She wanted to find him, wanted to be with someone who understood. Someone else who'd loved Mummy.

Alice had grown away from her adopted family, knowing them to be unlike her. It was the summer and she was working at the old people's home in the night, sleeping a lot in the day, avoiding her mother's tearful gaze and pleading: "Please, Alice, go and see Dr. Murray. He can help you." She avoided Lee and her puppy-dog devotion. No wonder she wanted to break free. To catch the piece of her that had been lost and make herself whole again. She felt like she'd been in pieces for years.

Her mother was a hoarder, and Alice knew she had a box in which she kept special documents. It was somewhere she never let Alice look and Alice guessed that she must have the details of her adoption in that box, maybe the address of the team that had dealt with it. It was hard to snoop with her mother always at home, and always so neat. She was bound to notice anything not returned to exactly the same place. But Alice was determined, and waited until she was in the kitchen, bleaching the floor. That always took at least two hours.

When Alice heard her mother's plastic shoe-covers on the kitchen lino she went to the bedroom, slowly opened the door into the stuffy boudoir of pink-valanced pillowcases, china girls in bonnets, and lace doilies on every surface. She knelt down by the melamine dressing table and slid open the lower drawer, the one that held tights and slips. The box Alice sought was navy and had once contained a man's shirt. It held documents her mother considered important, like report cards and the first pictures she'd drawn at school. She hoped it was where she would find the map to her real father.

She didn't rummage in the drawer, but lifted out skin-coloured underwear, nylon nighties, piling them neatly on the carpet, until she had the box. She wanted to snatch it and disappear to her room but knew that would be foolish. She should just look, and leave everything as she found it.

Sitting on the chintzy carpet she lifted the lid, slowly, and slid out a few papers. There were recent letters from the doctor's surgery acknowledging the 'assessment' appointment with Dr. Murray. A burst of anger erupted, and she felt justified in what she was doing. Everything in this box was about her.

She found her birth certificate, showing her adopted name, Dunn. The original would be stored somewhere, locked in a filing cabinet which Alice could only access when she was eighteen. It made her so mad. She didn't even know what her real surname was.

Under the papers, her hand touched plastic. She pulled the bag free, an old supermarket carrier. It was light and thin and warmth spread over Alice's heart. She slid her fingers into the box and touched the wool, fingers tingling with a blissful sensation like coming home.

She felt a stinging behind her eyes as she gently lifted out the lilac cardigan. The scrappy, badly knitted woollen cardigan that she knew so well. It had been her favourite. It was what she had worn, thrown on over a nightshirt, when she found Mummy in Mr. Wilding's room. That must be why it was there: the precious cardigan had arrived with Alice. She brought it to her face, nuzzling the wool, which bobbled and caught under her lips. It had been in the box for twelve years, yet it still smelled the same. It smelt of Mummy, of the bedsit they had shared.

She unfolded it on her lap, and then held it to her chest. The sleeves came to the crook of her elbow, and the cardigan stopped just below her bust. That was how small she'd been once. She studied the clumsy knitting, the dropped stitch that had grown into a hole, and knew that Mummy had loved her. She undid the one pearlised button and opened the cardigan, feeling the texture and remembering wearing it. Then she saw a white label, stitched at only one end and hanging loose. A name tag. Because Mummy had knitted this cardigan for her to wear to preschool, and all clothes had to be named. Her heart leapt.

The name tag wasn't printed, but homemade. It was the only time she'd seen Mummy's handwriting. It said Alice Mariani.

She knew who she was. She had a name: Mariani.

Alice had forgotten her name, only remembered that Mummy was called Matty. She was too young to remember her surname, but she liked it. It sounded Italian and sophisticated. 'Mariani' was so much more glamorous than "Dunn," which she'd been saddled with for twelve years, a heavy name that made you think of farms and labourers.

Alice put the reports and pictures back in the box, but not the cardigan. It was hers. It should never have been taken from her. She didn't waste a second. Hadn't she waited long enough? After hiding the cardigan in her bedroom, at the back of her wardrobe, Alice went to the hallway. From the low seat of the telephone table in the hall she could see into the kitchen. Her mother was mopping the last part of the floor, backing herself into a corner. Her face was wet with sweat.

There was no Mariani in the local telephone directory. But she didn't give up. She knew that the local library had directories for the whole country and would have checked them all if necessary, but she found what she sought in the sixth directory, the one for Norwich. A listing for Mariani. It even gave an address.

And it was that easy. She had a name, an address. She had a phone number and was just one meeting away from finding out who she was.

That telephone call was the hardest she'd ever made, but it was brief. Businesslike. As though her grandmother had been expecting her call, waiting for it.

Mrs. Mariani agreed to meet Alice.

Alice's grandmother was nothing and everything like she expected. She was younger, and Alice's memory of her in the bedsit fit like a missing jigsaw piece when she saw her fur coat, the expensive leather gloves. Her grandmother's face held Mummy's mouth. She wanted to kiss it.

There was no kissing. Her grandmother peered at her, perhaps seeing beyond the teenager to the dead woman she so resembled, and then nipped in her mouth. Her skin was tight across her brow and towards her ears, wrinkle free. She was smart and attractive and as unreadable as granite. Alice wished she would smile.

Her grandmother was dressed in black, tailored fabrics over a solid frame. Her impossibly dark hair was cut straight across her forehead, a fashionable but severe style, and any softness her face might have had been obliterated by sharp kohl and violent rouge. Harsh artist, she had erased any flaws that would have made her approachable.

Alice wanted so much, but most of all she wanted to know about her parents. Her memories were old. She wanted pretty tales to add to her scant store of love.

Her grandmother gave her nothing. Her words were cold and distinct. Her eyes quite dry as she spoke of her dead daughter: "Matilde was ridiculously young to have a child. By the time I found out it was impossible to do anything about it."

Me, thought Alice. Not it. To do anything about me.

"She was nearly seven months pregnant by the time we saw the doctor. We'd planned for an adoption. It would have all been so simple, she just had to go through with the delivery. But she got this notion in her head that she had to keep it."

Alice looked at her hands, which were pale and shaking. She felt invisible.

"She was in a home for teenage mothers, and I suppose she saw all the other girls keeping their babies, getting council flats, and she got this crazy idea that she would do the same. It was out of my hands then."

"You came to the bedsit. I remember you."

"Of course I came. A daughter of mine in those squalid conditions! I came to try and talk her out of keeping the baby. But she was always so surly, so pig-headed. Just like her father." She had the grace to look at Alice. "Of course, they would have found you a respectable family. But Matilde was determined, and would not be told what was best for all concerned." Her voice cracked like a dropped glass. "She was so clever. She could have gone to university."

"I want to go to university. I start my A levels next term." Her grandmother appraised her with new interest, then fought it down and looked away.

"I suppose you've got your brains from her. They certainly didn't come from me." Her grandmother ordered a second espresso. All Alice could stomach was water. Today she would discover who she was. "I have a cheque for you, Alice. I want you to take it and make something of your life. It is all I can offer you."

On the circular table was a silver pot of cubed sugar, and the older woman propped an envelope against it. Alice took it, peered into the open flap and saw the amount the cheque was made for. Her mouth went slack at such a huge amount. "Are you rich, then? You and my grandfather?"

"Yes."

"But you let us stay in that tiny bedsit." If this was the only time they would ever meet then she may as well say it. There was nothing to lose.

"Yes. That was Matilde's choice. She could always have returned home."

"Without me?"

"Without you."

Her grandmother dropped a cube of sugar into her coffee. It dissolved upwards, the sweet in the bitter. Alice sipped her Perrier water, welcoming the sparkle in her loosening stomach. "I want to know who my father is."

Her grandmother touched a red nail to the white tablecloth, to her pink lip. "Does it matter?"

"Of course it matters!" Alice's anger rose. "You've got no idea what it feels like to be raised by strangers. Just tell me, okay? Then I'll piss off out of your life forever."

A woman at the next table turned around, but Alice didn't care. She would never come back here again. Her stomach churned violently, but she couldn't risk a trip to the loo. Her grandmother may disappear, and with her any hope of her finding her father.

"I want you to promise," her grandmother replied, carefully, "that after today you will never contact me again. We've met. Our mutual curiosity has been satisfied. This must be the end of it."

Alice struggled to hold the rage within herself. She wanted to scream. She wanted to smash glass.

"Look, why not end it here? Stop searching. It can only lead to heartache. Go home, Alice. Settle for the family you have."

Alice was blind with tears. "I bet you sent him away, didn't you? I bet he loved Mummy—they would have made it work! It's your fault!" The lady at the other table was gawping but Alice didn't care. "It's all your fault!" She grabbed the pot of sugar and hurled it to the floor. Everyone in the room turned.

"Shut up!" The old woman didn't look controlled anymore; her face was pink and her teeth were very white. She leaned forward. "Shut up!" she hissed.

"Why? Because it's true? It is your fault! You turned my father away!"

"Be careful, Alice! Innocence is precious; once lost, it cannot be regained. Knowledge is a heavy burden."

"Don't lecture me, you sanctimonious bitch. You killed Mummy! It was you, wasn't it? Sending her away like that. It was your fault she died!"

In the silent room Alice's grandmother reached forward, grabbed her wrist, the silver pot still wheeling on the floor, "Your mother was a little whore!"

"No!" Alice pulled back.

"Oh, yes—Matilde made herself available!"

"You turned her out," Alice accused, "it's your fault she's dead—"

"And was it my fault that she seduced my husband?" "What are you talking about?"

"That's right, Alice. She was seventeen, she wasn't a child. Your mother was a little slut. And your father is also your grandfather."

Alice was drunk because she knew no other way to dull the pain.

Alice had been with her grandmother for as long as it took the old woman to drink two espressos, yet in that time her sense of self had fractured into a million pieces. She'd always been different, and she thought it was because she was adopted. Now she knew it was something worse that singled her out. She knew why she had always been on the edge of life.

It was the twinning in her genes, the thickness of her blood. Mummy had been raped, and she was the outcome. Worse, Mummy had been raped by her own father. And if her mother was a victim, and her father a monster, then what did that make her? Of course she was drunk.

Her grandmother's cheque was blood money. Family blood, too clotted, too rich. The cheque was for her to disappear, for the problem that she was to go away. Such a large amount. Enough to cover university, to buy a house. The price of her grandmother's guilt. The price she would pay for failing to protect her daughter, her only child. Alice had taken the cheque. You owe me this, she thought.

Back in her parent's home, the people who'd taken her on when she was only half-formed, she saw that this silent house was all she had. There would be no rescue. No fairytale ending.

In her bedroom, she smoothed the duvet and lay down, thinking: so this is it. You've woken up at last.

Such a lot of money, that cheque. It could buy her a castle to keep her safe from the wolf. From the axe man she feared may be outside her window. She would take something else, too. Just one more thing: the name. Her beautiful Mummy's name, and her father's name too. She would take the Mariani name to show what she was, to see if it revealed the poison inside her blood.

The wolf she'd always dreaded was already deep inside her nature.

36

I don't think I can do it, he'd said, I don't want to die. So I soothed him and kissed him and told him that he was strong. That if he wasn't, I would be strong enough for us both. To die with someone, you have to trust them, be able to feel vulnerable in their presence. It was just one week from Smith's chosen date, June 16th. Just one week and I needed to help him to prepare and remove any doubts. He needed me to show him that I was able to see it through. To prove my strength. After a day wandering around the heart of the village we had returned to my home where we drank a bottle of Pouilly Fumé and ate a light meal of bread and cheese. Smith was jittery, despite the alcohol. He wouldn't sit and was hovering around the kitchen counter, picking up my things, until I wanted to scream at him. When he touched my precious blue vase I tensed but sat still, my hands wedged between my thighs. He looked it over, put it down, started pulling petals off the flowers.

"Let's go out," he said, the idea sparking the corners of his mouth, a shock of a smile.

"There's not much to do around here," I said, even as he was heading to the front door, making a bid for freedom. I resented him opening the latch; it was my latch, my door. He was impolite in his haste.

Outside it was cool, the day's heat gone. The village was dead. Although tourists wander around the shops and houses, or read ancient stones in the churchyard, or sit in The Swan knifing clotted cream onto floury scones, when evening arrives they leave; entertainment beckons from other towns that come alive at dusk. They go to Ipswich or Colchester, where youths champion the night, hanging about outside the massive multiplex cinemas that show too many loud films, near the American chain restaurants that sell burgers and ribs and chips, chips, chips. I'd hate to live in a busy town. In daylight I can cope with Colchester, with its park and castle offering refuge from the chain stores and social security scroungers, but come evening I only want my own village.

How to entertain Smith was a problem.

Further down the road from my house, behind the pub, there was something going on. The community hall's entrance was propped open by a chair and a couple of women were leaning against the wall, smoking and laughing. I wondered what Smith thought of those silly laughing women, if he noticed their short skirts and pumped up breasts.

"Looks like there's a party going on," he said, a shrug and a suggestion all at once. I knew there would be nothing else to do and he needed to be distracted.

We walked over, and the women stopped laughing to watch us. "It's in aid of the church roof," one said. I recognised her from the delicatessen further down the high street. "Trying to raise money to fix it." I didn't want to go to a local village disco and would have preferred the hush of an art gallery, a museum, reading notes telling me what the artist intended. I was suspicious of the laughing women's motives, but Smith lead the way, pushing his glasses further up his nose as we crossed the threshold.

Inside the hall the stench of middle age desperation was thick. Divorced women, wearing clothes better suited to teenagers, dancing like they were having the time of their lives to songs about surviving. One woman who wore a black taffeta skirt with stiff netting looked over at Smith and winked, then saw me standing behind him and smiled at me knowingly. I was out of place in my cream pencil skirt and linen blouse. I had to be younger than the other women by more than a decade but I felt ancient. For a stupid second despair caught me up and I wanted to run out of the hall and cry. Smith went to the makeshift bar, a pasting table with boxed wine and cans of beer. He came back with a beer for himself, a glass of warm wine for me. It tasted like vinegar.

We perched on chapel chairs at a school desk, watching the women who were dancing like they were at a wedding. There were hardly any men in the room. After downing his can of lager Smith looked at me, frowning. "How do you know you can do it, if you can't even eat meat?" Two parallel lines appeared between his eyebrows making his glasses bob lower on his nose. "Robin, we need to know that you can inflict pain." He was nearly shouting over the blaring disco beat, but the middle-aged women were too lost in their dancing to hear him.

I understood his worry. His fear that, being a vegetarian, I was somehow squeamish about blood or flesh. But my decision wasn't because of moral scruples or an unwillingness to eat dead flesh. I simply found the lengthy process of chewing and masticating meat tiresome, preferring the simplicity of vegetables, the clarity of blandness. Meat repeated on me physically in a way I disliked. I didn't say this to Smith. I could see that worrying about the details was his way of preparing himself.

"So what do you want me to do? Wring a chicken's neck?" It was a joke, and my laughter matched the mood in the hall, the music providing a jolly backbeat. But Smith's mouth was a straight line, his cheeks crease-free and stern. I swallowed the last of the vinegar-wine and placed a firm hand on his wrist.

"Tell me what you want, Smith."

"I want to test you."

He said it was important that we bound ourselves together with a deed. A blood bargain. We decided on a knife. We just needed to find a sacrifice and rural Suffolk is awash with farms and smallholdings, middle-class ex-urbanites longing for idyllic days of Laura Ashley pinnies and organic milk, whimsical romanticism.

There was an allotment area around some outer fields, where village dwellers without sufficient gardens could rent a patch of earth to grow crops or—more to the point—graze a few goats or sheep. Many had hens, as I knew only too well from the shrill rousing I received at dawn if I forgot to use earplugs.

Smith was excited by the idea, and we left the village hall quickly, heading first into the house, collecting the knife from the kitchen, and then to my car. He was so pumped up that he misjudged the angle for the seat belt, and couldn't buckle himself in. I reached over and secured him, as if he were a child. He gave me a grateful smile, a look of guilty pleasure on his face. He enjoyed being mothered.

Initially, the allotments seemed familiar to me from those of my girlhood, although on closer inspection I realised that these allotments were nothing like Dad's. His was a solitary, male domain. A rickety shed, amidst smart rows of tomatoes. He'd lean against the shed, his back into the grain of the wood, considering his work. I went with him, also to escape the confines of home, but as I watched his satisfied smile and half-closed eyes, all I felt was boredom. Unearthing carrots or twisting tomatoes free from their vines became boring rather swiftly. When I hit puberty I stopped going to the allotment. I think he was relieved.

These allotments were a distant relation to Dad's, upwardly mobile from their humble heritage. The sheds were more like chalets with glass windows and wooden verandas boasting pine benches and polka dot Wellingtons. It was almost nine o'clock, and light had faded, so only a few people remained. Unlike the allotments of my childhood, the feminine touch dominated; curtains hung at the shed windows, rows of flowers rather than vegetables, and some sheds were painted in pastel shades.

"Bloody hell," said Smith, "it's like something from *Homes and Gardens.*" We took in the scene together, and then heard a rude snort behind us.

Turning sharply, we were surprised to see a black boar-like creature. Disorientated for a second, I had the mad thought that it was wild until I saw that a chicken-wire fence separated us from the ugly beast.

"A potbellied pig," whispered Smith, touching my shoulder. "Perfect."

The pig was friendly, pushing its snout through the holes to suckle my skirt. Its saliva darkened the fabric and I shoved my knee against it, pushed it away, but it was tenacious in its desire to be petted. There was a wooden kennel behind it, with a homemade sign over the door that read 'Boris.'

Boris chewed ferociously, the sound of gravel on teeth, watching with black beady eyes, its wet snout dripping. Its muzzle and brow were coarse with wiry black, like pubic hair. "I don't think I can," I said, feeling my nose wrinkle as I watched Boris take a long piss in the mud.

"Think of it as a gift," he said, extracting my kitchen knife from his coat, unwrapping the tea towel from the blade. "A sacrifice."

"To you?"

"If you like." Smith watched Boris, showing him the shiny steel to see if he recognised the danger; he didn't. "Or to God." I snatched the handle from him, just wanting to get it over with. For Christ's sake, I thought, this had suddenly gotten bizarre. To me, the act of killing the pig proved nothing. Smith's sacrifice was voluntary, but the pig had no consciousness, no choice, and no will. It was just a dumb animal.

I climbed over the netting, only high enough to keep the pig in, not intended to keep humans out, and approached the tame beast, the knife poised and ready.

My God, how it squealed!

I panicked, fearing we would be discovered, and plunged the knife into Boris' neck, feeling the layers of fat and gristle give way to unforgiving bone. I must have punctured an artery as blood started pouring out, and I wanted to heave but Smith was watching. This was my test and I had to prove myself worthy.

The pig flopped onto its fat side, still alive, a gaping mouth revealing black molars. I pulled the knife from its neck and, seeing the double row of nipples plunged into the centre, aiming for the heart. The pig screamed like a baby, but it was over. I leaned back on my heels, sick to the core. Who the hell called a female, Boris?

"I've done it. Now let's get out of here."

I stood quickly, longing for escape, giddy on my feet, and stepped back over the netting. Smith was rooted to the spot, his hands clasped to the wooden fence post.

"Are you okay, Smith?"

Was he disgusted with the violence? Had I gone too far? But when he looked at me his eyes were moist and dark. He took my hand in his, which was clammy with sweat, and placed it over his groin. I felt his erection, straining against the thin fabric and understood. Boris' death had made him feel alive and happy, the act of sacrifice sealing his devotion to the plan.

Later, I took Smith to the station in Colchester, and waited with him until his train arrived. We were bound together by blood, and didn't want to be separated, even for the few days until he returned. I touched him, soothed him, knowing this would be how he remembered me until then. I touched his cheek, stroked the soft skin, felt the irregular growth of stubble. I pulled him to me, kissing the place where his pulse throbbed in his neck. The intercom crackled and a woman's shrill voice broke the tender tension. 'The train about to depart from platform one is the seven o'clock service to London Liverpool Street.'

He leaned towards me, his mouth wet on my ear. "Robin," his voice stuttered, agitated, "I'm ready now. Make sure you're prepared."

His words stilled the world. It was all I ever wanted to hear. I could hardly breathe, my throat tight, and I found myself rocking, my heart suddenly running a sprint. He held me, and I fell into his embrace. His arms were tight and my heartbeat fast, my hands wet. The surgical detachment was gone. My head knew that I was having a panic attack, and that the driver in the seat of my emotions was my heart. His words hadn't been heard by Robin, the cool academic, they had been heard by the girl Alice who longed to be back again, in that room, with her still-warm Mummy. Who wanted that love back.

I hated Smith seeing me this way, but more than that I needed to be held. He supported me, arms around my tense body, until my breathing steadied. When my heart slowed I felt dizzy, as if I had just run a race. Smith pulled away. He was calm, as if my emotion has drained away his own. "I love you. I want us to be together. Always."

He placed his hand on my forehead, still wet with perspiration, "You shall eat of my flesh. Do this as a memorial of me. We shall be one flesh, one blood." It was a blessing.

He left me then, boarded the train. The train doors slammed closed as the conductor blew his whistle. I watched the train depart. I knew it would be the last time he would ever leave me. I was a convert. A disciple. I saw that everything before that moment had been a test.

Smith was ready to die.

37

I'm nervous as hell, with the sentencing just two days away. I feel sick and have a headache that refuses to die, even after four Nurofen. It's Lee's final day; tonight she flies back to Germany, her extended leave over. She wants to take me on a trip. I haven't been swimming for decades.

Not since I was four years old.

"It'll be fun," Lee says, grabbing my hand and pulling me behind her, through the silver turnstile, the gateway to the whorls of water and screams and slipping feet.

In the changing room are three women, of various ages, at opposite corners of the room. The oldest woman rubs sagging goose-bumped flesh with a patterned towel, the youngest woman is still dry, and adjusting the straps on her Speedo costume. She wears a plastic hat, and goggles are on the bench in front of her. A serious swimmer. But it's the third woman who captures my interest. I guess she's a similar age to me and she's helping her young daughter, a pale thing with limp bunches, into a red and white polka dot swimsuit. The girl is hopping, one foot to the other, like an excited sparrow in a birdbath. The mother looks my way and smiles, a distant greeting, a tired but happy face that makes my heart ache.

I lock myself into a cubicle while Lee changes in the communal area. I begin to remove my clothes, carefully folding them into a pile. Without my socks and boots the floor is wet and cold. I step into my new swimsuit, bought just moments ago in the small shop in the foyer. I hope it fits. It's strange, the feeling of lycra over my stomach, my breasts. I feel more exposed than when naked. It was a mistake to agree to this, I shouldn't have let Lee persuade me. When she said it would be fun she had no idea what she was asking of me. I haven't swum since I was a child, and maybe I only swam then with Mummy's help. What if I sink?

Lee is waiting for me, beyond the shallow footbath. She is simply waiting, in a plain navy costume, smiling. It's easy for her, she's relaxed here, after
all those years standing by the poolside ready to jump in if someone needed
help. Behind her, children screech as they hurl down the waterslide, landing
in a splash at the bottom, disappearing under the force of their own weight.
The echoing calls come to me as if from long ago.

I'm petrified and begin to shake.

"Come on, Alice. Let's get in. It's freezing just standing here." Lee takes
my hand. How is it that such a simple thing can steady me? "We'll go to the
children's pool. It'll be a lot warmer in there." She leads me, allows me to find
my way carefully on the wet tiles, stepping delicate as a flamingo.

The children's pool is as warm as a bath, and just as shallow. I'm grateful
for both. I watch as the girl in the polka dot swimsuit splashes around her
mother, her orange armbands like the wings of an exotic bird.

We sit, with the warm water just below our necks, and under the water Lee
keeps hold of my hand. She seems to be waiting for something to happen. I'm
not waiting, I could stay here for a long time. I even close my eyes. This is it,
I think. The moment I shall remember if I'm locked away. The thing I shall
think about from my prison cell. And I think back, to another time, another
swimming pool. I watch the young girl splashing, remembering that I, too,
was young once. Mummy was with me. Lee, by my side, anchors me. She
always did. "Now, Alice. The big pool. Come on!"

I follow, trusting her, still nervous of slipping. The silver steps take me into
colder water, and deeper. I'm grateful for Lee's hands on my waist, her closeness, but still the steps go down, lower into the deep water and then nothing.
I'm out of my depth.

"It's okay, Alice. I've got you."

I panic like a cat thrown in a river, scrabbling for the edge. She lets me
claw my way to her, supporting me as she treads water. "Don't hold my neck,
Alice. Hold my shoulders." Her shoulders are narrow and sinewy, but I can
feel the strength. Lee begins to swim, to move away from the side, taking me
with her. A graceful breaststroke, with me holding on. We rise in the water as
she pulls at each wave, my face just in the air, chlorine on my lips.

She swims like a dolphin.

I hold on, rescued, her shoulder a fin for me to grip. I trust in the strength
that takes me out into the middle, where the water is deepest. I will not
drown. I'm learning to swim.

I'm learning what it is to feel safe.

Back at home Lee cooks me supper. She massages my feet. She likes to do ordinary things. She likes to watch TV with a jumbo bag of popcorn. She likes to go to the Indian takeaway and order a vindaloo, even though it gives her wind. And she likes to ask questions. All the time, trying to fix me like some boat that's got a leak, dammit, and she'll sort that out, she'll make it sound. She won't stop, patching me up with normality. She's like a child rattling a pill bottle. She just won't get the message that the cap is designed to keep the contents safe.

And she's so restless. She won't keep still, even after sex when all I want to do is sleep. She props herself on an arm and annoys me with her stroking fingers, her probing questions: So how are your parents keeping? What good films have you seen recently? Are you still enjoying work? Peanut butter or marmite?

"Why do you care?" I snap, exasperated by the litany of interrogation, tired of feigning sleep. "You'll be back in Germany soon."

"I just want to talk, that's all," she says, bruised. Like a dog that's just been kicked, she shrinks away from me. I've just opened up my body for her, what more does she want? Isn't that enough? Apparently not.

"The thing is Lee, this time tomorrow you'll be in another country, and I don't see the point in us having this kind of conversation. Oh, and I hate both peanut butter and marmite. There. Now can we please go to sleep?"

She touches my chin, tentatively kisses my cheek. When she speaks she sounds sad, "Not like this, Alice. I don't want to force you to open up. I want you to trust me. You know I'd do anything to be with you. If you want me to, I'll leave the forces. Or you could come with me. Back to Germany."

"Ha! They're cool about lesbians in the military now, are they?"

Lee looks stung. "I'm not saying it would be easy. But it's possible. If you want to be with me, Alice, you can be."

I screw my eyes shut and wait until her breathing is low and even, and I'm sure she is asleep. I watch the flicker of her eyelids, her hand uncurling like an upturned crab after the tide is out. It's so easy for her. She doesn't have to appear in court in two days. Then, with the dark sky outside my only witness, I let a shoal of tears swim over my face.

Later, we kiss goodbye. She has to go to Colchester to pack, before taking a taxi to the airport.

I am abandoned.

38

Robin: Are you there?

Smith: Yes. Sleep well?

Robin: No. I'm restless.

Smith: Me too. I want to be with you.

Robin: You are. Always. Have you been thinking?

Smith: About death. I couldn't stand it to be too quick I want to be conscious when you taste me. I want to see you do it.

Robin: What should I use to cut you?

Smith: I'll do the cutting, Alice. I won't let you do anything that gets you into trouble later. I just want you to be with me.

Robin: But you want me to taste you?

Smith: Yes. That above all else. Raw human flesh must be quite tough so I'll have to have a good knife.

Robin: I'll see to that.

Smith: I was thinking about the Holy Communion—the part of me you will eat. It makes sense for me to cut loose flesh. I think there's one obvious choice.

The day before Smith died I went to a knife shop. Of course it wasn't just a knife shop. It sold many other things but that was why I was there so it was a knife shop to me. The knives were under the counter and a woman wearing a striped butcher's apron guarded them. The shop sold gadgets to baste and wedge and grate. The shop assistant waited patiently for me to decide. But I was pretending. I picked up designer crockery, touched the Alessi lemon zester, but what I really wanted was locked beneath glass, glinting like stars. "Can I help you?" she finally asked.

I tried to arrange my face into innocence, to keep my voice neutral. "I'd like to buy a carving knife please. A good one."

She turned and unlocked the cabinet, reached in, held one out to me. "This is a good quality all-purpose knife. What'll you be using it for?"

A difficult question. I thought of what to say, the closest approximation of the truth. It was simple. I needed a knife to cut flesh. I need a knife to kill. "For meat. Cutting chops." I didn't even know if that was right. I had never bought meat. Did people cut chops, or did the butcher do it for them? Did I need a cleaver?

She returned the knife she was holding into its wooden sheath. "This is the best one," she said, showing me a larger knife, a triangle of steel with a rosewood handle. "It's a Sabatier boning knife. Top quality."

I took it, measuring the weight as if expert in such purchases. Someone approached the counter, another woman, and I stood aside so she could purchase her Krupps espresso machine. I could wait. I was happy. I'd found what I sought and it felt natural in my grip, a perfect fit.

The knife was expensive. It cost a week's pay, but was worth it. The label boasted its credentials: sixty-three layers of hammered and folded steel, a hard yet flexible blade. Oh—and it was beautiful.

Do you want to put me in a box, just like the professionals? To call me mad or a freak?

I'm not mad. I'm like you, and, like you, I seek love. I'm someone who wants to be loved, who longs for devotion. But I don't trust it. The only love I've ever known, died. That is why. Unsatisfactory. Distorted. My apology. But I'm a flawed human being. Just like you.

An act is always more than what happens. Everything carries more weight as a totality, than as a sum of separate parts. And the separate parts are these:

I had a knife, shiny and new and of the highest quality. It was hidden in my bedside cabinet, a final gift.

We had a plan. Smith would take the second vial of GHB and as he drifted into unconsciousness he would cut himself. While we waited for his death, for the heart attack that would come from the overdose, I would eat his flesh.

39

Cate slides the memory stick into the computer and waits for Smith's diary to load onto the screen. In less than two hours she'll have her final meeting with Alice. By then she'll have decided what sentence to recommend. The report is already written, except for the final paragraph: the proposed sentence. She is thinking about a lengthy community order, maybe for two years, but most probably for three. She's spoken to Dr. Gregg, who will continue to work with Alice as an outpatient and he's agreed that she could be managed in the community as long as she's monitored. What would be the point of a prison sentence? Alice wouldn't get any kind of therapy or intervention, and her problems don't fit the standard 'one size fits all' treatments currently in vogue. At least working with her on an individual basis would give Cate the opportunity to look at Alice's distorted attitude to relationships. She could refer Alice to a grief counsellor; the loss of her mother had affected Alice's attitude to love and death and she had never worked through the trauma of finding her mother dead when she was just four years old.

Cate feels sorry for Alice. After reading most of David Jenkins' diary it's clear that he had wanted to die, and if Alice hadn't volunteered he would have found somebody else to assist him. Added to this is the horrible fact of Jenkins' illness and his desire to infect her with CJD. Who wouldn't feel sorry for Alice, knowing that? Alice must be told that she was at risk of having the disease. There was no doubt in Cate's mind that Alice, not Jenkins, was the real victim.

So, a community order was her preferred sentence. In court tomorrow she would argue strongly against prison. Backed up with a persuasive account of how Alice would be totally unable to cope with being locked up, Cate was sure she could convince the judge to be lenient. After all, assisting a suicide wasn't the same as murder. David Jenkins had wanted to die.

She clicked the icon titled Robin & Smith and prepared to read the last part of his testimony:

It's Friday night. Friday June 15th. My final night.

It was strange leaving the bungalow, surreal, saying goodbye to the bits and pieces that make up my life's journey—though my travels only amount to the daily commute to the office and a few holidays in the Lake District. I've surrounded myself with fossilised rocks, pictures of mountains I've seen but not climbed, menus from the local Chinese takeaway. This is the stuff of my life and, in the end, it's pretty pathetic. It'll be emptied into black plastic bags, maybe a few things will be taken to sell or give away, but most will end up in a landfill site. Forgotten. And that could've been my fate. Instead, I'll die a memorable death. And, through Robin, part of me will live on, until her death. (Jesus said, I am the Resurrection and the Life: he that believeth in me, though he were dead, yet shall he live.)

I packed a small suitcase, like I was going on a weekend away, a mini-break to relieve the stress, to break the monotony. I packed carefully. A clean shirt. Worn but comfortable beige chinos. New underwear. A bag for a journey with no return. The thought makes me sentimental, and I took a photo from the shelf, dusty and ignored for months. In it my parents are young and smiling. It's not how I remember them but I like it. It shows me how they were, how life was, before the car crash. The anniversary of my mother's death is tomorrow.

I was just eight years old. Remembering that day, I think of the stamp book I'd been looking at, the new stamps carefully inserted behind paper sheets with tweezers. I was busy with this when my grandma took the call. It had been my dad calling; his injuries were only minor. I still had the tweezers in my hand when I heard her slide to the floor, sobbing as she held the receiver tight to her ear, listening for better news about her daughter that would never come. I threw my stamp collection away that night, but Dad picked it out of the trash, kept it with the photo albums in the cupboard that housed the electricity meter.

In the empty bungalow I went to the meter cupboard, opening it to the scurry of a spider and an outbreath of dust. It was there, beneath the yellow pages, on top of an old holiday brochure: my stamp book. I took it out. It was smaller than I remembered, a cardboard collection with my scrawled name inside the dog-eared front cover in careful round letters, but the stamps were immaculate. I put the book into the case, along with my laptop and the USB stick, safe in an envelope.

At London Liverpool Street I bought a single ticket, one way, to Colchester. I walked past a Big Issue seller, a mangy greyhound lying at his feet, and gave him a tenner. He tried to offer me the magazine but I didn't take it. What good would it do me to read about the world? Instead, I stood and watched the board change, scanning for the town, until finally the name revealed itself. Platform twelve, the four o'clock service to Colchester.

The train was full, and I was forced to stand in the part where two carriages met and motion was jerky. I was next to the communal toilet, and the door kept opening in a belch of stale fags and piss. Next to me stood a weary mother with shopping bags and a young girl, who refused to stand. No doubt sick of being dragged around shops for hours, the girl silently rebelled by wiping her hand on the unclean floor, making shapes in the dust. Every time a traveller came to use the toilet the mother had to apologise and make a show of asking her daughter to get up.

I guessed the girl was about eight, and thought of myself at that age. I'd loved trains. I'd collected stamps from places I'd never been and would never go, though I didn't know that then. I thought the world was mine for the taking. How innocent I was. I didn't even know I was alive, never doubted that my eyes would open each day, that my lungs would take in air. I'd give anything for one hour, just sixty minutes, of that certainty now.

The girl had blonde hair, which was bright when the sun caught it, and green eyes like a kitten. This must have been what Robin looked like as a child; she was innocent once. Was innocent still, ignorant of the disease that's killing me. Five months ago I'd sat before a computer screen and set a plan in motion. All those ideas we'd tussled with on the screen, the words we played with which seemed more real than being on the train in a cramped carriage, as if I was already a ghost. The little girl, sensing me staring, looked up.

I felt dizzy and longed to sit on the dirty floor next to her, to trail my fingers in the dust. Instead I took off my glasses and rubbed the bridge of my nose, closing my eyes. I lurched as the train hurled around a corner and collided with the mother, stepping back on one of her shopping bags. "Sorry," I said, but she looked at me disapprovingly, maybe thinking I was drunk. I wasn't drunk. I was sick. Morbidly unwell.

The dizziness intensified and I sat clumsily on the floor, not caring that my clothes would get dirty. The girl looked at me, curious, and her mother's hand protectively touched her blonde head. No one trusts strangers anymore especially if they talk to children. But I had nothing to lose.

"Hello," I said, and she looked back at the floor, well taught in ignoring men she didn't know. She wasn't shy—her eyes kept wandering towards me, and she was bored. I reached forward unsteadily, unzipped my case. I could feel her mother watching me, sense her tension as if I was about to

retrieve a bomb. But I'm no hijacker. I just wanted to make a connection. I took out the stamp book and opened it on my lap, seeing that the girl was looking, too.

"Do you know what these are?"

She shrugged, the casual indifference of I'm-not-stupid. "Stamps."

"That's right. From all over the world. Places you wouldn't even dream of. See this," I pointed to a pink stamp depicting an alpaca, "that's from Peru. Do you know where that is?"

The girl shook her head.

"South America. A long way away."

"I've been to America," she offered. "We went to Florida. I swam with dolphins."

The girl's face lit up, and I wondered if Robin had ever swum with dolphins. If she'd ever travelled to America. "I'd like to go to South America," I told the girl.

"Then why don't you?" she asked.

A simple enough question, but I couldn't answer. When the train stopped at Chelmsford her mother started to collect her bags. I handed the stamp book to the girl. "Here," I said, "it's yours." She took it, no doubt to be told off by her mother after they got off. She'll look at it, and dream of other places that maybe someday she'll visit, and then may even remember me.

After Chelmsford I was alone in the corridor, and the toilet door swung against my foot, but I didn't stand. I occupied myself by picturing Robin as a little girl, and waited for the train to stop again at the terminus. The end of my journey.

Robin was waiting. It was a sunny June evening and she'd dressed up for me in a cream dress and strappy sandals. I worried that the grime from my clothes would mark her, but she ran over, not caring about my dirty clothes, and threw her arms around me. I should've felt supported, less likely to fall, but instead I had vertigo like I was standing at a great height and looking over the edge. If she noticed me shaking she didn't say.

We drove back to the house and she was unusually chatty, talking about the sun, and how everything looked beautiful. We stopped outside an off-licence and I watched her disappear into the shop, saw a man walking by give her the once-over. She did look beautiful, so why didn't I feel happy? After all, she was my girlfriend and soon she would be my lover. Everything was as it should be. As we'd planned.

She came back to the car holding a bottle of Belle Époque, stupidly expensive champagne with hand-painted flowers on the bottle. She slid into the driver's seat, pleased with her purchase. "It wasn't chilled, but I couldn't resist. It means 'beautiful age.' It's prophetic, don't you think?" The green bottle was heavy in my lap, and I thought of the pressurised gases, waiting to explode.

Her home was immaculate, as always, and I could smell the bleach. It smelt like a hospital. Death was close.

"I'll just put this in the fridge," she said, relieving me of the painted bottle. It was a party, and she was the hostess. I felt myself getting into the spirit, something like hope rising in my heart. When I closed my eyes I pictured clear blue water, and saw Robin by my side.

"I've cooked you a special meal," she said.

This was new. For all Robin's attention to domestic detail, she was no cook and we usually ate packaged food from Marks and Spencer. She placed a pot on the table, a blue casserole dish, and held the lid with a gloved hand, like a silver service waiter with a platter. I half expected her to say "ta-da!"

It was a stew, brown chunks of meat floating alongside carrots and other root vegetables. I would've preferred something from M&S but pretended to be grateful.

"It's a special treat. Can you guess?" I couldn't.

"I had to go to a very specialist butcher in Yoxford. It's a boar. In memory of Boris." I looked at her flushed face, the sweating bottle of champagne in the ice bucket, and felt dizzy with sorrow.

"Are you going to eat it?" I asked her. I'd never seen her eat meat, and her face grew serious. She pulled her white hand from the oven glove and kissed her finger, then touched my forehead, "Yes. I'm going to eat it. For you."

Another sacrifice, I thought.

I watched her release the cork from the champagne bottle. She frowned for a second as amber liquid drenched the white tablecloth, before she remembered that a stained cloth is nothing compared to the blood we planned to spill. I wondered if she ever doubted my motives, if she ever imagined that I would want to harm her. Despite her clever brain, Robin is as trusting as the girl on the train. I took the flute of champagne from her, thinking how she looked like a child on Christmas day.

I ate the meat, although it was gristly and felt too large in my mouth. Robin wanted me to eat the boar, and she polished off a large portion.

"For a vegetarian," I said, "you're quite a carnivore." She grinned at me, a sliver of gristle caught between her front teeth, and my shaking hand held

the fine flute too hard, shattering it into my palm. When I opened my hand I saw that the tips of my two fingers were bleeding.

"My poor love," she said, reaching over, gently removing the shards of splintered glass from my skin, dabbing at the cuts with her napkin. Then she did something I hadn't expected. She knelt on the floor beside me, still holding my hand, and took my two bloody fingers into her mouth. It was soft and warm, and her tongue licked and sucked. It turned me on until I remembered the disease in my body, the way some sufferers have been infected through blood. I pulled my hand away sharply, and Alice was surprised. She looked hurt. How could I tell her that I wanted to protect her?

Now, the sun is setting. Orange skies and tall shadows fall on the church and gravestones opposite, and as I stare out of the window I see a man walk by. He looks up, and then I see then it's not a man at all, but a woman. The leather jacket, the short haircut, fooled me. She must realise I've seen her because she quickly turns and walks away.

Downstairs I hear Robin moving around, the sound of water filling a kettle, the flick of a switch, the pop of air from a storage jar under pressure. I can picture her face, a serene smile on her lips, a light hum from deep in her throat. I enjoy thinking of her this way, thinking of our relationship as truly domestic. Is this how it would have been for us, if we had met under different circumstances? If I'd not been ill?

When I was a child, collecting stamps, I was certain that one day I would travel to those faraway countries. That boy is somewhere inside and kicking to get out, yelling that it's not too late to see the world.

We have a plan and it's too late for me. But it's not too late for Robin.

Why can't I feel more certain? This is our plan, the way we want it, but nothing feels as it should. The house is too clean, the food is too rich. Why doesn't anything feel right? Is it doubt, this nagging anxiety that keeps unsettling me? Can I change my mind now?

Even Jesus had doubts as the end drew closer—I just need to resolve myself. But still, I'm unsure . . . my head hurts. I can't think straight.

I take a coin from my pocket. Okay then, even though it's a certainty that I'll be dead within a matter of weeks, this will give me a 50% chance of living until then.

I take the ten pence piece and flick it high into the air, and I go to catch it but my hand is shaking so much that I miss, and it lands on the floor, rolling somewhere under the bed. I have to get on my hands and knees, watching it spin, waiting for it to drop, until I can finally get it.

I hold it tight, and try again.

This time, I throw lower and manage to catch it and slap it on the back of my hand, hiding it with the other. Still, my hands shake and I'm worried I'll drop it. If it's heads I'll stop all this—I'll tell Alice about the CJD. I won't put her at risk. If it's tails, I'll carry on.

I pray to God to intervene, to send me a message. Please, oh please, let this coin guide me in my decision.

Slowly I prize my hand from the concealed coin, not daring to look fully but squinting until I realise that I must see what God, or Fate, has decided. I force myself to look.

The coin is tails up.

I throw it on the floor, cursing, hearing it spin on the floorboards. My throat tightens; I must go ahead with my original plan. To die; to potentially infect Alice.

And then I know, from how fucked off I feel, that I've already made my decision. My reaction to the coin was the real sign. I wanted the coin to land heads-up.

I don't want to die today. I don't want to hurt Alice.

Cate re-read the final paragraph. David had changed his mind. But he had died and been eaten anyway. Cate felt a shift in her understanding as she wondered if the death had been, after all, against his will? Or had he changed his mind once more, deciding to go ahead with the plan? Then she thought of something else, other pieces of the puzzle which she could finally place. Opening her desk drawer she lifted out the handwritten note that Krishna had given her:

16th June

Krish,

I know you'll look after this. It's important. Sometimes things don't work out as we planned, as you and I both know. After all, we deal in improbabilities. By the time you get this I'll be long gone, but I want to travel light. Keep this safe for me.

I hope to see you again, either here or in another life.

Dave

Like a mist suddenly lifted by sun, Cate understood. When David talked in his letter about travelling light, he didn't mean it as a metaphor, he wasn't talking about the journey of death. He was talking about the actual journey he wanted to take, the travels he had decided to go on before the CJD finally killed him. And he no longer needed the memory stick, the diary, which was initially intended to exonerate Alice, because he no longer wanted to go ahead with the plan. He had changed his mind, so there was no reason to give the stick to Alice. He didn't want to take it with him. When he posted it to Krishna it was because he had decided to live.

Cate clicked the print icon on the screen, knowing the papers would soon spew out in the printer tray out in the lobby. She then opened the file containing her pre-sentence report and re-wrote her final paragraph. She now knew exactly what to write, what the judge must do. When it was written she emailed the report to the court office, attaching an explanatory note. It would be before the judge in minutes. Cate grabbed her bag, walked into the lobby to collect the printed copy of David's diary, and headed downstairs to the reception area.

"Dot, make sure this goes in the next hour," she said to the secretary, handing her the brown jiffy bag, sealed tightly, which contained the memory stick. "And address it for the attention of DCI Stephen West. It's urgent. He must get it today."

As she drove she thought, am I being stupid—why don't I just telephone Alice? But Alice didn't know about David having CJD, and Cate felt it was only right to tell her face-to-face. This was not something that could be relayed over the phone. Alice should be told about her possible fate in person. At the very least, she deserved that.

Cate would not fail David. But she would not fail Alice, either. Both of them were victims.

40

I promised you the truth and you deserve to know. I know forgiveness is too much to ask, so I simply hope for understanding. This is how Smith died.

As the minutes passed and midnight approached I was as excited as a child on Christmas Eve. I tried to capture the moment, not wanting to forget any detail. Smith was upstairs in the spare room, resting before his final sleep, catching up on dreams. I made us a midnight feast; I juiced some fruit, added honey to yogurt, fetched cheese from the fridge, a mild creamy goat's cheese and blue-veined Stilton, which we could have on crackers. I laid the table with white china and cut glass, a bottle of Sancerre. The two plastic vials of GHB in the fridge, one already partly used.

I arranged some poppies in my precious blue vase, the perfect centrepiece. It was a quarter past eleven. We had less than one hour to wait and the only sound from upstairs was the tapping of fingers on a keyboard as Smith completed his diary. The suicide note was sealed in an envelope and propped against the empty bottle of Belle Époque, from our meal earlier. We were both nervous and in his agitation Smith had broken a glass, but it had all been cleaned away. I'd put a plaster on each of his cut fingers.

I took a shower, anointing myself with papaya and mango, washing my hair with jasmine. I took my time, patting my skin, stroking in scented lotion, perfuming and oiling myself as if for an ancient ritual. I decided to wear only white, a long linen dress and simple, plain underwear. I dried my hair at the bedroom mirror, watching my reflection and thinking how peaceful I looked. I applied a tinted moisturiser, a cream eye shadow and a pale pink lip-gloss. Then I painted my nails a pretty shade of pink. I remembered how Mummy looked, the day she died. Her pale cool skin.

The Sancerre was getting warm on the table, and I began to feel impatient. I tapped on Smith's door. No answer. I opened the door.

He was gone. I turned, darted back to the bathroom, but he wasn't there either.

I called, "Smith! SMITH!" My voice increasingly loud and demanding. He had left me—disappeared while I was preparing. I caught myself in the mirror. I no longer looked radiant, I looked enraged. His bed had been made, the duvet pulled neatly over the mattress. I dashed to the window, then I saw, on the floor, his bag. His weekend bag was still there. Relief cooled my hot heart.

Outside, the moon was alone in the sky. There was no one around. I saw a movement coming from the dark shadows. It was Smith.

He had something in his hand. An envelope. Where would he have bought a card at that time of night? He slid the envelope into the post box across the road. He stood for several moments, his hand lost in the box, as if deciding whether to let go of his envelope. Who was that letter for? A goodbye to someone special? Eventually he retrieved his empty hand. The envelope was in the box, waiting to be collected.

I heard him open the back door. I smoothed my brow, forced a smile. I demanded of my face that it regain the poise it had lost and went downstairs.

He looked shy and acted like a guest in a hotel, polite and formal. "Alice, this spread looks great."

I flinched but didn't point out that he should call me Robin. He wolfed down two crackers in rapid succession, as if he'd not eaten for a week. His haste disappointed me, as I carefully dotted crumbs from my lips. He was skittish, his body moved in lively jerks, and his eyes darted from me. We were both strained in our conversation, skating on thin ice, afraid to initiate what was pressing for us both.

He cleared his throat to speak, and my hand froze on my knife, poised to slice the cheese in two. "Alice, we need to talk."

"Of course." I put down the knife. "But please stop calling me Alice."

"I won't call you anything but Alice." He looked shifty, his Adam's apple rose in his neck.

"But we agreed." I was angry. I preferred to be Robin. Alice made me think of my childhood, of a giant girl in a tiny house, of an outsized body in a Mad Hatter's world. I stood and gathered the dirty plates.

It was all going wrong.

I began loading the dishwasher, briskly cleaning away the mess, chipping plates in my haste. When the table was wiped and everything clean I looked at the clock on the wall. It was a quarter to midnight. Pouring two large measures of Islay malt I took the unopened vial of GHB from the fridge and opened it, tipping the liquid into one of the tall glasses, using the drug instead of soda to make a long drink. I stirred it with my finger, which I licked, satisfied that the drug wasn't detectable.

I went to the front lounge where Smith was seated looking out of the window and put my arms around his neck. "Let's talk upstairs over a nightcap. Maybe we should make love first?" I needed to make it right between us. It was time to begin and I watched him take a swig of the whiskey. He winced, "This stuff is so salty. Good though."

I held up my own glass in a toast. "To love."

He clinked his glass against mine and finished his drink. I took his glass from him and went to the kitchen, pouring him another whisky and adding the last of the GHB from the opened vial. I returned to him and led the way to my bedroom.

After Smith finished his second drink, I held him tight as we fell on the bed, took him closer than if he was bound to me by rope. He pulled back, removed his glasses, looking so different without them. The skin around his weak eyes was white and perfect, like a child's.

"God, that whiskey's strong stuff. It's gone straight to my head."

I kissed him, unbuttoned his shirt, stroked my hand over his smooth chest, felt his ribs under my palm, felt his heartbeat with my fingers. Such a thin body; when Jesus died on the cross his ribs could be counted. I stroked Smith like a pianist finding a tune. I found beauty.

"I feel a bit dizzy. Must be all the alcohol," he said, his voice already slurred as the drug coursed through his veins.

He was tense but allowed me to undress him, watching as I slipped off my knickers. We were soft and smooth, pale and clean, fitting together aesthetically, if not mechanically. The sex was awkward. His penis resisted my hand, my mouth, stubbornly flaccid.

"I'm sorry," he said, looking towards the window. "I'm so sorry, Alice. I don't want to die. I don't want to be a sacrifice. I want to live." I couldn't breathe. I felt rage like hot blood. How dare he change his mind? What kind of fool did he take me for?

"I want to travel, Alice. You and I together!"

"Travel?" I spat the word. "Where to?"

"To all the places I've never been. I've got money. There's nothing to stop us." Our plan, I thought, anger overcoming me until I wanted to break bones. What about our plan?

"I'm not going back to London, Alice. I've got my passport; I've got my American Express card. Anything else we need I'll just buy." He was swaying, sweat started to gather on his brow.

"You planned this," I said. "Why else have your passport?"

"For identification, when they found my body. It was the only thing with my photo in. Believe me, Alice, this is better for you, too. I only changed my mind tonight. It's a sign from God. I didn't plan this change of heart. I planned to die. I'd even written a diary to explain why I wanted to commit suicide. I was going to leave it here to exonerate you."

"Where is it now?"

"I posted it to a friend, on a USB. I won't need it anymore." He pulled me to him, his mouth grazing my shoulder then falling slack. I could feel the Band-Aid on the tips of his fingers grazing my thigh. The plan must go ahead. What he'd said was only words. His actions told me that he wanted to continue, even though he was now pale and his breathing was laboured as the drug worked its magic.

"Smith . . . this is our dream . . . this is what we both wanted." I took him on his back, made all the motions to drive us together. When his penis was in me I felt it harden, and I knew it wasn't too late. I looked at the bed-side clock—five minutes to midnight. As my own body tensed and began its incremental steps towards the great fall, he thrust into me with a sudden hunger. I saw his teeth, his closed eyes, and closed my own. He was deep inside me when he slurred, "Alice, change your mind. Come travelling with me."

I bit his shoulder. He still thought he could change his mind. He pushed into me with a boy's eagerness, oblivious to my needs. I was wooden in his embrace, and he was too inexperienced to notice or care.

"Oh, Alice," he moaned, taking me more firmly in his arms, thrusting faster.

It was nearly midnight.

I rolled over, pulling him with me so he was on top. Suddenly poised he shuddered, "Oh God, my arm. It hurts right up my arm." He looked ghastly, like marble, and every breath was a struggle.

I didn't let him rest, wouldn't let him pull away. He was grunting, close to orgasm even as his pale face twisted in pain.

"Kiss me!" I demanded, my hands holding his buttocks as he bucked into me. He was unable to do anything else but give in to the demands of his body, and his kiss was an open mouth, a gasp of pain. As he came I swallowed his scream, and felt his heart give way to palpitations.

There was a deathly stillness. He struggled, gurgling and gasping, as I pushed him off me. He was doubled in agony, his arm held straight as his whole body shuddered, his heart giving in to cardiac arrest.

"This was what you wanted, Smith, remember? To cease upon the midnight with no pain." He coughed, struggling to breathe. A war in his chest.

"The whiskey," he gasped, "you drugged it."

"You were afraid, but I helped you to see our plan through. You're glad now, aren't you?"

There was no fear in his eyes, and when they stopped rolling I saw peace. His body shuddered with the final tremors of life. I am a woman of honour. I didn't go back on my word, even when he'd done so. A deal was struck and I had agreed to taste him. I took the knife from under my pillow.

It wasn't easy to lay him straight and I wasn't so gentle as I would have liked, but his body was awkward. It was hard work to get the angle right so that my grip on the knife was firm. He was still conscious when I took the bloody blade and coaxed his shrunken penis from the pink shell of his foreskin. I held firm and cut away a slice of skin.

Who would have thought there would be so much blood? Such a small piece of meat—I must have cut a vein.

I sucked the blood. I tasted him.

It was like eating the dead skin from a scab. It was nothing. It was rubber and salt. Looking at him, I swallowed and his mouth made a shape that I believed was a smile. He was leaving me, disappearing into himself.

I took the blade to the side of his penis and in one strong motion cut across the flesh. It was swift and bloody, the white cotton sheet bloomed with red petals. My face was splattered. My cheeks were wet as if with tears. Smith's head hung to the side, a broken toy. His eyes rolled in their sockets, and a word of air came from his mute mouth. I wanted to close his eyes, which were fixed on me, the moon reflected in his iris was our only witness, but I was afraid to touch his face, afraid that he would suddenly right himself. How could I be scared after what I'd done? I looked down at the knife where beads of blood dripped onto the bedding. I lifted my finger to my lips, tasting salt and iron. Colour drained from his face like the beach at low tide, until he turned to alabaster.

I knew he was close to death.

"You're happy now, Smith, aren't you?" I whispered, "This is what you wanted."

I lay beside him and kissed his cheek, putting the knife in his hand. I had never loved him more.

I was no longer afraid. I placed my head near his heart, listened to the silence, the moon outside lighting us with her gaze. I closed my eyes, waited for his body to cool and for Mummy to come back to me. I was with her again.

My heart was finally whole.

41

As usual, Cate Austin is late. I'm upstairs when I hear the knock, and not yet at the top of the stairs when she knocks again. When I open the door she practically falls into the hallway. She's full of energy and she bounds into my home, breathless. I lead her into the breakfast room, and she perches in the same place on the pine bench that she took a month before. A lifetime ago. She's here to deliver her verdict and she looks tense, her fingers drumming on the table. She's frowning and breathing heavily. "How are you today, Alice? Looking forward to the finale tomorrow?"

There's something in her tone, hostility that I've not heard before. "I'll feel better when I know what you're recommending in your report."

"Ah yes," she says, her eyes glinting, "my report. I imagine you're expecting a favourable conclusion. After all, our meetings have gone so well. So very smoothly. I imagine you're dying to know what my report will say."

"Yes, I am." I confess, sitting opposite. "You know how much depends on it."

"And do you think you deserve a favourable report, Alice?" Her tone is taunting, and too loud.

"I've attended all our appointments, I even came to your dismal office. And I've talked to you."

She takes a sheaf of papers from her bag. The papers look too many to be a report. "You've certainly talked, Alice, that I won't deny. And I've listened. You've had the opportunity to explain your motives and persuade me to propose an alternative to prison. You've killed two birds with one stone, so to speak." There is an accusation in her narrowed eyes. I feel my colour rise. "He changed his mind, didn't he, Alice? He didn't want to die."

She pushes the pile of papers across the table. On the top sheet, it says, Robin & Smith. I know immediately what it is. His diary. I knew he was keeping one though I never saw it. How the hell did she get it? I feel suddenly light, like I might faint.

I see from the rise of her chest that her heart is beating a rapid rhythm but her voice does not betray her. "You killed him anyway."

I look at the pile of paper in front of me. I touch it with a finger, then pull away as if it's hot. I don't read the words, but look at Cate's face. It's as pale as a child's, and I recognise something new: she's furious with me.

"He advertised for a lover to help him die, remember?"

She breathes deeply, still maintaining her composure. "Yes, but that advert was in January. By the time he actually died he'd changed his mind. He didn't want to die. He wanted you to travel together. He wanted to be with you." I want her to stop, but she continues. "Read his diary, Alice. It's all there. His doubts. That he changed his mind." The new arrival of softness in her voice makes my limbs tense. "His illness."

"Illness?" I have no idea what she means, though my pulse heeds the warning, begins to jog. The dull ache begins at the top of my spine and I know the headache is returning.

Now she speaks softly, every syllable urging my heart to sprint, to break into the tearing pace that I know as panic. "The tragic thing is, Alice, he was dying anyway. You didn't know that, did you? It was ironic that you invented the story of the cancer for your parents when he actually was terminally ill. He had Creutzfeldt-Jakob disease, and maybe just a few weeks left to live. At first he thought that by choosing when to die he was taking control over the illness. Then he realised that he didn't want to put you at risk. He'd decided to protect you. He wanted you to travel with him, to South America. He wanted to swim with dolphins. He wanted to live."

"He was afraid, that was all." I can only manage a few words, my chest is so full, so large. My ears throb to an urgent rhythm and I hold the table to calm the first wave of dizziness. "He needed me to take control, to help him fulfill his destiny. When he drank the whisky he knew the drug was in it." My voice sounds unfamiliar, echoing itself, carved out of stone.

"So you admit you killed him? Oh, Alice."

"But he wanted to die! The diary must confirm that?"

"It confirms everything, Alice. Why he placed the advert and why he wanted to be eaten." She says the words softly, "CJD can't be transmitted by sex. But it can be passed on through blood, through flesh. You did eat part of him, Alice, didn't you?"

I nod, slowly. My head pounds in protest at the movement. "I'm no expert so I've briefed the court doctor. Tomorrow he'll be able to give you more information about the potential risk of you contracting CJD. But I didn't want you to hear it first from a stranger."

I'm the student now. I don't understand. I refuse to understand. If I tried to use words I would stumble. My palms are sweaty and I look to the door with longing.

"He wanted to infect you, Alice. That was his intention. That was why he asked you to eat him."

"No! He wanted me to eat him so that he could live in me. So he could live on."

"That's what he told you." She says sadly.

"He wanted me to catch the disease?" Is Smith watching me now, from wherever the dead go, enjoying this moment? Tears relay down my cheeks, surprising my mouth with their salt. I can't make sense of the jumble in my head. "But how did the diary get to be with you?"

"David wrote his final entry here, on his laptop, before he told you he'd changed his mind. He downloaded the diary onto a memory stick and posted it. He sent it to Krishna Dasi, a colleague he trusted, along with a note that said he wanted to travel. Krishna assumed he was talking about death, that it was a metaphor. I did, too, until I read the final entry in the diary.

"Krishna didn't hand the memory stick over straightaway because he didn't want to get involved. He knew he would be implicated if he did because he'd given David a drug dealer's name which was mentioned in the diary and he knew David had died of an overdose. Also, Krishna wanted to protect his friend, knowing that he had originally planned to infect you. Thankfully, in the end, he realised he had no right to keep it to himself."

"But how did you come to have it?" My heart is slowing now, exhausted with effort. My limbs are heavy and the headache is now reigning in my brain, waves of pain that make me want to lie down in a dark room.

"Krishna gave it to me, the last time we were at court."

I'm trying to listen. I'm trying to concentrate, despite the pain. Smith wanted to infect me with his disease. But then he changed his mind—he tried to stop it happening. In the end he wanted to save me. In going ahead with the plan I condemned myself.

"David thought he could stop the plan, call it off. But he was wrong, wasn't he Alice? You weren't going to let him go. You murdered him before he could do that."

"It wasn't murder. We had a plan. It had all been agreed." She's looking at me with disgust but also with pity.

"In the end he couldn't bring himself to harm you."

I see it suddenly, my mistake. My failure to recognise love. In the end Smith didn't want to harm me. He loved me.

"What happens now?" I ask, "I'm being sentenced tomorrow."

"My report reflects exactly what I've found out. It's already filed with the court, and the USB is now with the police. There will be a new trial, but with a new charge. You'll be charged with murder."

I remember the story that scared me so much as a child, the tale of the woman with the jigsaw puzzle. Of the axe man at the window. When I first heard it I was twelve and I cried and cried until Dad came to take me home. And now, over twenty years later, I feel like I'm twelve again. I can't stop crying. Only now I'm alone in my house and no one is coming to save me. I had the jigsaw laid out, and thought I knew what the picture was, but when Cate Austin came today she showed me that I was wrong. Then she put in the final piece. She showed me the real picture and it's horrible.

There has been a man at my window all along. Even worse, he'd already broken in and attacked me with a poisoned axe and I didn't even feel it. And now there could be disease in my veins. All the headaches, dizziness, sickness. . .

All these months when the police and the courts have been interrogating me, trying to discover if Smith wanted to die, deciding if I was a criminal, and all the time I was the victim. They arrested the wrong person. Smith has murdered me. He's condemned me to a life of watching and waiting for telltale signs of a disease that may never materialise.

I thought we had achieved so much. The best, the perfect moment of death. To cease upon the midnight with no pain. I thought he loved me when he wanted to die, but now I see that in wanting to live he was trying to protect me. But I failed to protect myself.

I can't bear this. I will not bear it. When Cate Austin has gone I reach for my telephone and dial, knowing there is only one person who can save me now.

42

I wait for my lover to arrive. My hair is loose and I wear a long white dress. I could be going to a wedding, if it was not for the fact that upstairs, hidden under the pillow, is a knife. I don't think I breathe until I hear the knocking on the door. Until I open it and feel Lee's arms tight around me. Her grip allows me to fall, the pain in my chest rising in my throat. There's no choice but to surrender, to let her love me. She guides me back into the house and closes the door.

"I thought I might be too late. That you would be on the plane to Germany."

Lee's lips are on my ear. "There was no plane, Alice, not tonight anyway. I was going to be in court tomorrow, in the viewing gallery. I didn't want to tell you that I knew everything. It had to be your choice, and you wanted to keep it from me. I respected that."

"But you knew?"

"I always knew. It's why I came back."

Of course, of course she knew. She knows me. She knows the weight of my silence. Lee wipes the tears from my chin, my cheek. She takes her fingers and strokes my face as she's done a million times, as if her only desire is to comfort me. She shows no surprise, only concern. No fear, only love.

"Have you never stopped to ask yourself, Alice, why it all happened last year? You're the same person you've been since you were a teenager—why then and not any other year?"

"Because that was when I found Smith."

"But it was also when you started looking—when you needed to find something, someone. Because, after being together since we were five years old, I'd left. Don't you see?"

"What?"

"It was me, Alice. Our love. That's what kept you stable. Kept you safe. But last year I was posted to Germany. That's when things went wrong."

I'm silent. Is it true? "I love you, Alice. I should never have left you. I won't leave you again."

I'm crying again, collapsing into her, letting her hold me like a strengthening force. Is she right? Was Smith's death not what I longed for, not the remembrance of love past, newly tasted. Lee will give me that. She gives me a sense of it already. It can only be her. I know she can make it right.

When I'm finally still she asks, "What has happened, Alice? Why are you like this now? Is it because of the sentencing tomorrow?"

Her arms are tight, holding me fast. Her mouth places kisses on my neck like pearls. I long to tell her everything but my mouth is a fortress, keeping it back. I can't tell her that I'm diseased.

"I know, Alice," she whispers. "I know about David Jenkins. Alice, Alice, my sweet love . . ." I struggle to turn from her, and she releases me slightly, but I'm still in her embrace, turned away. She rocks me. I give in to myself, let my weight be hers. I'm a child again and she is my parent. I close my eyes and allow it, feeling what it is to be loved. I must forget the disease in my brain, planted like a bad seed.

I remember my mother. I think of her cool skin, her freshly painted pink toenails. Being alone with her that final time, my head on her chest. I want it back, so much, that love. I want her back . . .

"Let's go upstairs," I say.

Lee leads me to the bedroom.

She undresses, watching me. I stand, in my white dress. I won't be naked. When she is under the sheets she reaches for me, gently pulling me onto the soft mattress, next to her. I slide under the new sheets. Despite the warmth of her smile, I'm shaking. "Kiss me," I say. "I want you to make love to me."

Lee strokes me, pushes her thigh between my legs. She closes her eyes and it is then that I remove the knife from the pillow. She looks at me and the blade flashes in her pupils.

"Alice, please . . . put the knife down . . ." The knife is still in my hand, but raised. The blade points to her heart. Now is the moment. "Alice, please . . ."

I'm Lot's wife, immobile and poised, pale as salt.

"It's over, isn't it, Lee?" The question comes from nowhere conscious, barely a movement, the sound of grains in an hourglass. "They'll lock me away for life."

She watches the knife as its blade touches her skin, my pale hand gripped to the wooden handle. "Whatever happens Alice, we can sort this out. I'll never go away again, but first I want you to give me the knife."

She moves slowly, as if managing a lion that has pinned her to the back of the cage. I could pounce at any moment, but our bodies are still close, alongside each other, her leg between mine. My heart palpitates and I'm sure she must see beads of sweat on my lip. Does she still find me beautiful?

Slowly, so very slowly, Lee covers my hand with her own and we hold the knife together. She pulls the length of the blade forward so it punctures her breast. "Is this what you want, Alice? To kill me?"

She coaxes my hand forward, the tip of the blade digging further into her flesh, towards her heart. A bead of blood blooms on the silver like a ruby, and Lee watches me, never breaking eye contact. "Alice, is this what you want?"

Like cracks appearing in marble, my composure dissolves, my voice loud and stuttering. "He betrayed me! He lied! I thought it was what we wanted. What I thought was love was his desire to infect me. I'm sick, Lee, I think I'm dying. Smith murdered me."

I pull the handle hard so the knife is over my own heart. The tip is razor sharp and cuts as it falls, but I no longer wield it. Surrendered, I crumple into the mattress. Finally, I cry like a child.

Lee holds me, still with the knife in her grip. Kisses me. I won't hurt anymore. She whispers, intimate words. This was the moment I sought all along. The gift of love. She loves me, even now. Even knowing I have killed a man. Even knowing I may be diseased. Unconditional, immovable love. I don't need her death to make love immortal: she won't abandon me.

She will never leave.

43

It is morning. Alice was to be sentenced today.

She lies on the floor, her pale skin almost translucent in the weak February sun, as her lover paints the last of her fingernails a pretty shade of pink.

Lee takes the cardigan from the chest of drawers. Hand knitted, lilac wool, with a precious pearl button. The blood from the wound on Alice's breast is dried, clotted dark. Lee touches it, feeling the bump of fresh scar tissue.

"Are you cold, my darling?" she asks, taking the cardigan and wrapping it around Alice's shoulder. "You're with your Mummy now. You won't be cold anymore."

Lee strokes her beloved's arm, kisses her, knowing that this time, this final time, there will be no bad dreams, no nightmares, to disturb Alice's sleep.

Ruth Dugdall studied English Literature at Warwick University before taking an MA in Social Work at the University of East Anglia. After graduating she worked for almost a decade within the criminal justice system, first as a youth justice social worker and then as a probation officer, before dedicating herself to writing novels.

Her first novel, *The James Version*, is a historical fiction based on the notorious murder of Maria Marten in the Red Barn, Suffolk.

The Woman Before Me, the first novel to feature probation officer Cate Austin, was published by Legend Press in August 2010. It won the CWA Debut Dagger, the 2009 Luke Bitmead Bursary Award, was shortlisted for the 2011 People's Book Prize, and longlisted for the New Angle Book Prize.

The Sacrificial Man is Ruth's third novel.